AMANDA BRITTANY lives in Hertfordshire with her husband and two dogs. When she's not writing, she loves spending time with family, travelling, walking, reading and sunny days. Her debut, *Her Last Lie* reached the Kindle top 100 in the US and Australia and was a #1 Bestseller in the UK. It has also been optioned for film. Her second psychological thriller *Tell The Truth* reached the Kindle top 100 in the US & was a #1 Bestseller in the US. All her ebook royalties for *Her Last Lie* are being donated to Cancer Research UK, in memory of her sister who lost her battle with cancer in July 2017. It has so far raised over £7,500.

Also by Amanda Brittany

Her Last Lie
Tell The Truth

Praise for Amanda Brittany

'Brittany reels readers in with this twisty, clever thriller that will have you second-guessing everything'
Phoebe Morgan, author of *The Doll House*

'Brilliant, pacey, and will leave you suspecting everyone is involved!'
Darren O'Sullivan, author of *Our Little Secret*

'Totally gripping'
Reader Review

'I had to keep turning the pages'
Reader Review

'A lot of twists and turns ... it didn't disappoint'
Reader Review

Traces of Her

AMANDA BRITTANY

ONE PLACE. MANY STORIES

HQ
An imprint of HarperCollins*Publishers* Ltd
1 London Bridge Street
London SE1 9GF

First published by HQ Digital 2019

1
This edition published in Great Britain by
HQ, an imprint of HarperCollins*Publishers* Ltd 2020

ISBN: 978-0-00-833118-4

MIX
Paper from
responsible sources
FSC
www.fsc.org   **FSC˙ C007454**

Printed and bound in Great Britain by
CPI Group (UK) Ltd, Croydon, CR0 4YY

To Liam, Daniel, Luke, Lucy & Janni.

Prologue

She lies on the sand dressed in yellow satin, a ring of sodden flowers clinging to her blonde hair like seaweed. The pendant around her slim neck says 'Mummy' – a gift from Willow.

Grasses stir in the howling wind and a mist rolls in from the Celtic Sea, moving over her lifeless body – ghosts waiting to take her hand and lead her away from this lonely place where seagulls cry.

A man will come soon. He walks his border collie at the same time each morning along the same sandy path that edges the sea in Bostagel, and today will be no different.

He will stride with the aid of his stick; grey hair flapping in the wind, calling after his dog. Content with his lot.

Then he will see her body, and her sister's wedding dress folded neatly on the rocks. The shock will stay with him forever.

He will call the police.

Sirens will pierce the silent air.

The youngest Millar girl is dead. Stabbed repeatedly.

'Rest in peace, young Millar girls,' they will say.

Chapter 1

ROSE

Now

'Willow! Thank God,' I say, my mobile pressed to my ear. She's disappeared before. In fact, her ability to take off without explanation is something we've learned to live with over the last few years.

'Rose,' she says. 'Rose I'm …' Her voice is apprehensive, and I imagine her twirling a strand of her long blonde hair around her finger, something she's done since childhood. 'I'm sorry I haven't called before.'

'Well, you're calling now. That's what's important,' I say, always aware how fragile she is. 'And it's good to hear your voice, Willow.' It's only been a month, but I've missed her.

I drop down onto the edge of the sofa, my eyes flicking to the photograph above my open fireplace: me at fifteen – lanky, with lifeless hair and acne; Willow, a beautiful child of three sitting on my knee, her expression blank, bewildered. It was the day I met her.

'We had no idea if you were OK,' I say, although there was

3

nothing new there. In fairness, she put a couple of generic updates on Facebook about a week ago. 'Where are you?'

'Cornwall.'

'Cornwall?'

'I'm staying at a cottage in Bostagel near Newquay ...' She breaks off, and I sense she has more to say, but a silence falls between us.

'Why didn't you call or text?' I ask.

'Sorry,' she says. 'The signal's erratic down here. And, if I'm honest, I needed to get my head straight before I spoke to any of you about ...' She stops.

'About what, Willow?' I clear my throat. 'About what?'

'It's ... well ... the thing is, someone paid for me to stay here until August.'

'Someone?'

'I don't know who, Rose. I got a message on Facebook and—'

'You just took off?' I can't hide the irritation at her naivety. 'Someone paid for you to stay in Cornwall, and you've no idea who?'

'No, but, hear me out, Rose. There's so much you don't know,' she says in a rush. 'But I can't tell you over the phone. You never know who's listening.'

'Who would be listening?' I say. My voice cracks. I love her so much, but she has no self-awareness – no sense of self-preservation. 'Listen come home. We can talk here.'

'I can't. I'm so close.'

'Close to what?' My anxiety is rising. 'Is everything OK?'

'Yes. I'm fine. Gareth is here.'

'Who's Gareth?'

'He's been helping me.' A pause. 'Please come to Cornwall, Rose. Please. I'll explain absolutely everything once you're here.'

A lump rises in my throat, blocking my efforts to say no, and a sudden strangling fear she could be in some sort of danger grabs me. I rise and pace the lounge, raking my fingers through my hair.

The sun beating on the windowpane hurts my eyes. I drag the curtains hard across the glass, and the room plunges into a depressive grey haze.

'Rose?'

'Yes. I'm still here.'

'Well? Will you come?' There's a tremor in her voice. 'I need you right now. Please.'

'Come back home then,' I try once more, but I know I'm losing.

'I can't,' she says. 'I just can't, Rose. And I know I don't deserve you – that I drive you all crazy. But I can barely sleep at night for all the stuff going on in my head.'

'I've Becky to think of.'

'Becky,' she says, a whimsical ring to her voice at the mention of my teenage daughter. 'Bring her too.'

'I'm not sure.'

'Please, Rose,' she says again. 'Come. I'm begging you.' I hear tears in her words and feel myself weakening. She has a childlike quality, often seeming younger than Becky. I've felt protective of her from the day I arrived at Darlington House eighteen years ago, when she was all curls and big eyes. She needed me then, and she needs me now.

It's over five hours from Old Stevenage to Cornwall, but I love driving. It won't be a problem. And I know I could battle with her for ages, tell her 'no' over and over, but, in spite of myself, I will go. It's impossible to ignore her cry for help – she's always had that power over me. 'OK, I'll come,' I say.

She sighs with relief. 'Thanks. You're amazing, Rose. I'll explain everything when you get here. There's so much to tell you.'

'I can't come until Saturday, Willow. I don't break up for the summer until Friday. Will you be OK until then?'

'Yes. That's fine … brilliant. I'm so grateful. I can show you the note.'

'What note?'

There's a loud knock in the background. 'I've got to go,' she says, and drags in a breath. 'I'll email you my address, and see you at the weekend, yeah? I can't wait. Love you, Rose.'

The phone goes dead before I can reply.

'Love you too,' I whisper, flopping back down on the sofa, and throwing my phone onto the coffee table.

After some moments, my eyes drift to the photo of Willow and me again, and I can almost feel her in my arms, smell the freshness of her golden hair.

*

Dad met Eleanor Winter in the August of 2002 at a conference about the destruction of the rainforest – something they both care about deeply, and bonded over.

I was pleased for Dad, really I was. When Mum died three years before, the weight dropped from his body like a jolly snowman facing the sun. I lost count of the times I caught him crying. He was a shadow of the strong dad who'd brought me up – and all that time I was grieving her loss too.

I liked Eleanor from the off. Softly spoken, tall with bobbed highlighted hair and small grey eyes, she was nothing like my chubby, tiny, fun-loving mum. It was as though Dad had gone out of his way to find Mum's opposite.

I admit unwanted feelings reached into my head at first – 'I want my dad to myself'; 'What would Mum think?' – that kind of thing. But mainly I was happy for him. At fifteen I was often out with friends, leaving him to wander lonely around our semi in Hitchin – the house I grew up in – feeling guilty I wasn't there for him 24/7.

That day, the day of the photo, was the first time I'd visited Darlington House in Old Welwyn, an amazing detached house built in the eighteenth century, set in picturesque grounds. I remember it looked even more beautiful that day because of the sprinkling of snow we'd had. I knew it would be a culture shock when we moved in with Eleanor and Willow; that it would never feel like home. But I was prepared to do anything to bring my old dad back.

Dad put down the camera, and Willow shuffled from my knee, and trotted towards her Duplo scattered over the carpet near the French windows. She dropped down onto her bottom, her curls bouncing.

'That's a smashing picture of you two girls,' Dad said, looking at the camera screen and smiling. 'Take one of me and Eleanor, will you, Rose?' he went on, handing me the camera. I felt awkward. Forced into another world I'd rather not be in. But still I rose and did as he asked.

As they leaned into each other, his arm around her waist, I knew they were in love. Dad had been through hell, and Eleanor was recently widowed; they deserved a second chance at happiness. I had to support them.

They headed into the kitchen to prepare lunch, and I padded over to Willow, and knelt next to her on the floor. 'What are you building?' I asked.

She looked up at me, her blue eyes seeming too big for her face. She'd lost her father six months before, and looked so fragile, as though she might break. She didn't answer, and I found myself playing with her curls, twirling them around my fingers. 'You're so pretty,' I said.

She looked up at me. 'Uncle Peter lets me stand on his shoes when we dance.' Her lips turned upwards.

'Does he?' I said, realising I knew nothing about Eleanor's family. 'That's nice.'

'Mummy's gone now,' she said. 'Uncle Peter's gone too.'

I glanced over my shoulder, to where laughter leaked from the kitchen. 'Mummy's here, she's making lunch, sweetie,' I said, stroking a wayward curl from her cheek.

'No.' She picked up two yellow bricks and stared at me through watery eyes. 'Mummy's an angel,' she went on, clicking the bricks together.

Chapter 2

AVA

1996

'You can't come with us, Ava.' Gail laughed, and her two friends, all three dressed in skimpy tops and shorts, joined in. 'Get the bus home.' With a flick of her blonde ponytail, Gail linked arms with her friends, and in perfect step they made their way through the tourists towards the arcades, the sun beaming down on them.

'Mum said ...' Ava began, but her sister was out of earshot. And what was the point, anyway? Gail never listened to her.

Mum always said they should meet up after school each day and catch the bus together. And they used to. They used to chat about their school day, as the bus weaved its way towards Bostagel. But their two-year age gap seemed to have grown bigger lately. Since Gail turned sixteen she hadn't wanted Ava hanging on like a dead leaf on a beautiful oak.

Ava made her way into Kathy's Café, the aroma of freshly cooked chips bombarding her senses. She couldn't afford food, so grabbed a drink from the fridge and paid for it.

From a window seat she people-watched. To her, Newquay

was just a nearby seaside town – to holidaymakers jostling on the pavement in their sun hats and beachwear, faces scorched from the sun, it was clearly magical.

She cracked open the can of cola and poured the fizzy liquid into a glass, her mind drifting back to Gail. She would start studying for her A-levels in September, and there was no doubting she would sail through them. She'd always been clever, and popular too. Mum's favourite.

'Is she your sister?' The Welsh male voice came from the table behind her. She glanced over her shoulder to see a boy of about sixteen. His light brown hair was parted in the middle, hanging like curtains about his pale face, as he played on his Game Boy.

'Who?' she asked, but she guessed he meant Gail. Had he watched them from the window?

He didn't look up from his screen, his thumbs moving fast over the controls. 'The girl who dumped you.'

'She didn't dump me.'

'If you say so.'

But the boy was right, Gail had dumped her – she was always dumping her. Ava turned back to the window and sipped her drink, aware of the boy's chair scraping across the floor. He was suddenly beside her, tall and thin, shoving the Game Boy into his jacket pocket. 'She's beautiful, your sister,' he said, thumping down on the chair next to her. 'My mate fancies her.'

'Everyone does.'

'Are you jealous?'

Ava shook her head, avoiding eye contact.

'You're pretty too, you know. She just makes more effort. How old are you?'

'Fourteen.'

'I bet you're sick of living in her shadow.'

She felt herself flush. She always did when boys talked to her. 'That's complete bollocks.' She gulped back the rest of her drink, slammed the glass on the table, and rose to her feet. 'You don't even know me. Move.' She thumped his arm. 'I need to catch my bus.' She squeezed past him and grabbed her rucksack.

'What's your name?' he said.

She tugged at the hem of her school skirt, as she flung open the café door, the heat of the day warming her face. 'None of your business,' she said.

'Well, I'm Maxen. And if you want my advice, don't let your sister ruin your life,' he called after her. 'Don't give her that power. Once she has it, you'll never escape.'

*

A bus drew up at the shelter and Ava jumped onto it. It was empty, apart from an old lady talking to a cat in a crate. 'We're nearly there, sweetie,' she was saying to the mewing feline, her voice too loud as if the cat was deaf. 'We'll soon be home.'

As the bus pulled away, Ava slid down in the seat. Perhaps Maxen was right. She needed to find herself – her own life – to move out from under her sister's shadow. Grow up and get as far away from Bostagel as she could.

She was the youngest of three children, and often felt like the runt of the litter. Never quite belonging. Wishing she'd been born into another family – a family who cared about each other and didn't spend most of their time arguing.

When she was ten, she'd dreamed of having a brand new mum who baked lemon drizzle cake, and a dad who made everyone laugh, and a golden retriever called Butler, that they walked every day. Ava's life was a long way from her fantasy. Her mum was cold and unreachable, and her father had taken off just after Ava was born. Gail told her once that it was her fault they no longer had their dad with them – that she was the reason their mum was miserable most of the time.

The bus rocked and jolted on its way, and she looked through the window at the sea spreading endlessly. A flock of oystercatchers had gathered on the rocks and beach, wading through the shallow waves, dipping orange beaks into the sand for food.

Unexpected rain speckled the window like tears, blurring the view. That wouldn't please the holidaymakers. Ava rested her head on the glass and closed her eyes, imagining the fun Gail and her friends would be having in the arcades, wishing she was there too.

Chapter 3

ROSE

Now

I get up from the sofa and straighten the cushions and tartan throw. Willow's call has unsettled me, and as I go over her words, trying to make sense of them, a shiver runs through my body.

I pad towards the window and pull back the curtains to let the sun fill the room once more. The small square of grass looks patchy. It hasn't rained for some time and the plants are wilting. Our house is a new-build, and like most new-builds we haven't got much garden to worry about. I feel guilty that I've neglected such a small area, but I never seem to have the time.

In fact, I'd been looking forward to the days stretched ahead of me once school closed for the summer. I'm fully aware it won't be a complete break, as there are still lots of things to do that involve the school, but I'd seen it as time out; time to breathe and make up my mind if my school headship is exactly what I want from life.

I'd hoped for plenty of time to work on the garden too, time to paint the staircase, and buy curtains for Becky's room. I'd hoped to go swimming, read more, and get in touch with old friends. But now my head is consumed with thoughts of going to Cornwall. A strange little laugh escapes me at the absurdity of driving all that way to see Willow, when she should come straight home.

Sudden memories of Willow storming out of Darlington House a month ago, without looking back, fill my head. The raised voices that day. Willow's pale face as she opened the study door and ran out in tears, leaving Eleanor alone, her shoulders rising and falling in sobs.

Later, I tried talking to Eleanor, to Dad too, but they said together, as though they'd rehearsed it, that it was something and nothing. *You know Willow*.

I pick up my mobile, and head into the hallway where I pull on my black, low-heeled shoes I'd worn all day at the school and grab my keys.

'I'm heading out, Becky,' I call up the stairs, trying to make myself heard above my daughter's music. 'Back soon.'

She appears on the landing in black straight-leg jeans and a baggy, grey T-shirt. Her tightly curled black hair hangs to her shoulders. In some ways she reminds me of myself at almost fifteen. Thin and tall, a little awkward in her own skin. But she hasn't inherited my youthful acne, or my lank, lifeless hair that still needs far too much product to make it even remotely bouncy. Her smooth, unblemished dark complexion and hair are like her father's, her eyes as brown and appealing as his. There's no doubt she's inherited my ex-husband's looks.

'Where are you going?' she says, nibbling her nails. She does that when she's bored or anxious or just trying to annoy me.

I fiddle with my keys. I want to tell her about Willow later, when my partner Aaron gets home. I intend to call a family meeting, like the day the hamster looked to be on his last legs, or when I got the headship at Mandalay Primary. There will be a small window before Aaron flies out again, and that's when I'm aiming for.

'I'm popping over to see Grandpa and Eleanor. I thought we might grab a takeaway later, when Aaron gets home.'

'Chinese?' she says with a smile, the glint of her braces telling me she will soon have perfectly shaped teeth.

'If you like.' I turn and reach for the door latch, but her heavy footfalls on the stairs behind me tell me I'm going to have company.

'Wait up!' she calls. 'I'm coming with you.' I sigh as she thumps down on her bottom at the foot of the stairs and pulls her Doc Martens over mismatched socks. I have to turn away. Socks that don't match unnerve me. 'I haven't seen Grandpa and Eleanor for ages,' she goes on, getting to her feet with the aid of the banister.

She opens the door and I follow her onto the cobbled drive, slipping on my sunglasses.

We're halfway to Darlington House when I say, 'Can you look up from your phone for a second, sweetheart?' I glance at her out of the corner of my eye.

'Let me answer Tamsyn first, Mum,' she says. She's slumped in the passenger seat, thumbs racing over the screen. 'George dumped her, and she's thinking of eating her bodyweight in salted caramel ice cream.' She looks up at me, and with a serious tone says, 'I can't let her do it. I don't want her to get as fat as me.'

'Why would you even say that? You're perfect, darling.' She is. Too thin if anything, and I worry about how she sees herself. Worry that Willow has been her role model for too long.

Moments later she drops her phone into her lap. 'So, what's up, Mother?'

'It's just, well … Willow called,' I say, deciding to come straight to the point.

'Oh my God. Is she OK?'

'I think so, but—'

'That's amazing,' she cuts in. 'Is she coming home? Can we see her? Oh, please say we can see her.' She presses her palms together as though praying. She adores Willow. 'Please.'

I note how accepting she is. No questions about why Willow hasn't been in touch for a month. But then she's like the rest of us. We all know Willow.

'She's staying in Cornwall. I'm going down to see her at the weekend.'

'O-M-G! That's the best news ever. I can't wait to see her. It will make the time go quicker until America.'

I still have doubts about her going to the US alone in a few weeks' time. Her dad is directing a film out there and has invited her over. At first my motherly instincts kicked in. I wanted her to stay at home where she's safe, and I know Aaron has doubts too. But then he can be a bit overprotective at times. Eventually I agreed she could go, knowing how much she adores her dad. And he's a good man. He'll take care of her.

'The thing is, Becky,' I say as we make our way down the motorway, 'I thought I'd go and see Willow alone. Maybe you could stay with Grandpa and Eleanor.'

'What? Why?' She folds her arms across her chest, and her glare burns my cheek.

'Because it will be easier, that's all.'

'How? How will it be easier? I can't believe you would just dump me.'

'I'm not dumping you.' I glance at her, but she's flicked her gaze to the front window, her face set in a scowl.

'Then let me come,' she says. 'Or give me one good reason why not.'

I can't. My head spins as I indicate and turn left.

'*Stop!*' Becky yells, and I slam my foot on the brake, almost hitting the car in front.

'Jeez, Mother, it looks as if you pretty much need me to come to keep an eye on you.'

I'm losing the battle. And the truth is I want to spend time with her. 'OK,' I say.

'OK?'

'You can come.'

'Fab!'

'Hang on though, there's something you need to know first.' I think out my next words carefully. 'The thing is, Willow sounded worried about something. I don't know how she'll be when we get there.'

Her phone pings, and she picks it up, and reads the screen. 'For God's sake, has Tamsyn any idea how many calories there are in three tubs of ice cream?'

I've lost her once more.

Chapter 4

AVA

1998

It had become a habit, following Gail and her friends to the arcade. Watching them flirt with boys – laugh – have fun. Although Ava only ever stayed long enough for the thump of the music to get under her skin, for the games machines – clunking and whizzing and flashing coloured lights – to heighten her senses.

Despite Maxen's advice, she was still hiding – too self-conscious, her self-esteem low, getting her thrills from watching Gail enjoy life. Wishing she was like her.

It was September, and the holiday season had dialled down a notch ready for winter – the arcade seemed empty compared to previous months, and there weren't so many places to hide. Gail had left school after her final exams in May, but, so far, she'd made no attempt to get a job. 'She worked so hard on her exams,' Mum had said. 'She needs some time out.'

Ava had left school too, with no qualifications. 'You need to get a job, Ava,' Mum had said. 'Pay your way.'

Today she watched from behind a slot machine, 'Candle in the Wind' playing loud through the speakers as she sipped cola from a plastic cup. Suddenly Gail looked in her direction and she stepped backwards, bashing into someone. She spun round to see a handsome lad of around eighteen, with cold blue eyes and tousled dark hair.

'Christ!' he said, brushing cola from his black leather jacket. He had a confident air about him, his jaw set tight. 'Watch where you're fucking going next time! Idiot!'

'Sorry,' she said, as he pushed past her, almost knocking her over as he headed towards her sister.

'Hey, beautiful,' he said as he flung an arm around Gail's shoulders, and she planted a kiss on his cheek.

'His name's Rory Thompson.' It was Maxen, appearing beside her. She'd seen him about, but he hadn't spoken to her since that day in the café two years ago. 'He's going out with your sister,' he said. 'Did you know?'

Ava shook her head. Gail hadn't mentioned him, but then she never told her anything anymore.

Maxen's eyes were fixed on the couple, who were now kissing as though they were in a blockbuster movie. 'He gets his looks from his Italian mother,' he said. 'He's rich too, just inherited three international IT companies and several properties from his father who kicked it a couple of months back.'

She stared up at Maxen – at the splattering of acne across his pale cheeks, the way he was huddled into his khaki jacket, various badges pinned to the pockets.

'And now he's going out with your sister,' he said.

She clenched her fists. Why did everything good happen to Gail?

'Why are you telling me all this?' she said. But she didn't wait for an answer – she turned and rushed from the arcade and out into the dull grey day.

She hurried along Cliff Road, eventually turning a corner

towards the sea, and shuffled a packet of cigarettes from her denim jacket pocket.

The cliff edge was deserted, apart from a teenager with his back to her looking out to sea, his hands in black trouser pockets. She dropped down on a bench and stared at him as she lit a cigarette. He turned as though sensing her there. She vaguely recognised him from school – although he hadn't been in any of her classes. He looked somehow wrong in a creased white shirt that had clearly been taken straight from the packet, and a black tie.

'Hey,' he said, raking his fingers through white-blonde hair. 'Couldn't spare one of those, could you?'

She threw him the packet, and he took one and threw it back. 'Got a light?' he said, approaching. She handed him her lighter as he sat down beside her. He smelt of cheap aftershave.

He dragged on the cigarette and blew smoke circles upwards. 'My mum died,' he said after some moments. 'I've just been to her funeral. Carried the coffin. Life's shit, don't you think?'

'I'm so sorry,' was all she could think to say.

'Me too.' He sniffed, looking up and into her eyes. 'You look a bit like one of those china dolls,' he said. 'My mum used to have one. It freaked the life out of me when I was little.'

'Oh …' She touched her face.

He laughed. 'You're all right. I didn't mean you're freaky or nothing. Just pale and fragile, and your hair's all curly and that.' He smiled. 'Do I know you?'

She shrugged. 'I think we went to the same school.'

'Yeah, that's it. And you live in Bostagel, don't you?'

She nodded. 'Ocean View Cottage.'

'Yeah, I thought I'd seen you about. I live in Cranberry Close.' Another sniff.

'How did your mum die? If you don't mind me asking.'

'Fucking cancer,' he said. 'She'd been ill for ages. We all knew it was terminal, but it was still a shock, you know.'

She met his blue, watery eyes. Her family was useless, but at least they were alive. 'I'm so sorry.'

'Cheers for that.' He turned from her gaze. Kicked a stone. 'Dad's taken it bad. She was his rock – mine too.'

'I'm so sorry,' she said again. She felt an urge to lean over and hug him, but beat it down.

They sat for a while, looking out. The sea and sky were the same shade of grey. It was impossible to tell where one ended and the other began. Boats bobbed on the waves and a feeling of peace washed over Ava, and her stomach twisted as she looked at the lad, and quickly looked away again. She liked him.

Nearby seagulls wailed, breaking the quiet.

'What's your name?' he said, and she turned back to see his eyes were fixed on her.

'Ava.'

'Nice – suits you. I'm Justin.' He rose. 'Well, Ava, I'd better get back to the wake. Dad's been necking the spirits, so I need to keep an eye on him. I reckon he's full of grief and guilt and shit.' He threw the cigarette to the ground and pummelled it with his trainer. 'Maybe I'll see you in the village sometime.'

'I hope so,' she said, as he walked away, hands deep in his pockets, shoulders hunched, not looking back.

Chapter 5

AVA

1999

Ava stared at the ceiling, eyes wide. She hadn't slept for two nights. Not since she bought the pregnancy test on Thursday. Not since it told her she was having Justin's baby.

It had been a weak moment – that night they went back to Cranberry Close when Justin's dad was out. She hadn't meant for things to go so far.

'She's seeing Justin Havers, Mum.' It was Gail's voice – her tone high-pitched, carrying up the stairs. Ava sat up. She'd kept her relationship with Justin from her mum for almost four months, knowing she would disapprove of him. Think he wasn't good enough. How the hell had Gail found out?

'Ian Havers' son?' Jeannette cried.

'Aha. That's the one. Talk about scraping the barrel.'

'Oh my God, no.' Jeannette's voice was high and tense. 'She can't go out with him. For goodness' sake, that girl will be the death of me. Whatever is she thinking?'

Ava dived from her bed, and raced down the stairs in her

pyjamas to where Jeannette and Gail sat in the lounge drinking coffee. They looked up.

'I love him,' Ava blurted from the doorway.

'You have no idea what love is, Ava. You're only seventeen,' her mother cried, slamming down her mug. 'And Ian Havers' son of all people – sometimes I think you go out of your way to upset me.' She sniffed, pulled a tissue from her sleeve, and dabbed her nose.

Ava stepped into the room and sat down on the chair, glaring at her mum and sister. She took a deep breath and blurted, 'I'm pregnant.'

Jeannette gasped and covered her mouth with her hands.

'Jesus, Ava,' Gail said. 'Just when I thought you couldn't stoop any lower.'

'You failed all your exams, you smoke, you drink …' Jeannette released the slide clipping her fair hair back, as though it might relieve her tension. 'And now you're pregnant,' she continued. 'You'll have an abortion. There's no doubt about that. I'll book you in privately. And don't for goodness' sake tell anyone.'

'No!' Ava yelled.

'No?'

'I'm keeping the baby. I know when I tell Justin he'll be pleased, and we can move in together.'

'Ava, for Christ's sake stop being so naïve,' Gail said. 'He's seventeen. And not only that, he's a total loser. I saw him with one of the Bristow brothers the other day, and they're a bad lot – into drugs and joyriding and—'

'You're lying,' Ava cried.

'No, Ava, I'm not lying. And a baby will ruin your life. Think of your future, you must have an abortion.' She sounded almost kind. 'Rory could get you a little job in admin where I work.' She leaned forward and placed her hand on Ava's. 'Let me talk to him.'

'No!' Ava snatched her hand away. 'I'm going to be a mum,

and I'll live with Justin. He's not into drugs. He's going to be a singer, and we'll be rich one day.'

'A singer?' Jeannette laughed, a hard, fake laugh.

'He's got a great voice, Mum.' He had. He'd even written a song for her.

Jeannette rubbed her face and with a deep sigh said, 'You need to see a doctor, Ava. He could have given you something awful.'

'Like a baby,' Gail muttered.

Ava shook her head. 'I'm his first, Mum.'

'Oh for God's sake, wake up, Ava,' Gail snapped. 'Please.'

Ava rose. 'I'm keeping this baby,' she said, holding her stomach, a feeling of nausea swirling. 'Whether you like it or not.' And with that, she turned and left the room, leaving Gail to comfort their mother who burst into tears.

Chapter 6

ROSE

Now

My phone rings as we pull onto the drive outside Darlington House. It's Aaron.

'Go ring the bell, sweetheart,' I say to Becky, and she clambers from the passenger seat and hurtles towards the front door. I answer the call.

'Just landed,' Aaron says, as though he is a passenger on a flight, rather than the pilot. I admit it's what hooked me in when I met him a year ago. Although I'm not sure if, at the time, I equated a pilot's uniform with being alone so often. But when he is home he's the best partner there is, so I mustn't complain.

'That's great,' I say. 'I thought we might have a takeaway tonight. I've picked up wine.'

'Sounds good. I should be home in a couple of hours.'

I will only see him for two days before he takes off again. I don't like it, but I guess I'm getting used to it. I love him and the times we spend together mean everything. And there's always the bonus that absence is a great aphrodisiac.

'I'm at my dad's at the moment,' I say into the phone. 'But I need to tell you something when I see you.'

'What?' He sounds alarmed. 'You can't leave me hanging. Nothing's wrong, is it? Is Becky OK?'

'She's fine. Nothing's wrong. It's just that ... well, Willow called.'

'Willow? Is she OK?' He's met Willow several times, and they seem to get on well, although he does find her a bit flaky, and frankly I'm not surprised.

'Yes. Yes, I think so. I'll tell you everything when you get home.'

'Did she say why she hasn't been in contact?'

'Of course.' I don't want to get into a conversation about it right now. 'She's staying in Cornwall, apparently. I'm going down there when school breaks up.'

'What's she doing in Cornwall?'

'It's a long story, Aaron.' I bite down on my bottom lip. 'Listen, can we talk at home? I'm at my dad's,' I repeat.

'OK, yes, I'll see you soon,' he says.

He rings off, and I drop my phone into my bag.

As I climb from the car and stride towards Darlington House, I notice Eleanor's jeep isn't on the drive. Dad will be alone. The house is too big for two people, but Eleanor refuses to sell up and move somewhere smaller – she says her memories are here. She told me once she still hears Willow's childhood laughter echoing around the walls.

Becky has left the front door ajar, and I step inside out of the bright day, and into the dimly lit hallway that feels cold, whatever the weather.

'Hi,' I call out, placing my bag on the antique cabinet by the door.

'In here, Mum,' Becky calls back, and I make my way into the lounge, where three sofas – that have been there since we moved in and are now a little worn – hug an open fireplace that hasn't been lit since last winter. Sun pours in through the huge bay window, and I blink, my eyes adjusting to the sudden light. Becky

25

and Dad sit in the middle of one of the sofas, her head on his shoulder.

He peers at me over his glasses, 'Rose, darling. It's lovely to see you. How's the headship going?' He's so proud – part of the reason I accepted it. 'I was telling the boys at the Fox and Hound how well you're doing.'

'Fine,' I say, looking about me. It isn't strictly true –I'm not sure I'm cut out to manage a school. 'Where's Eleanor?'

'Shopping with the girls,' he says, with a small laugh. 'They call themselves "the girls" and yet they're almost sixty.'

I want to say I know. That he tells me that every time I visit. I bend and kiss his silver-grey hair, his familiar aftershave tickling my nostrils, making me smile. 'Shall I make some tea?'

'Not for me, dear,' he says, and Becky shakes her head, giving me a look as if to say *tell him, tell him Willow called.*

'It's such good news,' Dad says once I've told him. His irises look far too blue, as though he might cry, showing however many times Willow takes off, it still worries him. He loves Willow as though she is his own daughter.

Becky takes her grandpa's hand in hers and squeezes. 'We're going to see her at the weekend. We'll bring her back. Promise.' She fumbles in her pocket for a tissue and dabs his cheeks. 'Everything is going to be just fine, Grandpa. You'll see.'

*

Aaron's Mercedes is on the drive when we get home, and a fizz of excitement runs through me.

'Call me when the Chinese is here,' Becky says once we're inside and she's unlacing her Doc Martens and tugging them free. She jumps to her feet and bobs her head around the lounge door. 'Hey, Aaron,' she calls, raising her hand in a wave.

'Hey, Becky,' he says, waving back.

'I'll have beef and broccoli with boiled rice.' She's done her

26

research online for the healthiest Chinese takeaway options, and always has the same thing.

She drops her boots and heads up the stairs. I bend to pick them up and stand them neatly on the shoe shelf.

I enter the lounge. Aaron is watching *The One Show*. He looks up, points the remote control at the TV, and presses pause.

'Hey, beautiful,' he says, rising and heading towards me, taking me into his arms. He's showered – smells of Jimmy Choo. He's worn it ever since I bought him a bottle at Christmas.

'It's so good to see you,' I say, nuzzling into his shoulder, breathing him in. I suppose the only consolation of this difficult way of life is we never seem to get bored with each other. My heart still races when I see him, and he says his does too. I'm guessing if we'd seen each other every second of the last year, things might be different – more static, normal. But I guess I'll never know. He suggested once that he could change careers, said he hated that we were apart so often, but I knew how much he loved his job – still does. It wouldn't have been fair to ask him to throw it in for me.

'It's so good to see you too,' he says, placing a kiss on my forehead, and releasing me. He sits back down, patting the seat next to him.

I grab my laptop, and as I lean back, opening it up, his arm falls loosely around my shoulders, and I feel safe. 'I'd better order the Chinese,' I say with a smile.

'Pork in black bean sauce for me, please' he says, pointing the remote control at the TV again and unfreezing Matt Baker, his smile dimpling his cheek as he glances at the menu with me.

An email notification appears in the corner of my laptop screen. I click on it. It's from Willow, telling me her address in Cornwall – and a brief message:

I can't wait to see you, Rose. I need you so much, Willow.
X

Chapter 7

AVA

2001

Ava screwed up her face and wiggled so the bridesmaid dress rustled. It was floor-length, yellow satin, like her daughter's – although Willow looked like child-sized sunshine, and Ava most definitely did not.

But in seven weeks Gail was getting married to Rory, and Ava would be their bridesmaid.

'I look stupid, Mum,' Ava said, strutting around the lounge, bashing her leg on the coffee table, as her mum looked on. 'This headdress would look better on our front door this Christmas.'

'You look fine, Ava. Now stop with your whinging,' Jeannette said, pinning her with a stare.

Ava pulled the fake floral headdress over her eyes. 'Ah, I can't see.' She held out her arms like a zombie and took pigeon steps across the room. 'I reckon Gail pinched this thing off a gravestone.'

'Enough. Stop that stupid talk.' Her mum reached up and straightened her daughter's headdress. 'Your sister wants you and

Willow to look beautiful. Why would she go out of her way to make you look stupid on her wedding day?' She took short, sharp strides away from Ava, retreating into the kitchen.

'Because she hates me, that's why.' Ava had no doubt of that. 'She's only having me as her bridesmaid because you told her she had to, and Rory wants Willow as their flower girl.'

Her mother reappeared in the lounge, and folding her arms across her slim body, said, 'She doesn't hate you, Ava. She despairs of you, as we all do. There's a difference. And this is Gail's big day, not yours. So can you please stop thinking about yourself for once, and be happy for her?'

The words stung. Ava rarely thought about herself.

Ava followed her mum as she headed back into the small, impeccable kitchen. 'I'm pleased for Gail, really I am,' she said. It wasn't true. She wasn't pleased for her sister. The only plus she could see was that Gail had finally moved out of the cottage. It had taken a while for the move to happen, as Rory had had problems getting rid of his lodger, but now her sister had moved into Rory's Edwardian detached in Newquay.

Gail and Ava had always shared the bigger room – neither wanting to sleep in their brother Peter's old room when he left for Australia when he was eighteen. They both claimed it smelt funny. When Willow was born, the young women had fought over the limited space. Gail had never had any patience with Willow – said she wasn't cut out to be an auntie and didn't want kids herself. But now Gail had gone, and it was bliss for Willow and Ava to have the room to themselves.

'Do you like Rory, Mum?' Ava asked, taking two mugs from the cupboard. She wasn't sure what she felt about her soon to be brother-in-law. He had the looks, the charm, but she'd seen him grip Gail's arm a little too tightly on occasions, and the aggressive way he'd treated her in the arcade two years back when she'd bumped into him, still stayed in her mind. 'You're sure Gail's making the right decision marrying him?

'For Christ's sake, stop, Ava.' Her mum raised her hand. 'Rory is handsome, intelligent, witty, well-off—'

'Too good to be true?'

'He'll make your sister happy.' She turned and shoved the kettle under the streaming tap. 'Sometimes I think you're jealous of Gail.'

'Maybe I am,' Ava whispered, out of her mother's earshot. Gail was marrying a rich, handsome man, while Ava struggled to hold on to Willow's father. Some days she felt as though she might lose her mind stuck in this isolated part of Cornwall, with no means of escape.

But she had her beautiful daughter. Willow made things right.

And while she didn't have many friends, she drew comfort from being close to the sea. From her bedroom window she would watch the tides rise and fall, and could be on the beach within moments; smell the salty air, feel sand between her toes. It kept her sane. Gave her hope. Hope that one day everything would be different. One day she would give her daughter a perfect life – the life she'd never had.

She looked down at the yellow dress once more. 'Right,' she said, putting the mug back in the cupboard, deciding she didn't want a hot drink. 'I'm getting out of this.'

She climbed the stairs, unzipping the dress as she went, and once in her room, she pushed it from her shoulders, letting it drop in a heap around her ankles. She stepped from it, and grabbed her robe, and pulled it on over her bra and pants, and flopped onto her bed wishing she was a million miles from away.

'I'm heading out, Ava,' her mum called up the stairs later. 'Do you need anything from the shop?'

'No, thanks,' she called back.

The door slammed shut, and a cry came from the bed in the corner of the room. Willow was stirring.

As Ava padded over to her, she glanced out of the window to see her mum, wrapped in her winter coat, hurrying down the uneven road towards the local shop – her head down. She always avoided eye contact with dog walkers, neighbours, holidaymakers, and now she was quickening her step as she passed a lad with a yellow baseball cap pulled low. He stopped, turned, and watched her mum dash onwards until she was out of sight. Suddenly his gaze flicked up to the window where Ava stood. Before she could register his face, she moved out of sight with a jolt. When she looked again, he'd gone.

Willow had drifted back to sleep, lids closed over blue eyes, her thumb in her mouth. Ava stroked a strand of hair from her daughter's face. 'You deserve so much more, darling girl,' she whispered. 'One day your life will be perfect, you'll see.'

Chapter 8

YOU

Always surrounded by friends – so popular – but then you had a charm, didn't you? A charisma that drew people in, so much so you could make them do almost anything.

When I was young I imagined, as I watched you from a distance, what it would be like to be part of your network of friends. What did you all do when you went into the woods at night?

Mystery and darkness shrouded you and I suppose that made you all the more intriguing, fascinating – made me want to be a part of your world even more.

You didn't see me following you everywhere. See me watching you.

I thought about you constantly – wished for the day when you would wrap your arm around my shoulders, pull me close, and kiss me.

But you never did. Well, not at first anyway.

I was so young when I made it my mission to infiltrate your world. You were so beautiful to me – I had to be close to you. But it was later – much later in fact – when you finally noticed me. You glanced over and smiled, and I don't mind admitting, my stomach flipped. You had such a winning smile – those dimples making you look so innocent. No one could have imagined what was beneath that smile – not even me. Not back then.

Chapter 9

ROSE

Now

I stand in the corner of the staffroom gripping the stem of my wine glass, the sun beaming through the small Georgian windows behind me, bringing on the makings of a migraine. I'm exhausted. It's been a difficult first year at Mandalay Primary School. Some days I feel like running back to my old school and begging them to take me back. I loved being a teacher. I hate being a head.

And secret-gift swapping with staff is far from my idea of fun. In fact, as I said to Aaron when he picked me up for lunch earlier, the whole thing is quite bizarre.

'It's like a Secret Santa, but in the summer,' the school secretary told me a few weeks back, coming into my office brandishing a too-bright smile. She thrust a tartan cap full of pieces of paper towards me. 'We've been doing it for years,' she went on. 'It was John's idea.' It was an obvious nod to the previous head who I knew she preferred. 'We normally give gifts around the ten-pound mark.'

It was one of those many moments when I wanted to say, 'I

34

think some of these silly traditions need changing.' But instead I pulled out a name and smiled politely.

I'd studied to be a teacher when Becky was young, after Seb left. I was living with Dad and Eleanor at the time, and I know, without their support, I wouldn't be where I am. I guess that's why I'm here, in this role, continually trying to prove their faith in me was worth it.

A shriek of laughter brings me out of my daydream, and I stare at the gift collection box in the middle of the room. It has stood outside my office for the last month, with staff dropping parcels off, and children and parents nosing inside. Even Becky, when she met me last week after work, asked who the gifts were for. 'Sounds cool,' she said when I explained. But then at fourteen, it probably did.

I sip red wine and wince. Not one for drinking in the day, I put the glass down, deciding not to touch any more. I'll be driving soon, so shouldn't anyway, and I know it won't help a migraine.

Several members of staff are red-cheeked already, enjoying the fact the children have gone home to their families for six weeks, and chatting and laughing together after a long term.

I'm struggling to fit in here, and I try telling myself that being a headteacher isn't about making friends. I must accept I will be slightly removed from the staff – on the outside looking in.

Ralph Martin, a trainee teacher who looks young enough to be brought to school by his mum, stands up and claps his hands. My heart sinks as the chatter fades. I hate surprises. They make me feel out of control.

'It's pressie time,' he says, sounding upbeat, clearly enjoying the excitement. 'Do you want to do the honours, Rose?'

'No!' The word shoots from my mouth sharper than intended, and everyone looks at me. 'You go for it, Ralph,' I say, trying to smooth the edges from my words.

The presents are distributed quickly. Wrappings are ripped off, flying everywhere, and the room fills with laughter and overexcited 'oohs'. The gifts range from saucy pink, furry handcuffs to sensible silk scarves.

The teaching assistant who receives my gift doesn't look too thrilled by a book of poetry, but I didn't know what to get a man I barely know. And he is attached to literacy after all.

'Rose,' Ralph says. 'This one's for you.'

I take it with a fake smile, and pull free the gold wrapping paper, like I'm ripping off a plaster. Inside is a set of body oils. 'Thank you,' I say, flicking my eyes around the room, wondering who sent me such a thoughtful gift.

'Just one left,' Ralph says, lifting out another parcel. I see the tag is torn. 'Another one for you, Rose,' he says, arching his eyebrow.

'That can't be right, can it?' I look at everyone in turn. 'Wasn't it one for each of us?' I take it from him, feeling too warm in my short-sleeved polo neck top. The room's too noisy. Too crowded.

In my hand is a green box, tied with a yellow silk ribbon. I feel a slight dizziness, a need for air. 'Betsy,' I whisper.

'Sorry?' Ralph says.

'Listen, I'm just going outside for a moment,' I say, turning to head for the door, unsure what's wrong with me. Is it the stress of the long term? The worry I'm not cut out for a leadership role? Thoughts of Willow?

'Aren't you going to open it first?' someone says, and an echo of 'Go on,' follows.

'OK,' I say. My fingers tremble as I run them over the lid. I'm being ridiculous.

Ralph takes the box from me. 'Shall I open it for you?'

'OK,' I say. I have no choice. Everyone's eyes are on me.

'Chocolate biscuits,' he says, lifting the lid, and handing it back to me. 'They look delicious.'

I let out a breath I didn't know I was holding. 'Biscuits,' I whisper, placing the box on the table next to my barely touched glass of wine. 'Just biscuits.' *But who sent them? I've already received my gift.*

I go to leave, and as I head for the door I glance over my shoulder just once. Why did I react so stupidly? Am I on high alert? Fight or flight mode because I'm in a situation I'd rather not be in?

'Help yourselves, everyone,' I say, raising my hand and fluttering my fingers. 'And enjoy the holidays.'

A chorus of goodbyes follow me from the staffroom as I dash down the corridor, the walls stripped of the children's colourful paintings, making the school feel a little sad.

I fling open the door and breathe in fresh air, before heading for my car. Once inside, with the doors central-locked, I stare through the front window at the school, my mind drifting to the day we buried Betsy.

*

Willow had been five when she gripped my hand and looked up at me with sad eyes. The rain had poured down earlier, and the grass squelched under our feet as we walked down the garden, the moisture still in the air formed tiny bubbles on Willow's curls.

'Will Mummy look after Betsy when she gets to heaven?' she asked me.

I'd known her for two years now, and over that time she had mentioned her mummy being an angel a few times, but it was always put down to her over-active imagination. Willow would make up the most outlandish stories even then. 'My daddy is a bad man,' she told me once, and I'd wondered if she was talking about Eleanor's first husband – she certainly couldn't have meant my dad.

We'd put Betsy the guinea pig in a green box tied with a yellow ribbon, and now Dad was saying a few words, as Eleanor lowered the little coffin into the ground.

'We all loved Betsy,' he said. 'She lived a long and happy life with Willow caring for her so well.'

I swallowed down tears, as Eleanor sprinkled soil over the box, and Willow squeezed my hand. She looked up at me bewildered, and within moments released my hand and ran into the house. She cried in her room for hours.

I slip the key into the ignition and start the engine. I'm about to put the car into gear when a knock on the window startles me. It's Ralph dangling a torn gift tag close to the glass.

From Jasmine Year 3 x

I buzz down the window and stare at it for some moments, before taking it from him, and turning it over in my hands. It's the other half of the tag that was on the biscuits.

'It was in the bottom of the box,' he says. 'Jasmine must have put your end of term gift in there by mistake.' He pauses. 'Are you OK, Rose? You seem a little—'

'I'm fine,' I cut in, snapping to my senses and smiling. 'Just glad to be breaking up from school for a while, that's all. It's been a long term.'

'Yes. Yes, it has.' He scratches his head. 'It's just you seemed bothered by the biscuits.'

I shake my head, putting the tag down on the passenger seat. 'I'm fine,' I repeat. 'I've got a lot on my mind, that's all.'

'Of course, you're off to Cornwall tomorrow, aren't you? Have a wonderful time.' He raises his hand in a wave and steps backwards.

'Thanks. Enjoy the rest of the afternoon.' The site manager is locking up later than usual because I want to get home, and don't want to spoil the end of term fun.

'Thanks, Rose.' He takes another step away from the car, as I pull away.

Chapter 10

AVA

2001

Peter stood at the foot of the stairs, his holdall at his feet, looking at Ava through round-rimmed glasses. The siblings weren't close in age, and he'd taken off for Brisbane when he was eighteen, almost ten years ago. The void between them was that of strangers.

His dark, tangled hair rested on his shoulders, his colourful striped trousers were creased, the fur collar of his purple jacket matted. She felt sure he hadn't looked so dishevelled when he left home. In fact, the photos of him on the dresser in the lounge, that Mum had put out just before he arrived, showed a cute kid, and a good-looking teenager.

Peter lifted his holdall and climbed the stairs, knocking pictures as he went. He was almost at the top when he glanced over his shoulder. 'Grab my rucksack, will you, Ava, and bring it up?' he said, disappearing from view. She looked about her, spotting a tatty rucksack covered in sewn-on badges, by the front door. She picked it up and headed up the stairs.

Peter stood in the doorway of his old room, which was rammed with junk – his old guitar, a music centre, massive speakers. In fact, it was just as he'd left it: posters of wrestlers pinned to the wall, and dust-covered models of horror movie villains lining the shelves.

He threw his holdall on the bed and Ava dropped his rucksack to the floor.

'Ta,' he said, looking about him. 'It hasn't changed at all, has it?' he added, and she picked up his Aussie twang for the first time.

'Mum keeps the door shut, mostly,' she said, her eyes flicking over the dusty surfaces, vague memories of Peter spending most of his time alone here, floating in. There had been arguments too between her mum and her brother – lots of arguments.

He took off his jacket and threw it on the bed next to his holdall. He gave the room one last scan, and left. She followed, closing the door behind her.

'So tell me, little sis,' he said, lumbering down the stairs, knocking another picture with his shoulder. 'What have you been up to since I've been away? Gail told me you got pregnant. Bit careless of you. Never heard of condoms?'

She followed him into the lounge. 'Her name is Willow.'

'You what?' he said, dropping into the armchair.

'My daughter – your niece – her name is Willow. She's the best thing that's ever happened to me.'

'Whatever you say,' he said, tipping a cigarette from a box and lighting it. He dragged hard on it, and blew smoke towards her. 'Want a ciggie?' he said, offering the packet.

'I don't smoke anymore,' she said. She'd given up when she found out she was pregnant with Willow. 'And Mum doesn't allow smoking in the house. You should stand on the doorstep, or in the back garden.'

'Mum's not here though, is she?' He jokingly glanced under the chair. 'Take it easy, Ava, you're like a wound-up spring. It's just the one. I need it after that bloody long flight.'

'So what made you travel all this way for Gail's wedding?'

'Rory paid for the trip. Gail wants me to give her away. So I thought I'd make a long break of it. Nothing much keeping me in Australia.' He took another drag on his cigarette. 'Rory seems like a great bloke.'

'Yeah, I suppose.'

'You don't like him?'

She coiled her hair around her finger. Sometimes, in her darkest moments, she thought she might like him too much – hated that he could get inside her head like that. 'He's OK. Seems to make Gail happy.'

'You don't sound convinced.' He took another long drag on the cigarette, eyeing Ava. 'So, are you pleased to see me?'

'I barely remember you,' she said, her voice void of emotion. 'You pissed off when I was a kid.'

'Cheers for that,' he said with a sarcastic tone. 'I remember you. You were always bawling as a toddler.'

'I was not.'

'Yeah you were.' He closed his eyes. 'Christ, I'm knackered,' he said, his cigarette burning between his fingers. 'Bloody jet lag.'

'So what have you been up to in Australia?' she said, sitting down on the sofa.

His eyes sprung open. 'This and that.' He stubbed his cigarette out on one of Jeannette's ornamental dishes, and Ava cringed. 'I was married for a bit. Still am legally, I guess.'

'What? You never let us know.'

'It only lasted six months, Ava. I wanted kids. She wanted to wait a few years. That was that.'

'Did you love her?'

'Yeah. Still do. But we're on different pages. Couldn't make it work.'

'Maybe you should have waited for her to catch up. Maybe she needed to know the time was right to have kids.'

'You know nothing about it,' he said. 'You're just a kid yourself, forced to be a grown-up.'

41

'I'm nineteen, and I know marriages are give and take – any good Disney film tells you that much,' she smiled.

'Perhaps,' he answered her smile. 'I bet you're a good mum, aren't you, Ava?' His tone had softened, his bravado falling away. 'I remember you playing happy families with your dolls.'

'And do you remember Gail stabbing them all with a kitchen knife?' It had scarred Ava for months – perhaps longer. 'She was never maternal even then.'

'Yeah, I remember.' He shook his head. 'She was pretty feisty at times.'

'I can think of better words to describe her.' Ava looked down at the palms of her hands, remembering. 'I only wanted to play with her – be part of her world. But she rarely let me. Always blamed me for Dad leaving.' Tears burned behind her eyes. 'Anyway, enough about the past,' she said in a rush. 'How long are you staying?'

'I'm not sure I'm going back.'

'You're staying in Cornwall? Here? With us?' She couldn't hide the surprise in her voice.

'Yeah, for a bit anyway.'

'What do you do? For a job, I mean? My wages won't stretch to another person, Peter, and you know Mum hasn't worked since Willow was born.'

Jeannette had been in a high-powered position in forensics before Ava was born, but when their father left, she never returned to it. Instead she took a part-time job in a factory office, working alone most of the time – which she said she preferred – and rarely socialised out of work. When Willow was born she insisted it was Ava's turn to work – that she'd done her bit for *this* family. She would stay home and look after the baby. Ava had tried to argue, wanting desperately to be with Willow. But her mother was firm. 'You work, or you leave.'

'Well, I've been doing a bit of plumbing,' Peter said. 'A bloke over in Australia took me on as an apprentice. I'm pretty good, so once I get a bit of freelance work, it'll take the pressure off you a bit.' He broke off for a moment before saying, 'So you're going to be Gail's bridesmaid?'

'Mmm, only because Rory wants Willow to be their flower girl – apparently he loves kids. Not sure he's twigged Gail doesn't,' she laughed.

'So where is Willow?'

'Upstairs asleep … in fact, I'd better check on her.' She rose, studying her brother once more. As her eyes met his, another memory invaded. She could see herself huddled against the kitchen wall, gripping her knees, and Peter is yelling, his body shaking, his eyes bloodshot, face streaming with tears. 'I hate you. I hate this house. I'm leaving,' he spat. 'And I'm never coming back.'

Chapter 11

ROSE

Now

'Hi beautiful,' Aaron calls from the lounge as I lumber through the front door, and dump my briefcase, laptop, and the gift I received onto the table at the foot of the stairs. 'Bet you're glad that's over until September.'

I am, although I know I will be in and out of school working throughout the holiday. I take off my shoes, and slip my feet into my slippers – sighing with relief as I pad through to the kitchen.

Aaron appears from the lounge, and kisses my cheek before sitting down in front of his open laptop.

'You OK?' he says, smiling, and I think, as I always do, how handsome he is, never fully shaking the feeling he's out of my league.

We met a year ago. I was out with friends when he walked into the bar in his pilot's uniform. Confident, tall, dark-haired – perfect. Us girls were giddy on wine that night, and gave a collective swoon, followed by a flurry of laughter. He looked over and smiled. But it was me he focused on – staring for a long moment. And it was me he chatted to later, when I pushed my way to the bar to order more drinks.

'Fancy escaping?' he said, and I looked over at my friends who were now up on the dance floor, giggling – happy.

'I can't,' I said, although I desperately wanted to, despite not knowing him. 'It's a friend's hen night.'

'Another time?' he suggested.

We exchanged numbers. A week later he called. He was landing in Luton again.

'So, tell me about yourself,' he said, when we met up at a bar on Old Stevenage High Street, and sipped wine.

'Well, I'm a teacher. I have a thirteen-year-old daughter.' I took a gulp of wine. It seemed funny to sum up my identity with two short sentences. But that was my life. Still is. Although now I'm with a man I love – who loves me back.

I went on to tell him about Willow, and waffled on about how wonderful Eleanor was. How I loved my dad more than the world.

'I'm a tiny bit OCD,' I continued after another sip of wine, straightening some beermats into a neat row for effect, and he laughed. 'I'm kind to animals, and hate surprises.' It was nerves causing my inability to shut up. Nerves because somehow, in less than an hour, I knew I was falling for him.

'I'll keep that in mind when I want to send you surprise roses,' he said. 'Or want to whisk you off to Paris.'

I laughed. 'Well, there are exceptions to every rule.' I felt myself blushing, my stomach tipping. 'So tell me about you,' I said, and drained my glass.

'Well, I've travelled *a lot*,' he said. 'I've lived in Paris, Stockholm, Naples, Sydney, New York – the list goes on and on.' He paused and with a smile added, 'I'm presently living in Luton.'

I laughed at the contrast, as he got to his feet and took my glass. 'Let me get you another one of those,' he said. 'You'll need it when you hear more of my life story.'

Once back at the table, he told me how his father died when

he was young. That he was close with his mum. That he hadn't had any serious relationships *because of my job*. That his favourite film was, and still is *It's a Wonderful Life*. 'Oh, and I can't get enough of Frank Sinatra, and enjoy a bit of classical if the mood is right,' he concluded.

Now he closes down his laptop, rises and takes me in his arms.

'I'm glad I got to see you before you take off again,' I say, laying my head against his chest.

'Me too.' He lifts my chin and kisses me tenderly, before releasing his grip. 'This is so bloody hard,' he says, not for the first time.

'Well, I knew what I was getting into when I met you. I don't know what your excuse is.' I laugh, and he laughs too.

'I just wish … well … you know what I wish.'

I head for the kettle. 'Coffee?' I ask, picking it up and filling it, but when I glance over my shoulder he's shoving his laptop into his bag.

'I haven't got time,' he says. 'Sorry.'

My heart sinks. 'You're going already?' It's a daft question. I know his schedule. Planes don't fly themselves.

'Sorry,' he says, putting on his jacket. He's always sorry. 'I'll call you when I get there, like always,' he continues, approaching, and his lips brush against mine once more. 'I hope all goes well with Willow.'

He moves towards the door, grabbing the handle of his pull-along case.

'I'll give her your love, shall I?' I call after him.

'Yes, please do.' His tone is upbeat, as he looks back again before leaving. 'Bye, Becky,' he yells up the stairs to no answer.

As he closes the front door behind him, a sudden sadness creeps in. I head for the window and wave until his car disappears around the corner. Am I kidding myself that I'm used to this life?

Once I've made some coffee, I sit down at the kitchen table, and blow on the steaming mug before taking a sip. I need a caffeine jolt before I finish packing. I'm unsure how long we will stay with Willow, but I need to be prepared for a week, just in case. I look beyond the windowpane into the back garden, where washing blows in a light breeze.

I walk to the bottom of the stairs. It's silent above me, no music blaring out. Perhaps Becky is out. I grab my laptop and head back into the kitchen to print off a map of the area. I'll use my satnav to get to Cornwall, but I want to get an idea where Willow's staying.

I key the address into Google maps. It's about twenty miles north of Newquay, near the sea, and one of a handful of cottages just outside the village of Bostagel.

'Hey, Mum.' I jump, not hearing Becky's approach. She sits down, opens a bottle of black nail varnish, and begins painting her nails. It hardly seems worth it. Her nails are almost bitten away. 'I've been packing a few things,' she says. 'Will I need stuff for America too?'

'No, we'll be back before then. Take enough for about a week, and we'll see how things go. We may only stay overnight.' I close Google maps, and nod towards the garden. 'Thanks for hanging out the washing.'

'Wasn't me. Must have been Aaron.'

'Ah!'

'He'd done it before I got home, Mum. I would have hung it out.'

'I know, love.' I pat her arm, unsure if she would have. She's going through a lazy stage. But I know she could be a lot worse, so I'm rolling with it.

'Have you seen the parcel?' she says, screwing the lid back on the bottle of varnish, and blowing on her nails.

'What parcel?' I glance around the kitchen, which Aaron has cleaned until it sparkles. Sometimes I think he's the one with OCD.

Becky races into the lounge, and I follow. 'I opened it, sorry,' she says. 'It was addressed to Ms R Lawson. I thought it was the Blu-ray I ordered, but it isn't. It must be for you.' She picks up a cardboard box from the coffee table – the kind Blu-rays come in – and hands it to me. 'I glanced inside,' she says. 'It's photos.'

'Photos?'

'Mmm. Did you order any?'

I shake my head and, sitting down on the edge of the sofa, I look inside the box. She's right. It's photographs. I pull them out one at a time, and lay them in a row on the coffee table. There are four – all of men I've never seen before.

'Who are they?' Becky says, sitting down by my side. 'Do you know them?' She tucks her wayward curls behind her ears as she stares down at them.

I shake my head again. 'I've no idea.'

'So who sent them?' I hear a twang of apprehension in Becky's voice. 'Why have you been sent them, Mum?'

'I'm sure there's an explanation, sweetheart,' I say, although I don't know what it is. I turn the photos over one at a time, looking on the backs, hoping to find names.

There's a colour photograph of a boy of about seventeen, with white-blonde hair styled back from his face with gel, and blue eyes that seem a little too close together. I take in his baggy pale blue jeans, the way his hands are stuffed in the pockets of a black bomber jacket. I turn it over. 'It says Justin, 1999.'

'No surname?' Becky asks, and I shake my head. 'He looks a bit spaced out to me,' she goes on, taking the photo. 'A bit like Foggy Marsden in my class when he's high on coke.'

'Please tell me you're talking about the brown fizzy stuff.'

She rolls her eyes.

'You mean cocaine?' My heart, already thudding at the sight of the curious photographs, picks up speed.

'It's OK, Mother. I would never touch the stuff. My body is a temple.' She puts the photo down.

I pick up another photograph. This man looks like a throwback from the Sixties. He's nice looking enough, but too pale with dark shadows under eyes framed with Harry Potter style glasses. He's in his late twenties, I would think, with dishevelled hair to his shoulders. 'Peter Millar,' I read from the back of the photo.

The next picture is of a man with dark brown hair. He's good-looking, and kitted out in an expensive suit. I move the photo closer to my face, before flicking the photo over. 'Rory Thompson.'

The final picture isn't as clear as the others. It's taken from a distance, possibly without the man's knowledge. He's wearing a yellow baseball cap pulled low over what looks like brown hair, and a white hooded sweatshirt over black jeans. There's no name on the back.

'Why has someone sent you these?' Becky asks. 'Are you two-timing Aaron?' She tries for a laugh – she knows that would never happen. She's trying to make light of it. It isn't working.

I pick up the cardboard box once more, and search inside. Squashed at the bottom is a sealed envelope. I pull it free and rip it open. Inside is a piece of paper. I recognise Willow's handwriting instantly.

My eyes widen as Becky and I read her words.

Dear Rose,

I'm sending you these photos because one of these men killed my mother eighteen years ago. Her name was Ava Millar. I've been asking questions, and now someone is hanging about the cottage. They want me to leave, but I'm not giving up.

I'll explain everything when you arrive. But Rose – if anything happens to me, please keep digging until you find the truth.

Love, Willow X

My hands shake, and my heart bounces in my chest, as I try to push the letter back in the envelope. I'm in shock that Willow would send me a letter with such potency. That she would worry me that something could happen to her – tell me to take the baton if it did.

'Christ! What's going on, Mum?' Becky says. She's nibbling her nails, and her eyes look browner and wider than ever.

'I have no idea,' I say, the words of the letter jumping around my head, 'but the sooner I get to Cornwall the better.'

'This is so freaky.' Becky pulls her phone from her pocket. 'I need to tell Tamsyn.'

'No! Don't tell anyone.'

She rolls her eyes. 'OK, Mother.' A pause. 'But I just can't believe we're going to Cornwall to catch a killer.'

'You're not going at all,' I say. 'It's no place for you. You can stay with Grandpa and Eleanor.'

'But Mum!'

I raise my hand like I'm the traffic police. 'And I don't want to hear any more about it.'

Chapter 12

ROSE

Now

Becky thunders up the stairs and slams her bedroom door. With a deep sigh, I plonk down on the sofa and grab my laptop. Trying to block out her teenage tantrum, I open it up.

I key in 'murder' and 'Cornwall' into the search engine. There are almost 100,000 hits. As I scroll down the websites: unsolved murders, mysterious murders, frenzied killings, sadistic killings, my stomach turns over – and I pray nobody ever looks at my search history.

I spot an article about a rape and attempted murder of a young woman near Crantock in 2001, but Willow said her mother was murdered.

With determination, I do the same search and include *Ava Millar*.

Oh God, it's there in front of me within moments. Ava Millar. Murdered in 2001.

With shaking hands, I press the link. It takes me to a newspaper article:

The Cornwall Journal

December 22nd 2001

The body of nineteen-year-old Ava Millar was discovered early this morning by sixty-year-old Stephen Patterson while he was walking his dog along Beach Road, Bostagel.

Stephen told the Cornwall Journal that the attack on Ava was horrific, and finding her would live with him forever. It has now been confirmed that she was stabbed eight times.

Near the body a bride's dress, thought to belong to Ava's sister, Gail Thompson, was found folded neatly with what appeared to be a suicide note.

The last sightings of Ava and Gail were at Bostagel Village Hall yesterday evening. Police are keen to talk to anyone who may have seen Ava or Gail between ten o'clock and midnight last night to get in contact on the numbers below.

Ava leaves behind her two-year-old daughter Willow.

'Oh God,' I whisper, covering my face with my hands. Trying to comprehend the terrible tragedy. Imagining Willow doing the same online search. Reading this article. I can't bear to think of the effect it would have had on her. *Why didn't she turn to me sooner?*

I struggle to believe that Eleanor isn't Willow's real mother, that she kept it from us all. But as the idea settles, I wonder if there were signs I missed over the years. *Mummy is an angel.*

Later, as I stir fry chicken and vegetables, I try calling Willow, the phone wedged between my ear and shoulder as the food sizzles and spits in the wok, but her phone rings and rings, finally going to voicemail. I leave a short message. 'Call me, Willow. Please.'

'Becky, dinner's ready,' I call, as I serve.

She thumps down the stairs. 'I'm not hungry,' she says, disappearing into the lounge. So I sit alone, pushing food around my plate, unable to eat, my mind full of Willow.

Later, I grab my jacket from the rack, and call my dad. 'Hey! Is Eleanor home?' I say when he picks up.

'She's right beside me, love. Do you want to speak to her?'

'I thought I might come over, if that's OK. It's just I really need to chat with her in person.'

'Of course, is everything OK? You have that tell-tale wobble in your voice.'

'Do I?' He knows me so well. 'I'm fine, honestly. It's just … well I'll tell you when I get there.'

'OK, love. Drive carefully.'

'Yes, will do. Love you.'

I end the call and tug on my jacket, slipping the phone into my pocket. 'I won't be long,' I say to Becky, who is sprawled on the sofa, her long legs stretched out in front of her, a throw around her shoulders. She's watching a dark series on Netflix, and grunts, still sulking.

'Should you be watching that?' I say.

She keeps her eyes on the screen. 'How old do you actually think I am, Mum? No wait – I remember – you think I'm a baby.'

I glance at the TV and catch sight of a blood splattered wall, a decapitated body on a factory floor. I cringe and squeeze my eyes closed. 'I know how old you are, Becky.'

'Well stop treating me like a kid then.'

I duck out of the doorway, before we start bickering again, or I see another gruesome scene. I'm sure she shouldn't be watching disturbing programmes, but if I say anything she'll claim Aaron and I are overprotective. She doesn't seem to realise it's an awful world out there and we need to keep her safe.

*

I drive towards Old Welwyn, the sun setting behind the trees. Dusk has settled on the warm day by the time I pull onto the drive at Darlington House.

The grounds are still and quiet and, probably due to my mood, I feel uneasy. Dad and Eleanor have had a few offers over the years from film directors wanting to use the place as a setting for horror or supernatural movies, but they've always declined, insisting *this is a happy house.* And it is. Mostly.

I knock, and Eleanor answers the door within moments. She turned sixty at Christmas, but could easily pass as forty-five.

'Rose, darling,' she says, stepping forward and wrapping her arms around me – coating me with her expensive perfume. She's softly spoken, pronounces her vowels. 'Your father said you wanted to talk to me.'

Once she's released me, I follow her into the lounge. There's no sign of Dad, and as though sensing me searching for him, Eleanor says, 'He's popped to the Fox and Hound. Said he thought you wanted to see me. Decided to give us space. Drink?'

I shake my head. 'I'm driving.'

'Tea? Coffee?'

'I'm fine. Thanks.'

I spot two cases in the corner, and suddenly remember. 'Oh, I forgot you're going away.'

'Yes.' She aims the remote control at the TV, muting a wildlife programme. 'We're heading for Scotland in the morning. Your dad said we shouldn't go. That we should be here for Willow.' She stares deep into my eyes as though asking me what she should do.

'Dad needs a break,' I say. He's been suffering with angina, needs some time out to relax.

'Yes, and we're only going for the weekend. We could be back in a flash if needed.'

'You must go,' I insist, sitting down on one of the sofas opposite her. 'Dad's never been to Scotland. And let's be honest, if we stopped living every time Willow took off we'd never go anywhere.' She still looks a little unsure. 'She's got me, Eleanor. I'll keep you both updated.'

'Yes, of course you will. Thank you, Rose,' she says.

Photographs in silver frames of the family are everywhere. Expensive ornaments, mostly wild animals, are displayed in an oak cabinet. A bookshelf full of hardbacks – non-fiction mainly: biographies, books about birds, the rainforest – stretches across one of the walls.

'So what did you want to see me about?' she says. She cups her chin with her left hand, places her index finger on her cheek. 'Is everything OK?'

Deciding to come straight to the point, I say, 'Do you know why Willow took off like she did?'

She moves her hand from her cheek and examines her neat nails for some moments. 'Yes. Yes, I do.'

'Are you her biological mother, Eleanor?'

Tears appear on her lower lashes. 'You know about that?'

'That her real mother was murdered? Yes, I know.'

'I brought her up, Rose. She is my daughter.'

'You adopted her?'

'She's had a far better life with me – us – than she ever would have.' She sucks in a sigh, as a resting tear zigzags down her cheek. 'You may as well know how it came about.'

'Go on.' I lean back, feeling a tension in my shoulders, and the beginnings of a headache forming.

She presses the heels of her hands against her eyes and takes a deep breath. 'So you know Willow's mother was murdered.'

I nod, feeling fuzzy, as though I'm not in my own body. As though none of this is real.

'Her name was Ava Millar,' she goes on, and I don't stop her, even though I know that much. 'I knew the Millars from my time as a social worker. In the early Nineties Ava's older brother was a difficult boy, and her mother couldn't handle him. There was concern for the safety of Ava and her sister, Gail. They were eight and ten when I was assigned their case.

'Although things calmed down when the brother took off to Australia, I kept the family on my radar, and heard when Ava got pregnant at seventeen with Willow – the father was a useless article.

'When Ava was killed, I visited her mother. Jeannette Millar

55

was a mess. Anyone would be after losing two daughters. Gail killed herself you see, after supposedly killing Ava.'

'Supposedly?'

'I never quite believed she was capable. She was a self-centred girl but, in my opinion, not a killer. Although the evidence was there – the note – her wedding dress folded neatly – the knife.'

My mind drifts to the photographs I was sent. 'So if you don't think she killed her sister, who did?'

She shrugs. 'There were other theories. Ava's brother-in-law, Rory, was suspected for a short time, but he had a sound alibi.'

I think back to the photos. 'So Rory was Gail's husband?'

She nods. 'It happened on the night of their wedding.'

I cover my mouth. 'Oh God,' I say into my hand. 'That's awful.'

'It was, yes.' She shakes her head. 'A terrible tragedy.'

'And the other theories?'

'Well … there was Justin, Willow's father.'

'Her father?' My mind is racing. 'Is he still alive?'

'I've no idea. He was a useless man. I hope Willow never meets him if he is.' She takes a deep breath, and fiddles with her earring – a simple sleeper, she never wears fancy jewellery. 'There were so many stories kicking around that part of Cornwall at the time, Rose. But I doubt we'll ever know the truth, not after all these years.'

'So when Ava Millar died, you adopted Willow,' I say, bringing the conversation back to where we began.

'Not right away – as I said Jeannette Millar couldn't cope, and Willow's father was useless. Willow ended up in care. I fostered her, and being part of social services, pushed for a quick adoption.'

It doesn't seem possible we are talking about my stepsister – the young woman staying in Cornwall hunting for a killer.

I stare at Eleanor for some moments, before reaching over and taking her hand. 'So why tell Willow now?'

'I didn't. Someone contacted her on Facebook. Told her everything.'

'Who?'

'Willow didn't recognise the name, and there was no profile photo. They attached an article about the murder of her mother. Willow didn't believe it, of course. She came to me, hoping I would tell her it was an elaborate lie.' She lifts her head, dashes a tear from the corner of her eye, her voice crumbling. 'But I couldn't lie to her. I always said I would tell her one day, and it felt like the right time. But she took it so badly.'

I can't believe I don't know any of this, that Eleanor kept it a secret all these years. 'Did Dad know? Does Dad know?'

'He does now. He wishes I'd told him sooner.'

'Maybe you should have.'

A silence falls, as she rises to pour a brandy. 'Are you sure you won't have one?'

I shake my head and get up too. 'I should go,' I say.

'You do understand why I didn't tell Willow, don't you, Rose?' she says, 'Why I kept it quiet for so long. What good would have come of her knowing her mother was murdered?'

It seems vital to her that I understand. 'Of course,' I say, and turn to leave.

*

By the time I get home, I'm emotionally drained. What I'm not up for is a full-on argument with my daughter, who, going by her stance as she stands in the hallway, is ready for one.

'OK,' I say, before she can say anything.

'OK?'

'You can come,' I go on, as I tug off my shoes. What I don't say is her grandpa and Eleanor are going away, so I have no choice but to take her to Cornwall. That the last thing I want is her hanging about at home without supervision. 'But if things get tough, Becky, we're coming straight home.'

'Thanks, Mum,' she says, lunging at me, and hugging me. 'Yay!'

At that moment it hits me that I need her with me.

Chapter 13

ROSE

Now

My eyes are closed, but I've barely slept, my mind far too busy with thoughts of Willow – the nips of guilt that I should already be in Cornwall waking me on the hour, every hour; the heat of the night making it difficult to drop back off.

I reach across the bed. I know Aaron isn't here, but I imagine he wraps his hand tightly around mine, and wallow for a few moments thinking of him, before prising open my eyes and pulling myself to a sitting position.

My mouth is dry from the fan whirring on my bedside table. I click it off, knocking a photo of Aaron to the floor. I pick up my phone, and rub sleep from my eyes, trying to focus. It's 6 a.m.

I grab the glass of water that's been standing on my bedside table all night and swallow a gulp of the warm liquid before trying to call Willow. It goes straight to voicemail.

'Hey, Willow,' I say into the phone. 'Can't wait to see you later. Call me as soon as you can.' I end the call, trying not to worry. She's a late riser. That's all.

I need coffee, always my go-to first thing in the morning. And then we need to get going as early as possible.

But still I sit, my eyelids drooping.

The sun's fingers reach in through a gap in my flimsy pale-blue curtains, picking out Becky's life so far in photos that jostle for space on the far wall. My daughter is beautiful. I wish she could see what I see when she looks in the mirror.

My eyes fall on a study of Willow at sixteen, her naturally curly hair straightened to shiny sheets of gold – the face of an angel.

She was spotted by a scout and picked up by a big modelling agency at sixteen. In no time her beautiful face was bounced from magazine cover to magazine cover. Her tall, slim body shuttled from fashion show to fashion show.

At first she revelled in it. Enjoyed the attention. Her eyes sparkling as cameras flashed. Although thrilled for her, it was strange seeing her face everywhere – from billboard posters to national newspapers – not looking quite like the Willow we knew and loved. We were worried too. Worried about the effect it was having on her.

'I wish I looked like Willow,' Becky would say, just nine years old at the time.

Willow was almost seventeen when I took one of my monthly trips by train to London to meet up with her. She was renting a huge apartment with three other models, which looked out over the River Thames.

We met in an Italian restaurant in Leicester Square, and as we hugged hello, I felt how dangerously thin she was, noticed how sallow her cheeks were, how the sparkle had disappeared from her eyes that now rested on dark cushions of flesh.

'So how's it going?' I said, trying for upbeat as we studied the menus.

'Great,' she said, not looking up.

'You look tired, Willow.' I reached across the table, rested my hand on hers.

'I am,' she said. 'I barely sleep.'

'Have you tried lavender?'

She nodded. 'I've tried everything from hypnosis to sleeping tablets. Nothing works.'

'Then take a break? Come home for a bit.'

'I can't, Rose. They've got so much lined up for me over the next few months. Anyway, I love it. I love everything about it.' Her words didn't match her lifeless tone. 'Let's order, shall we?'

She barely ate that day, and it was a couple of weeks later she disappeared. It was all over the tabloids. We were in such a state.

She was found a week later in a motel in Scotland. A wreck. A mess. Addicted to prescription drugs. Suicidal. The whole experience had been too much.

I cried so hard when we got her back, holding her tightly, never wanting to let her go. Blaming myself that I hadn't done something when I'd seen her last. That despite spotting how dreadful she looked, I'd done nothing.

She gave up modelling and came home, and seemed her usual upbeat self far too quickly, but there was something different I couldn't quite put my finger on. Then she took off again, refusing to tell anyone where she was – saying she needed to escape, needed time out. It was the first of many escapes. Something we've got used to over time. *It's what Willow does.*

Even now I sometimes Google her name and they are still there – thousands of images of Willow Winter. I want to rip them all down. Stop people ogling. Tell them to leave her alone. Leave her in peace.

*

Once we have showered and dressed, Becky and I load our hold-alls into the boot of the car, and climb in.

Becky plugs her earphones into her ears, and her thumbs tap her phone screen. I start the engine, but before I pull away, I notice a voicemail on my phone from Willow. She must have called when I was getting ready.

I listen to her strangled voice. 'Rose. Rose. Pick up, please.' A pause. 'I know who killed her. I know who killed my real mum. I've worked it all out.' The message ends, and despite the warm day, my body goes cold.

I try to call back, but it goes straight to voicemail. 'Willow, I got your message. Is everything OK? We're on our way now but call me when you get this. Please.'

'What's up, Mum?' Becky says, pulling free one of her earbuds.

'Nothing,' I say. Deciding not to worry her, I put the car into gear with a shaky hand and pull away.

*

We are halfway to Cornwall, when I pull into a service station. My head is throbbing and although I'd rather keep driving, I know I have to take a break, have something to eat to up my sugar level. Becky's feet are up on the seat and she's cradling her knees, listening to music. I find a space and kill the engine.

I take off my sunglasses and put them in the well between us. The sun has disappeared behind fluffy white clouds, after streaming through the window for most of the journey. The telltale zigzags and blurs of a migraine niggle. I've no doubt it has partly been brought on by the stress of Willow's call.

'Shall we have some coffee?' I say, nudging Becky, who removes her other earbud, and looks up at me.

'What?'

'I said, shall we get a drink or a cake or something?'

Becky straightens up in the seat and lowers her feet to the floor. 'OK,' she says. 'But no cake for me, I'll have some fruit or something.'

Once we've collected a cup of coffee and a chocolate muffin for me, an apple and a bottle of mineral water for Becky, we find a table in the corner. Once seated, I give it a quick clean with a wet wipe, and take a couple of migraine tablets.

'Are you going to be OK to drive, Mum?' she asks, as I massage my temples. 'You're, like, really white.'

'Once the tablets kick in, I'll be fine,' I say, leaning over the table to twirl a straying curl over her ear. She bats me away with her hand and I laugh. 'Are you looking forward to seeing Willow?' I ask.

'Yep. You?'

'Of course.' It's true, but I feel jittery about the photos, and her message is playing in a loop in my head.

Becky smiles, and a dimple forms in her cheek, disappearing as quickly as it came. 'You know I still can't get my head round Willow sending you those photos,' she says.

'Nor me. I'm hoping she'll explain more when we get there.'

She pushes sugar granules across the table with the tip of her finger, her earphone back in, and hums a tune I don't recognise. I realise how glad I am that she's with me, and watch her, trance-like, for several moments, before saying, 'Are you OK, sweetheart?'

She looks up. 'Mega worried about Willow, is all. You don't think she's in danger, do you?'

'I'm sure she's fine,' I say, trying not to think about her last voicemail. 'It's Willow, don't forget, we know what she's like. And we'll see her in a couple of hours, won't we? She can tell us everything.'

'Yeah, I guess.' Her phone buzzes, and she pulls it from her pocket. Her face lights up. 'It's Dad,' she says, answering it. 'Hey, Dad.'

Her eyes sparkle, and I know already what he's telling her. He called me a few days ago to let me know he was getting married. That he wanted to tell Becky himself and would ring her soon.

'Oh my God!' Becky squeals into the phone. 'That's fantastic.'

Her dad has been serious about his latest partner Jack, a lawyer from Florida, for a while now, and I smile. They are good together. I'm happy for them – but my head is spinning.

'Do you think he'll let me be their bridesmaid?' Becky says, once the call has ended, her face lit up by a wide smile.

'Of course,' I say.

'Will he let me wear my DMs, do you think?'

'Probably.' Becky could wear a sack and he would let her get away with it.

'We should get going.' I glance at my watch, a sense of urgency bringing me to my feet.

She rises too, and links arms with me. As we head across the café I glance back at her uneaten apple.

Chapter 14

AVA

2001

From the moment Gail and Rory pulled up outside Ocean View Cottage in his red Ferrari, tension had crawled across Ava's shoulders.

Although Gail had finally moved out, it was as though she was still there. Constantly visiting to discuss the wedding with their mum, over and over and over. And now they were having a family gathering to welcome Peter – the prodigal son – back from Australia.

Gail sat on the two-seater sofa next to her brother, scooping her blonde curls behind her ears as she turned the pages of her bridal book. Peter swigged beer from a bottle, his eyes closing briefly each time he swallowed.

'We're having the reception at the Jester Hotel in Newquay. It's five-star with Jacuzzis in every room and everything. But we can afford it, can't we Rory?' She sounded like a spoilt child.

'Of course,' he said, looking up from shuffling through a pile of CDs.

'And I'll be expecting you to get a new suit, Peter,' Gail continued. 'And you'll need a haircut.'

'I'm up for a new suit,' he said, 'but nobody touches my hair.'

'Well, you'll need to put a comb through it,' she said, reaching up and ruffling it.

'Get off,' he said, smacking her hand away and laughing. Was Peter really as absorbed as he seemed by her wedding plans?

'You do know marriage is the chief reason for divorce, Gail,' he said, and laughed. Ava met his eye and smiled.

'Not in our case.' Gail had completely missed his humour, rarely laughing in the abandoned way she had as a child.

Ava was kneeling on the floor, a glass of white wine clasped in both hands. Gail and Rory had brought two bottles with them, Gail bragging how expensive it was, and nagging Ava for drinking it way too fast. Truth was, Ava wasn't even keen on the taste, but she enjoyed the numbing effect it was having – each gulp making her care less and less that she'd been thrown together with her family.

She glanced up at Rory fiddling with the CD player. He looked good in a black tailored shirt and jeans. She couldn't help admiring how well they fitted.

'Hey, Gail,' he said, lifting up an Eric Clapton CD. 'You look wonderful tonight.'

She smiled and blew him a playful kiss – she looked happy. Ava bit down on her envy. They seemed besotted with each other. She should be pleased for her sister.

'What music will you have at the wedding service?' Jeannette asked.

'Vivaldi, Winter,' Rory said. 'For when Gail walks down the aisle.'

Gail smiled. 'Rory likes his classical music,' she said.

'Only Italian composers, Vivaldi was my mother's favourite.'

'And at the end of the service, we're having "Candle in the Wind",' Gail said.'

'Like at Diana's funeral?' Peter said, with an air of sarcasm.

Gail didn't take the bait. 'It's our song,' she said, her cheeks glowing. 'And our first dance will be "Yellow" by Coldplay.'

Ava's eyes moved to the open kitchen door, to where her mum was putting the finishing touches to a plate of sandwiches.

'Need any help, Mum?' she called through.

'Bit late for that, isn't it?' Rory said. She looked back at him. He nodded towards the table laden with food and laughed. 'Pretty sure you waited until everything was done before offering.'

'I didn't see anyone else offer,' she said with a half-smile, as her mum appeared with the final plate.

Rory pressed play on the CD Player. 'That looks great, Jeannette,' he said to her mum, as she placed them on the table.

Jeannette threw him a wide smile. 'It's so lovely that we're all together again. It's been so long,' she said, dropping into the armchair, and tapping her knee to Eric Clapton.

'When can we eat, Mum?' Peter said, as though he was eight years old.

'You haven't changed a bit,' she said. 'Always liked your food.'

He rose – his purple cotton trousers creased from sitting too long – and grabbed a plate.

Gail closed her wedding book and slipped it down beside the sofa. She picked up her glass of wine, taking a delicate sip. 'Do you like the wine, Mum?' she said.

Jeannette took a mouthful and winced. 'Lovely.'

'We're having it at the wedding,' she said, as Rory sat down beside her.

'Are you having Asti Spumante?' Jeannette chirped in. 'I do like a drop of fizz.'

'I'm getting a box of champagne, Jeannette,' Rory said. 'For the toasts.'

'Well, as long as there's beer,' Peter said, grabbing a handful of sandwiches, and looking around for somewhere to sit.

The room was small and square with patio doors opening

onto the wintery garden. The walls were papered with two different Laura Ashley patterns, separated by a dado rail, and photographs and ornaments cluttered every surface.

Claustrophobia washed over Ava. There were too many people – too much noise. The room swam before her eyes. Oh God, had she drunk too much wine? She got up to leave.

'Where are you off to, Ava?' Peter asked.

'I thought I heard Willow, that's all.'

'Well, don't be long,' Gail said. 'Mum's gone to a lot of trouble.'

'Yes, yes I know. I'll be back in a minute.'

She took the stairs two at a time and entered her bedroom. The room was in semi-darkness, red curtains pulled across the window. She clicked the door closed behind her – glad of her sanctuary, now Gail had moved out.

But it hadn't been all bad sharing with Gail, had it? A happy memory brightened her thoughts. Ava sitting at Gail's dressing table, flicking her sister's mascara brush over her fair lashes, leaving them gloopy.

'Not like that,' Gail had said, laughing, coming up behind her, and pulling up a stool. 'Let me show you.'

Gail had made up Ava's face that day – narrowing her eyes and biting the tip of her tongue as she applied foundation to Ava's fair skin, red lipstick to her lips, shades of grey and silver shadow onto her eyelids.

'You look amazing,' Gail had said, giving Ava's shoulders a squeeze, as their reflections looked back at them.

'I look like you,' Ava whispered as her sister left the room, knowing if Gail had any idea she had planned to meet Justin that evening, she wouldn't have been so kind.

Now, Willow was asleep in the single bed in the corner, covered with a quilt, her head nestled against the pillow, her hair like a golden halo. She hadn't really woken. Ava had needed an excuse to escape.

She would go back downstairs again soon, she knew that, but

they wouldn't miss her. Not immediately anyway – far too full of wedding talk to notice how long she'd been away. She thumped down on her beanbag, rested her head against the red and white striped wall, and closed her eyes.

Her parents had bought the house in the early Eighties, and the small mortgage was paid off a long time ago. Their father, wherever he was, had never asked her mother to sell the place. They weren't well-off, but they managed with her mum's savings and Ava's wages.

She opened her eyes and picked up the photo of Justin on her bedside cabinet. She took in his white-blonde hair, his eyes – the piercing blue of them. Gail said once his eyes were too close together, but they weren't. He was perfect. And one day they would get married. Buy a little house with roses around the door. They would own a golden retriever and have a little brother or sister for Willow. And Justin would have his own music studio – be famous one day.

'He's applied for *Popstars*,' she'd told her mum a few weeks back, trying to make her see he was doing his best.

'Never heard of it,' Jeannette had said.

'It's a TV talent show,' she'd gone on, but her mum wasn't listening. She'd made it clear from the beginning she didn't trust him. She hated that Ava was mixed up with *that family*. And the truth was, deep down Ava was beginning to doubt him too. He hadn't been round for ages to see her or Willow, and wasn't answering her calls or messages. She wasn't sure how much longer she could believe in him. But if she didn't have Justin, she had no one. The few friends she had were at university, or spending money on booze – having fun in Newquay at the weekends. She was stuck. Stuck in Ocean View Cottage in what some described as the most beautiful part of Cornwall, but she sometimes thought of as the loneliest place on earth.

She kissed the frame. Justin wouldn't let her and his daughter down completely, would he?

She put the photo back on her bedside unit. She would ask Justin to Gail and Rory's wedding as her plus one. Gail hadn't put his name on the invitation, saying she didn't want 'his type' there, and that he wouldn't come anyway. She'd told Ava he'd been sleeping with half of Cornwall. But she was lying. Justin wouldn't do that. Once he'd got his life on track, he would call her.

Her eyelids dropped over her eyes, the wine making her tired, and before long she'd drifted off to sleep.

A sudden noise on the landing woke her, and her eyes flew open. The bedroom door stood slightly ajar – hadn't she closed it? She blinked, a shudder running through her body. Through the crack in the door someone hovered.

'Who's there?' she called, unable to tell who it was. She pulled herself upright. 'Hello?' But whoever it was moved away.

'Mummy?' She turned to see Willow sitting up and rubbing her eyes with her fists. 'I need a wee wee.'

She jumped to her feet and headed towards her daughter, glancing over her shoulder, a tingle running down her spine. Outside on the landing a floorboard creaked before footsteps descended the staircase at speed.

Whoever it was had been watching them.

Chapter 15

YOU

'He's homeless, for fuck's sake,' you said, barricading the barn door with a piece of wood, your eyes fired with excitement. 'Nobody will miss him. His life is meaningless.' You turned and glared at me, before grabbing the can of petrol. 'Are you with me, or against me?'

I was with you. I loved you – pure and simple. And I'd thought I would do anything for you, if you would stay in my life.

The man was in his seventies. I'd seen him sitting on the street with his little white dog. He slept in the barn in the wood at night, and I often saw him begging on the streets in the day. Dad would give him a pack of sandwiches and a coffee sometimes, or food for the dog.

I lifted onto my toes and peered in at him through the window. He was swaddled in a grubby duvet, his mongrel dog close by.

'The dog,' I said, looking over my shoulder at you.

'What about it?'

'It's an innocent. I'm not burning a dog alive.' Truth was I wasn't willing to kill the old man either.

This was the first time I stood up to you, the first hint that things were getting out of hand.

70

I'd done everything you asked of me, just to be near you. I'd stolen for you. I'd lied for you. I'd put laxatives in your enemies' drinks. I'd been your foot soldier. But I wasn't prepared to kill an old man and his dog.

You began sloshing petrol around the door, and up the walls. 'I'll do it myself,' you said.

I should have been stronger. I should have told you no. But I feared I might lose you.

The fire spread quickly. 'Come on,' you said, dashing away – soon out of sight through the trees.

The flames licked the building, and I'm not going to lie, I cried. I couldn't get close to the door.

I ran around to the back of the building – there was an area where part of the building had broken away. I tugged at the wood, pulled it free, and the little dog shot out.

'Hey! Mr!' I called through the hole. The smoke was filling the barn, and he looked over at me with sad eyes. 'Come on,' I yelled.

He crawled across, and I helped him out. The dog raced to his side, as he lumbered away from the building, and propped himself against a tree, catching his breath. 'Thank you,' he said, lifting the dog into his arms.

You never did find out how badly I let you down that day.

Chapter 16

ROSE

Now

I drive down narrow country roads. Houses are now a rare sight between endless fields.

'Is that it?' Becky says, pointing out a cottage in the near distance.

'I don't think so,' I say, noticing the satnav insists we have over half a mile to go to the village, but I slow up anyway. It's a beautiful cottage, picture postcard perfect, with roses around the door, and my hopes rise that it is where Willow is staying.

'Floral Corner,' I say, seeing the sign, and putting my foot down on the throttle once more.

'Shame,' Becky says, looking back. 'It looks well nice.'

I pull up outside Ocean View Cottage at three o'clock, tired and achy from the drive, though thankfully my migraine has shifted, for now at least. The cottage is pretty with jasmine climbing the whitewashed walls. It's perched on a hill looking over a small deserted bay, a short walk from a country pub and a little shop at the foot of the hill.

I've parked in a layby, and we get out of the car, and grab our holdalls from the boot, before walking up the rustic road towards a wooden gate. It's so peaceful here; just the sound of birds chirping in the trees, and the distant crash of waves on the beach. The sun is warm on our backs and, once we're on the path leading to the front door, the stunning view of the sea fully opens up in front of us. I stop for a moment, and the sea gives the appearance of winking at me as the sun glints on the silvery blue water. The sand is a burnt-orange colour, and I imagine pulling off my socks and trainers, and sinking my feet into its warmth, and wonder if Willow has been down there – reading, paddling. But then I think of the letter with the photographs, the last call from her. She was lost in finding her mother's killer – had she even noticed her surroundings?

By the time we reach the door my stress levels have lowered. I love the sea air, and memories of childhood holidays in Cornwall with my parents drift in. I wish we were here under different circumstances – a holiday with my daughter, perhaps Aaron following on in a few days. 'It's beautiful,' I say.

The front garden is laid to lawn, though browning due to the hot summer we've had so far, but it's neat, with a freshly painted fence, and a wrought iron bench under the window. Had Willow sat here, trying to work out who took her mother's life?

'It's so quiet,' I say. *As though the world has ended.*

'A bit too quiet, if you ask me,' Becky says, looking around.

I ring the bell three times, before bending to look through the letterbox. 'Willow! Are you in there?'

Becky steps across the grass towards the window, and cupping her hands around her cheeks, to block the sun, she looks in. 'I can't see anyone,' she says.

I clench my fist and rap my knuckles against the door. 'Willow, it's me. Rose,' I call out.

'She could be in the garden,' Becky says, pointing to a six-foot gate leading to the rear of the house.

'Yes, good idea.' I take the initiative and open the gate. Leaving our holdalls on the front doorstep, we walk into the back garden. 'She's probably out in the sunshine,' I add, but as soon as I see the tiny garden – a square of neatly cut grass, also faded by the sun, I know Willow isn't here.

After looking in through the patio doors at the rear of the house, we head back to the front door.

'Who's that?' Becky says, and I turn to see a teenage boy wearing a yellow baseball hat at the bottom of the path, staring our way. 'God, do you think it's the boy in the photo?'

I take the picture from my bag of the man in a yellow cap, and study it. It's difficult to tell, as it was taken so far away. 'I'm not sure.' I look at him a little longer before calling out, 'Hello!' He stands waxwork still. 'Excuse me, but have you seen Willow?'

He turns, and races down the road.

'Wait,' I call after him, dashing down the path, but he's young and wiry – soon out of sight.

'That was odd,' I say, walking back up the path, and stuffing the photo back in my bag with the others.

'Freaky,' Becky agrees.

There's a stone ornament by the door – it's a rabbit wearing a waistcoat, meant to portray the White Rabbit from *Alice in Wonderland*, I suspect. As a child, my dad would often leave keys under garden ornaments if he or Mum weren't going to be there when I arrived home from school, something he and Eleanor would do too. I lift it. Sharing a home with a beetle and several worms is a brass key.

'Yay!' Becky says, grabbing it. 'Thank God for that.'

'But where is she?' I say, taking the key from Becky and sliding it into the keyhole.

She shrugs. 'The shop perhaps? Maybe she's getting things in.'

I turn the key and open the door. But I'm not convinced she's gone shopping. She still hasn't replied to my voicemail from earlier. Something isn't right, and my stomach churns – my stress levels, so successfully lowered by the sight of the sea, creeping up again.

'Willow!' I call out as we step inside, despite my certainty that she's not here. 'Willow, it's me, Rose,' I go on as we head through a narrow hall, and into a small, square lounge. The floor is wooden, with scattered rugs in primary colours. A bright orange sofa and armchair are angled around a wood burner, and a twenty-inch flat-screen TV. The walls are painted cream, and there are a few pictures on the walls of generic scenes I recognise as Cornwall. On the coffee table is a pile of tourist magazines.

I pick one up, and flick through it, memories of visiting the places inside as a child, flooding in. 'I think it's a holiday let,' I say.

I go into the kitchen, where there is barely enough room for one person, and there's a vague smell of something spicy in the air. It's got plenty of cupboards for its size, a cooker, fridge, kettle, and microwave.

I stream water into the kettle, not sure why. I don't want a hot drink. In fact, I could do with something stronger.

Despite that, I flick on the kettle out of habit, and head back to the lounge, where Becky is looking out through the patio doors, into the back garden. I look about me. There's no sense of Willow's presence. She's always been messy, leaving her clothes everywhere and driving me crazy – but it's clean. Spotless. Too immaculate, in fact, as if the owners have cleaned it ready for the next holidaymakers. But Willow has possession until August, that's what she said. Then why does it feel as though Willow has never been here?

'Do you want a cup of coffee?' I ask.

Becky turns. 'Let's look upstairs first,' she says, heading for the door.

Before I can reply, she dashes by me, and I follow her up. There are three bedrooms and a bathroom, but it's not until we get to the third bedroom that I sigh with relief. Willow's red leather jacket is lying on the floor in the corner – typical Willow. I race over to pick it up, pressing it against my nose, breathing in her perfume. 'She must be out,' I say, looking through the window at the lonely bay below. But things still aren't right. There should be piles of her clothes, make-up, bottles of perfume. I open the wardrobe. It's empty. A shiver tickles my spine, as I glance out of the window to see a cloud cover the sun.

'Where is she?' Becky says, as the feeling of unease grows, settling heavy on my shoulders.

Chapter 17

AVA

2001

Ava descended the stairs, Willow in her arms.

Seeing the front door open, she put Willow down, and ventured outside, where the air was freezing.

'Peter?' she called into the darkness, wondering if he was outside having a smoke. 'Peter, are you out here?'

There was no reply, but a sudden noise on the road startled her. A glimpse of yellow, as a figure ran down the road. She raced inside, slammed the door, and dragged across the bolt. She stood, shaking, trying to calm her racing heart.

'Mummy?' Willow was looking up at her, eyes wide.

'I'm OK, darling girl,' she said, taking her daughter's hand, and making for the lounge. As they stood in the doorway, Ava tried to summon the strength to reunite with her family. Her eyes flicked over each of them in turn. Had one of them peered at her while she slept? Or had the figure – whoever he was – come out of the darkness and crept up the stairs? She shuddered.

'Ava, you're back!' It was Peter, leaning against the table, knocking back another bottle of beer, and grinning over at her.

A memory pushed its way in.

'You're just like your father,' her mum is yelling, blood dripping from her fingers.

But the memory – so short, so confusing – disappeared as Rory spoke.

'Hey, Pete,' he said. He was sitting in the armchair. 'I'm having a stag do,' he went on. 'Gail says I've got to have it long before the wedding. Apparently I need six weeks to get over a hangover.' He laughed. 'Anyway, how are you fixed for November 10th?'

Peter raised his bottle towards Rory. 'Sounds good to me.'

'We'll do a pub crawl around Newquay, have a curry – pick up a few women.'

'Rory!' Gail cried.

'Joking, sweetheart!'

'Well, you can count me in,' Peter said. 'Should be a laugh.'

Gail hadn't mentioned a hen do. But then she wouldn't have invited Ava anyway.

'Did you take the money into the hotel earlier, Rory?' Gail asked him.

'Shit.' He slapped his forehead. 'I knew there was something I'd forgotten.'

'Please say you're messing with me.'

'No, I totally forgot.' He sounded unconcerned, a half-smile on his face.

'But the balance deadline was yesterday, Rory. They've already given us an extension. They told me they have another couple waiting for our slot. Please say you paid it.'

'I'll take it in tomorrow, Gail,' he said, giving her a hard stare. 'They won't have a problem. Calm down, for Christ's sake. They're just trying to panic us into paying.'

'Don't worry, love,' Jeannette said, patting Gail's knee. 'The village hall is nice, and always available.'

'The village hall?' Gail sounded close to tears. 'I don't want my wedding in the bloody village hall.'

'Well, let's hope it doesn't come to that,' Jeannette went on, patting Gail's knee once more. 'Now why not show me this cake of yours.'

Gail looked down at the book open on her lap, and with a sulky tone she said, 'Well, this is the picture I gave to Margo's of Newquay.'

'Oh my, you're using Margo's of Newquay?' Peter said, in a silly high-pitched voice, widening his eyes and covering his mouth flamboyantly with his hand. 'Whatever next!'

'Tell him to shut up, Mum,' Gail said like a child, as she placed the book on her mother's knee.

'Did anyone come upstairs while I was up there?' Ava said, twirling her hair around her finger, struggling to be heard over the chatter and music. Willow looked up at her with wide blue eyes, and then at the room in front of her. She opened her mouth and let out a piercing scream that lasted several seconds. Everyone stopped talking. The only sound now was Britney Spears singing 'Oops … I did it again' through the speakers.

'Willow!' Jeannette yelled, pushing the bridal book towards Gail.

'There is no way I'm ever having kids,' Gail said, covering her ears with her manicured hands. 'They're demons in disguise.'

'Whatever are you screaming for, Willow?' Jeannette said. 'Ava, you need to control your daughter. I would never have let any of you behave in such a way. Quite honestly, I sometimes worry about the way Willow is wired.'

Willow looked up at Ava and smiled. 'Mummy talk,' she said.

Ava returned Willow's smile and squeezed her hand. 'Did anyone come upstairs when I was up there?' she repeated.

'I think we've all been up there at some point in the last ten minutes,' Peter said, and with a grin, added, 'Mum's sandwiches go straight through you.'

'Not me,' said Gail. 'I haven't moved from this spot since I arrived. What's this about, Ava?'

'I went to the loo,' said Rory, raising an eyebrow. 'Didn't realise I had to sign in and out.'

'Ava?' Gail's eyes were firmly on her.

'I just thought—'

'What?' Gail's voice was sharp. She tapped an elegant fingernail. 'What did you think?'

'Nothing. It doesn't matter.' She finally stepped into the lounge and sat on the floor in the corner, pulling Willow onto her lap, wishing she had an invisibility cloak.

'She's such a pretty girl,' Rory said, staring down at Willow. 'Looks so like you, Ava.'

Ava felt herself flush. She received so few compliments that when she did she didn't know how to respond, but she knew she was flattered – stupidly flattered.

'Did you look like Willow as a child?' he asked her, his eyes, definitely his best feature, meeting hers.

'We both did,' Gail said, glaring his way. It was true. Ava and Gail were alike when they were children. But today they couldn't look more different: Ava was pale, her features dainty – whereas Gail's fake tan, expertly made-up face, and collagen-filled lips, had changed her from the girl she once was.

'I looked just like Willow when I was little, didn't I Mum?' Gail said.

'You both did,' Jeannette said.

The sudden thought of her sister claiming even a tiny part of Willow was unthinkable. Ava may have made a mistake getting pregnant, but Willow was hers. Gail wasn't going to share even a tiny moment of that. 'Willow's more like me, I think,' she said, pulling her daughter closer, the child's hair tickling her nose.

'So, she gets her good looks from you, Ava?' Rory said, swallowing a mouthful of wine, his eyes meeting hers again.

'What?' Gail glared at him. She was the confident sister, she'd always gone through life with her tribe of friends. Boys, and later men, had practically fallen at her feet. It was clear she wasn't happy that Ava was in the spotlight.

There was a painful silence as Britney Spears stopped singing, and the CD player clicked to standby.

'I was just saying Willow looks like Ava, that's all, Gail.' Rory narrowed his eyes, fixed them on Gail.

'But you said you think Ava is pretty.'

'I think Willow looks like her mum, Gail. That's all.'

'That's not what you said, though.'

'Enough, Gail.' He glared at her. Ava hadn't seen his eyes flare with so much anger since she'd bumped into him that time at the arcade. She pushed herself further against the wall.

Gail looked down at her hands. This was the most submissive Ava had ever seen her. 'We should leave,' Gail said, her voice quivering. She grabbed her bridal book and held it close against her chest. For a moment, Ava felt for her sister, wanted to get up and hold her close, but she knew she never could.

'Don't go,' Jeannette pleaded. 'We were having such a lovely time. Ava, why not take Willow upstairs for a little while?'

Ava wasted no time in jumping to her feet. She lifted Willow into her arms. 'Pleasure,' she said, and left the room once more.

Chapter 18

ROSE

Now

After searching the house and coming up with nothing, and trying Willow's phone several more times, we sit in the lounge, bewildered and at a complete loss.

'Are you hungry?' I say, although I'm far from it. 'Becky?'

She looks up from her phone. 'Not really,' she says, turning up her nose, the sparkle gone from her eyes. 'My stomach's all churned up. This is so weird, don't you think? Where is Willow?'

I lean over and touch her knee. 'She'll turn up, you'll see.'

'Will she? Her clothes have gone, Mum.'

'I'm sure once we've had a good night's sleep, we'll be able to think more clearly.'

'I'm not sure I'll be able to sleep.'

'We mustn't overreact. Don't forget what Willow can be like.' I'm not sure who I'm trying to convince, Becky, or myself.

My mobile vibrates across the table. It's Aaron.

'Hey,' I say into the phone, trying to inject brightness into my voice.

'Hey, beautiful, how's things? How's Willow?'

'She's not here,' I say. 'We're not sure where she is, but hopefully she'll turn up soon.' I omit that the only clue that she was ever here is her jacket.

'Well send her my love once she turns up, won't you?'

'Of course, yes.'

'You OK?'

'I'm fine,' I say, trying to sound positive. 'A bit tired from the journey, that's all. It's beautiful here, though. We're right next to the sea, and the weather is amazing.'

'Well, it's peeing it down in Germany. I wish I was there with you.'

'Me too.'

'And Becky, is she OK?'

'She's fine.'

She glances over, and I smile. '*Aaron?*' she mouths, and I nod. She reaches out for the phone. 'She wants a word,' I say to him. 'I'll pass you over. Love you.'

'Love you too.'

As Becky tells Aaron about her dad getting engaged, transforming into an excited teenager once more, I head for the kitchen to search out some bread, and grab some cheese and butter. The fridge is full of fresh food. Willow must have been here recently. *Or someone else.* The photos, her letter, and voicemail, the fact none of her clothes are here spin around in my head. Something is wrong. Something is very wrong.

A calendar hangs on the kitchen wall. I lift it down.

At the top is a picture of a guinea pig, and the month is July. It's packed with jottings in Willow's handwriting, and my eyes flick over them, attempting to take them all in at once. I finally settle on July 20th. Today.

Rose and Becky arrive.

She was clearly expecting us.

I make some sandwiches, before finding a bottle of white wine in the fridge. I pour a large glass. It's not the best idea. It may aggravate my head. But I'm willing to risk it.

I take the wine and sandwiches into the lounge, the calendar wedged under my arm, and drop down onto the sofa next to Becky. She's finished talking to Aaron, and my phone lays abandoned on top of the magazines on the coffee table.

I study the calendar, and Becky leans her head on my shoulder. 'That's Willow's handwriting,' she says.

'Yes. It was in the kitchen.'

There are lots of dates where a Gareth visited her, or she met up with him. I recall how she mentioned him when she called me.

'Look,' I say, pointing out an entry from a week ago. 'It looks as if she's visited Ava's mother, Jeannette Millar, at somewhere called Green Pastures in Newquay.'

'And Justin too,' Becky says, pointing at an entry two weeks ago. I'd told her earlier what Eleanor had said. That Justin was Willow's father. Had Willow really met up with him?

I yawn and stretch, my tired mind struggling to make sense of everything, before picking up a sandwich and taking a bite. I've got to keep my stamina up. 'Have one, Becky,' I say, gesturing to the plate.

'I'm not hungry, thanks. I feel a bit sick actually.'

'Because you haven't eaten,' I say, taking another bite, before standing up, and padding towards the front window. I stare out, willing Willow to skip up the path with her radiant smile and a flick of her golden hair. But despite the beautiful, sunny evening, a dark sense of foreboding washes over me – and a dreadful fear I may never see her again.

*

Maybe it's the long drive, or the fact I drank two glasses of wine quickly, but I nod off on the sofa, waking much later to find the house in darkness.

'Becky?' Disorientated, I pull myself up straight, and rub my eyes, before fumbling around on the coffee table for my phone. It's almost ten o'clock.

I hear the flick of a switch behind me, and the room fills with light. I turn to see Becky in her PJs, her hair damp, heading into the room. 'I thought I'd let you sleep,' she says. 'You were exhausted.'

'Thanks,' I say, stretching my arms above my head, and yawning. 'I must have needed it.'

'I'm in the box room. I didn't want Willow's room. I'm a bit freaked by it, if I'm honest.' She drops down next to me, smelling fresh and flowery. 'The fact Willow was in there, and now she's not. I'm being silly, I know.'

I wrap my arm around her shoulder and hug her close. 'And this is the girl who binge-watches horror movies.'

'That's different. This is real. Where is Willow, Mum?'

I tuck a straying curl over her ear and she pushes my hand away – hating her hair being touched. 'I don't know, love,' I say. 'But we will find her.'

'Promise?'

I take a deep breath. 'I'll do everything in my power to find her, Becky. I can promise you that.'

Chapter 19

AVA

2001

Peter's laughter, the shrillness of Gail's voice, and the feeling that her family hated her, coupled with the heavy bass of the music, and the wine in her system, made Ava's head throb.

She looked down at Willow playing with a Fisher Price phone that had once been hers, and despite her daughter looking content, jabbering into the receiver, Ava wished again that she could give her a better life.

She crouched and stroked her daughter's hair, catching a curl around her little finger, the silky softness somehow comforting, and Willow smiled up at her, trying to hand her the receiver. 'Mummy crying?' she said, tilting her head.

Ava hadn't realised she was, and swiped away the tears with the heel of her hand. She lifted Willow from the floor, and held her close, sniffing into her hair.

'Let's go out,' she said. It was time to do something proactive. She would go and see Justin. Confront him. Find out if he wanted her and Willow in his life. If he didn't, it was time to move on.

Once downstairs she snuggled Willow into her pink coat and hat, and pulled on her own duffle coat and scarf.

She opened the door and the cold air rushed in, stinging her face. Was she doing the right thing? She'd seen the figure running down the road earlier. What if he was still about?

Convincing herself he would be long gone, she stepped out into the dark night, and strapped her daughter into the buggy that always stood by the front door, then put on her gloves. She attempted to push thoughts of the figure from her mind. Had he really been watching them as they slept?

She hurried down the narrow, uneven road, lit only by a full moon that was slowly disappearing behind heavy clouds.

It would take about ten minutes to get to Justin's place, and as she raced along, she tried to stay hopeful. Hopeful that Gail was wrong, that Justin wasn't seeing other women. He hadn't answered her calls or messages for ages, she reminded herself. But Willow was his daughter. And he'd told Ava more than once that he loved them both. And she loved him too, didn't she?

'Dark. Dark. Dark. Dark,' Willow was saying, her gloved hands over her eyes, her legs bouncing up and down, slamming against the buggy.

'Yes, it is dark, darling girl,' Ava said, her eyes flicking to and fro at the bushes and trees either side of them. 'But we'll soon be at Daddy's house.'

'Daddy.'

'Yes, Daddy.'

'Dark. Dark. Dark. Dark.'

As Ava reached Cranberry Close, the moon vanished behind a cloud. 'Not far now, Willow,' she said, wishing she'd brought a torch. She pushed the buggy towards the house Justin shared with his dad and the Bristow brothers. She remembered them from school – when they bothered to attend. They were a bad lot, who were into drugs and petty crime. She hated them. Hated that Justin had got mixed up with them.

Outside the house, Ava looked up to see Justin's bedroom light on. She crouched in front of Willow. She didn't want to take her daughter inside – that's why she hadn't been before – but she couldn't leave her out on the lonely street. Maybe this wasn't such a good idea, after all.

'Daddy,' Willow said, bouncing her legs against the buggy and giggling.

'Yes, Daddy.' Ava lifted her out, and they walked hand in hand up the path to the front door. It had once been a beautiful house – a 1930s bay-fronted semi, with a heavy oak front door. But now there were signs it wasn't being cared for. The front garden was overgrown, empty beer bottles and cans sharing space with nettles and wildflowers, and the paintwork was chipped, curtains sagged at the window.

She knocked on the door and waited.

Eventually one of the Bristow brothers opened the door. She couldn't tell them apart – both tall and too skinny with cropped black hair. 'Ava,' he said, a smirk stretching his yellowing skin. 'Come to see Justin?'

'Is he in?'

He smirked again as he stepped back and gestured for her and Willow to enter. 'He's upstairs. I'm guessing he isn't expecting you.'

She looked into his vacant, staring eyes. 'I'll go up, shall I?'

'Be my guest.' He staggered away, disappearing through a door that led to the lounge.

She picked Willow up and climbed the stairs, passing the toilet, the door standing open, an unpleasant smell of urine reaching her nostrils. The house was filthy.

'Justin?' she said, tapping his bedroom door. But before he could answer, clarity hit her like a fist. She didn't want this life for Willow either. She wanted so much more for her darling girl.

She was about to turn to leave when the door opened, and Justin poked his head out, his white-blonde hair standing on end.

He was naked, and made little effort to hide the fact. His floor was littered with empty spirit bottles and cans, and the smell of weed and tobacco smoke mingled with the stench of grubby sheets, made her feel sick. He'd changed so much from the boy she met in Newquay.

'What are you doing here?' he said, eyes wide.

Ava lifted Willow up into her arms, and the child looked deep into her face, touching her cheek. 'Mummy OK?'

'I just thought ...' But she had no words – what she'd planned to say had gone with the realisation she no longer wanted Justin in her life.

'Who is it?' A female voice came from inside the room.

A tiny pang of pain came and went. She didn't want Justin for Willow. She didn't want Justin for her. She'd been such a fool waiting for him to give her the perfect life she'd always dreamed of – and now it hit her hard that he never would.

Justin glanced over his shoulder. 'Nobody.'

Nobody. 'I've come to say you're off the hook, Justin.'

'What you on about?' He sighed deeply, closing his eyes, swaying.

'I don't want you in Willow's life. I don't want you in mine.'

'What? No. Willow's my daughter, Ava. I have a right to see her once I can get my act together.'

'Let's face it, Justin; you'll never get your act together. You haven't bothered to see her for months.'

'I've been busy with my music, and stuff.' He went to touch Willow's cheek, and Ava slapped his hand away.

'Don't touch her. Don't ever touch her again,' she yelled, turning and racing down the stairs, afraid tears would come before she could get out of this disgusting house.

The Bristow brother stood at the foot of the stairs, blocking her way. 'If he doesn't want you, love, I'll give you a quick one.' He went to grab her, but she pushed him hard with her free hand. He tumbled, cracking his head against the wall.

'Fucking bitch,' he said, as she flung open the front door and ran down the path.

*

Tears rolled down her face as she flew along the lonely road, holding Willow against her, dragging the empty buggy behind them, her vision blurring. She hated that she was running from one nightmare back to another. Why had life always been so awful? What had she done wrong in a previous life?

'Wee wee,' Willow said into her ear. 'Wee wee, Mummy.'

'Oh Willow, please wait until we get home, darling girl,' Ava cried. 'It's too dark to stop.'

'Wee wee, Mummy. Wee wee, Mummy. Wee wee, Mummy.'

'OK, OK.' She let go of the buggy and raced into some nearby trees, Willow in her arms.

*

It was as she took her daughter's hand and led her back to the road, twigs crunching under their feet, bushes catching on their coats, that she noticed a truck had pulled up next to the empty buggy, and a prickling sensation ran down her spine.

Chapter 20

ROSE

Now

I'm awake, but my eyes are closed. Shades of orange burn through my eyelids, and the distant caw of seagulls, reminding me of childhood holidays, tell me it's morning.

I don't want to open my eyes, even though I'm aware it's another beautiful day. In fact, I don't want to be in this strange cottage with no idea where Willow is. Tears bubble up, but I know I must snap myself round. If Willow doesn't return, or at least get in touch, I need to contact the police.

One, two, three, I prise my eyes open to see the sun's rays streaming through a gap in the embroidered curtains that sway in a light breeze.

'Where the hell are you, Willow?' I whisper, imagining her flinging open the door, and in her upbeat, crazy way, racing towards me, knocking me off my feet as she takes me in her arms. *'Had you worried,'* she says in my fantasy. Like the time she hid in the garden behind the summerhouse when she was about eight. We hunted for her for ages, even contacted the police, Dad and

Eleanor crying – in bits that they couldn't find her – only for her to jump out and giggle, barely seeming to realise the effect she had on us all.

I lay for some time staring at the ceiling. I didn't notice how low it was when we arrived. Now it presses down on me, making me feel slightly claustrophobic. Trapped, unable to escape. The cottage is pretty, there's no doubting that. This room is painted pastel blue, with cream shabby chic furniture. But there's something in the ambience here that makes me feel uncomfortable. As though I'm not safe.

I look at my phone – it's almost seven – and throw back the quilt. I twist my legs round and push my feet into my slippers, before venturing onto the landing with my wash bag, black leggings and a funky, purple top Becky bought me for my birthday a few weeks back. The door to Willow's room stands ajar, but Becky's door is closed.

Once I've showered and dressed, I tap on Becky's door. 'Sweetheart,' I call softly. After a few moments she opens up, her dark curls spiralling out of control, her brown eyes half open. 'It's a bit early, Mum,' she croaks, stretching her thin arms above her head and yawning.

'I thought we should get an early start. I'm going to contact the police.'

She tilts her head. 'OK.'

'And I thought we might try finding Willow ourselves. Ask around if anyone has seen her. Make sure she's not just spent the night somewhere.'

'But surely she wouldn't have taken all her things for one night. And why hasn't she contacted us, Mum?'

My head spins. 'I don't know,' I say, massaging my temples with my fingers. I have no answers. 'Listen, have a shower and when you come down we'll decide what to do,' I say, turning and heading away.

'Your top looks great, by the way,' she calls after me.

'Thanks,' I say over my shoulder, as I take the stairs two at a time. 'Someone with great taste bought it for me.'

I enter the kitchen and fill then flick on the kettle. I don't know where to begin looking for Willow. Should I ask around the village – see if anyone's seen her? The local shop might be a good place to start.

As I pour boiling water over coffee granules, the photos and Willow's note flash into my head:

One of these men killed my mother.

Had she really worked out which one was a murderer?

Boiling water overflows the mug, as I lose sight of what I'm doing. 'Damn,' I say, as it puddles and drips down the cupboard door and onto the floor. I slam the kettle down and grab a tea towel to mop it up. I'm wringing it out when the doorbell rings.

'I'll get it,' Becky calls, as she thumps down the stairs. My heart picks up speed, and for a reason I can't quite explain, I call, 'Be careful.'

I hurry from the kitchen into the lounge and hear a friendly male voice at the door.

'Come in,' I hear Becky say, and my heart thuds faster. I race across the room, and perch on the armchair, arranging myself to look what I hope is nonchalant, rather than like the stress ball I really am.

The door swings open, and Becky, her hair still wet from her shower, and wearing a long, loose, black T-shirt over ripped jeans, leads a man, who looks to be in his fifties, into the room. He's tall, and his neat grey hair is combed back from a smiling, bearded face. He peers at me over gold-rimmed glasses.

'Mum, this is Inspector Jones,' Becky says, raising her eyebrows. 'He's looking for Willow. I've told him she's not here at the moment.'

'Oh, I see. Well, I'm Rose ... Willow's stepsister.'

'Good to meet you,' he says, sticking out his hand, and I half-rise to take it, breathing in his expensive aftershave.

He pumps my hand up and down for some moments. 'Call me Gareth,' he says.

'Well, Gareth,' I say, recalling how Willow said a man called Gareth was helping her – how I'd seen his name on the calendar. 'As my daughter said, Willow's not here at the moment.'

'Ah, yes, she mentioned she may be going into Newquay,' he says. 'She was following something up. She didn't say what.'

I sit back down, feeling a twinge of relief at his words, followed by panic. Has something happened to her in Newquay? 'Well, I'm sure she'll be back soon,' I say, attempting to keep my voice even. 'Can I give her a message?'

'No, no, I'll give her a call.' He's Welsh – sounds a bit like Rob Brydon, his voice rising and falling in a pleasant singsong way.

'I'm not sure she'll reply. I keep trying her phone, but it always goes to voicemail.'

'Well, I'll give it a go. If she turns up here in the meantime, can you ask her to give me a call?'

Words bubble up, and before I have chance to arrange them coherently, I blurt them out. 'Actually we're a bit worried about her. She asked us to come here, but seems to have disappeared. She's taken all her clothes too, which is a bit odd, don't you think? Especially as she was hunting for her mother's killer.'

'Mum!' Becky says, throwing me a surprised look. As though I shouldn't be sharing.

I ignore her and fix my eyes on the inspector. 'I'm sure the inspector already knows that already. You were helping her, weren't you? Your name is all over her calendar.'

He stares at me for some moments before nodding. 'I told her to be careful,' he says, dropping down onto the sofa, and shaking his head.

'I'll make some coffee, shall I?' Becky says, heading into the kitchen.

Inspector Gareth Jones cradles a mug of coffee. 'I worked on Willow's mother's murder case back in 2001,' he says. 'It was a terrible tragedy.' He looks about him. 'This is where they lived,' he says. 'The Millars.'

Despite the warm room, I shiver, a chill running through me, as though someone walked over my grave. 'So whoever booked this place for Willow would have known that?'

He nods. 'Too much of a coincidence otherwise, I would think.' He pauses to sip his coffee. 'I only spoke to Willow yesterday. As I say, she told me she was heading into Newquay. She'd tracked down her Uncle Peter in Australia, which was no easy feat. He was coming over to the UK. Maybe she was meeting him? As I say, she didn't tell me her reasons.'

Peter. 'Peter is Willow's uncle?' A memory floats in of Willow talking about him when she was a child.

He nods. 'Yes, he's Ava's older brother. I can't be sure it was him she planned to meet, but it seems likely.'

'He was in one of the photographs she sent Mum,' Becky says. 'Photographs?'

'Yes,' I say. 'She sent me four photos. She was certain one of the men in the pictures killed her mother. Peter's in one of them.'

'I wondered about him at the time of Ava's death,' Inspector Jones says. 'He dashed back to Australia shortly after her funeral.' He pauses for a moment. 'Have you got the photographs with you?'

'Yes.' I reach for my bag, search inside, and hand them to him.

He shuffles through them. 'I gave these to Willow. This is Peter Millar,' he says, staring at it for several moments. 'And this is Justin Havers – Willow's father. I still believe he killed her, despite his fairly sound alibi.' He flicks to the next photo. 'And this is Rory Thompson – Ava's brother-in-law.'

He studies the final photograph. 'I didn't give her this one,' he says, shaking his head. 'But then it's hard to tell who it is anyway.'

'Taken from a distance,' I say, stating the obvious, as I take the photo of the lad with the yellow cap from him.

He hands the rest of the photos back to me.

'She told me she knows who the killer was,' I say. 'That's what she said in her last voicemail.'

'Did she?' Becky says, raising an eyebrow.

'I'm sorry I never told you, sweetheart,' I say. 'I didn't want you to worry.'

'Yes, she told me that, too,' he says. 'But she was getting herself wound up to the point where I suggested she went home. I was worried about her. She seemed to suspect them all at one time or another. In fact, a few days back Dexter Powell was her prime suspect.'

'Who?' I flick foolishly through the pictures, knowing I won't find him.

'There's no photo of anyone called Dexter.'

'That's odd. I could have sworn I gave her one.' He furrows his forehead before shaking his head. 'Maybe I didn't.'

My mind drifts to the box lying open on the coffee table at home – had I dropped one without realising?

'We interviewed Dexter at the time,' the inspector goes on. 'He worked with Ava for a while at a DIY store in Newquay. They went out together briefly. He was at her sister's wedding the night she died, but he took off early evening. His mum gave him an alibi.'

All this talk of murder is making me anxious, and a rush of anxiety runs through me, as I try to take in everything he's saying.

'I think Willow may have visited Jeannette Millar a week ago at Green Pastures, whatever that is. It's on the calendar,' I say.

He nods. Rubs his chin. 'Yes. Green Pastures is a warden-controlled place in Newquay. Willow went to see her grandmother, but it was a waste of time. She was never close with Ava.'

'Surely our main concern at the moment is finding Willow, Mum,' Becky says. 'We don't want to start digging into an old murder case, do we?'

'You're right,' I say, snapping myself round. 'It's not up to us to solve an ancient murder, even if Willow thought it was hers.' I'm lying to myself. The death of Ava Millar is getting under my skin. I know it's connected to what's going on with Willow.

'Yes, you're absolutely right,' Inspector Jones says. 'I'd love to get to the bottom of it all, but if I couldn't solve it eighteen years ago, there's even less hope now.' He sighs deeply. 'I'll let them know at the station that Willow is missing. Get the ball rolling. Right then ...' He slaps his knees, before getting to his feet. He rams his hand in his trouser pocket and fishes out a card with his contact details on. 'Call me if you hear from her.'

I take the card, and he turns and heads for the door.

If Willow's in Newquay why hasn't she contacted us? Why has she taken all her clothes? This isn't just my unpredictable, flaky sister taking off on a whim. I've no doubt something's happened to her.

I follow the inspector into the hallway – glancing back once to give Becky a reassuring look – and out through the front door. I pull the door ajar behind me.

'Have you been searching for Ava's killer all these years?' I ask.

He shakes his head. 'The case went cold a long time ago, but it's always bugged me, you know. Ava was a lovely girl. But when the leads dried up and it stopped being a priority, I didn't have time to devote to it, what with other cases I was working on. It was Willow turning up asking questions around the village that piqued my interest once more. I visited her – offered to help if I could.'

'I see.' Part of me wishes he hadn't encouraged her. That he'd sent her home.

As though reading my mind he says, 'I tried to tell her all the leads had come to nothing eighteen years ago, but she was desperate to find out the truth.' He stares into my eyes for some moments and I see speckles of black in the blue in his. 'We'll find her, Rose,' he says, and places a comforting hand on my shoulder. 'Why not leave it to us? Head home. God forbid Willow's in any danger, but if she is, you'll be safer there. I'll keep you updated.'

Tears sting behind my eyes, as I watch him go. 'Inspector,' I call after him, as he reaches the gate. He stops and looks back. 'Did you know Willow visited Justin?'

'Yes,' he says, opening the gate and heading through it. 'Justin Havers – yes. He was recently released from prison.'

'Oh my God,' I say, covering my mouth.

He rubs his hand over his bearded chin. 'He went down for armed robbery a long time ago.' A pause. 'To be honest, it bugs me that the moment he's released she disappears.' With that, he raises his hand, gets into his car, and drives away.

Chapter 21

AVA

2001

Ice-cold rain started to fall, soaking Ava and Willow as they peered through the trees. The truck's headlights illuminated the bare, spindly trees that stretched across the road from both sides forming an arch. It was impossible to see who was sitting behind the wheel, but Ava recognised the battered truck, knew who it was.

She picked Willow up and dived towards the buggy, heart thumping as she attempted to strap her in with shaking hands. She had to get away from here. But *he* threw open the truck door and stormed towards her, grabbing her arm.

'Justin, let go of me,' she cried, trying to shake free, but his fingers pressed hard into her arm.

'You're not taking Willow away from me,' he yelled, and the child burst into tears and wiggled in the buggy.

'So now you want her?' Ava cried, rain stinging her cheeks. 'Now you can't have her, you panic.'

'I've always wanted her, Ava.' He lessened his grip. 'I just haven't had the time – what with my music.'

'And other girls, and drugs, and basically being a total waster.' She pulled away from him and unbuckled Willow, lifting her crying from the buggy.

'Who I sleep with is up to me, Ava.'

'Fuck's sake, Justin – you said you loved me, that we'd be together, the three of us. But you haven't done anything to make that happen, you haven't paid a penny towards bringing up Willow. Have you any idea how hard it's been?'

'I will help. As soon as my music takes off.'

'I've heard it before, Justin. It's too late.'

'I'll fight for her. She's my daughter too.' He made a grab for Willow, whose sobbing had taken on a new level.

A car engine rumbled nearby and a Ford Sierra rounded the bend, headlights blinding them. Ava ran into the road, screaming and waving, while holding tightly onto Willow with one arm.

Justin raced back to his truck. 'You won't take her from me, Ava,' he said before ducking into the driving seat. He slammed the door closed, and pulled away with a screech of tyres, as the other car pulled to a stop, windscreen wipers ticktocking.

'Inspector Jones?' Ava whispered, when he flicked on the interior light and buzzed down the window.

She'd seen him about the village. He'd even been in the DIY store where she worked. She'd helped him pick out some magnolia paint and some decent paintbrushes.

The inspector was in his late thirties, his pleasant face comforting as he leaned out of his car window, his gold-framed glasses getting splattered with rain. 'Is everything OK?' he said, looking concerned. His blue eyes were friendly, his dark hair cropped short – with a hint of army rather than police force.

She knew she looked a sight. Her face, still wet from tears, must have been red and blotchy, her eyes puffy, her hair soaked from the rain and clinging to her skull. 'Not really,' she said, squeezing Willow so close they were practically one person.

A sudden memory of the inspector coming to the cottage

when she was a child, just before Peter took off for Australia, came and went. He'd made her a hot chocolate that day – yes, she remembered that.

'You couldn't give us a lift home, could you?' she said.

'Of course.' He unclipped his seatbelt and within moments he was by her side folding the buggy. She sighed with relief as he put it in the boot. 'Climb in the back,' he said with a smile aimed at Willow, who was holding onto Ava's neck, as though she was on a log in rapid waters.

'Thanks,' Ava said, opening the door. 'I live at Ocean View Cottage.'

'Yes, I remember.'

Inspector Jones carefully took the bends in the roads, his headlights picking out the occasional rabbit on the grass verge, classical music playing softly on the radio. 'Whoever he is,' he said, meeting her eyes in the rear-view mirror. 'He's not worth it.'

She smiled, comforted by the inspector's soothing Welsh accent, his kindly words. Part of her didn't want to leave the security of the back seat.

'I know,' she said. 'I've been a total idiot.'

'Get him out of your life, love. If he makes you feel like this, he doesn't deserve you.'

'I will. I mean I have.' Tears pricked. 'I went round his house hoping to sort things out. But he had some woman with him. I've told him he can't see Willow anymore.'

'He's Willow's father?'

'Uh-huh, for his sins.'

Before too long the inspector pulled up outside Ocean View Cottage, tugged on the handbrake, and killed the engine. He flicked on the courtesy light once more and looked over his shoulder at Ava unbuckling the seatbelts.

'He doesn't deserve my darling girl,' she said, opening the door. 'And you know what else, I'm going to make a better life for

Willow. I really am. I'm going to get a better job, save money, and …' A tear rolled down her face. She sounded ridiculous. How the hell was she going to make that happen? 'Well, thanks for the lift,' she said, climbing out of the car.

'Why not study from home?' he said, his tone serious. 'I bet you're a bright girl, Ava. You've stumbled, that's all. But with time and hard work you can make that life you want for you both. With qualifications you could get a good job.'

The idea bounced around her head. 'Maybe,' she said.

'My son's done a few courses and we've still got all the details. I can drop them off sometime, if you like.'

'Yes. Yes, I'd like that,' she said, the idea taking shape in her head. 'Thanks, Inspector Jones.'

'Call me Gareth.'

'OK, Gareth,' she said with another smile, as she climbed from the car. She stood for a moment with Willow in her arms, looking up at the cottage, fine rain tickling her cheeks. Peter was standing outside the door in the porch light, a cigarette glowing between his fingers.

Gareth buzzed down his window. 'Who's that?' he said, nodding towards the house.

'My brother.'

'Peter? He's back?'

'Yes, for Gail and Rory's wedding.'

'Ava!' Peter was strutting down the path, huddled into his fur-collared coat. 'Where the hell have you been?'

'I'd better take off,' Gareth said, starting the engine and pulling away.

Peter reached her side. 'Who was that?' he said with a slur, watching Gareth's car disappear into the darkness.

'What do you want?' Ava said, pushing past him, heading towards the house. 'You're drunk, and I've had a crap evening.'

He followed. 'Listen,' he called after her. 'Wait up, please.'

She stopped, glanced over her shoulder. 'What?'

He was rubbing the cold from his arms, his eyes wide. He looked suddenly vulnerable, like a lost little boy. 'The thing is, I wanted to say sorry.'

'Sorry?'

'Yeah. I've been a bit of a dick since I arrived.'

'You're fine, Peter. I'm just tired, and it's cold out here,' she said, continuing towards the front door.

He raced after her, grabbed her arm, squeezing.

'Let go of my arm,' she said, as Willow started to cry.

'Sorry,' he said, releasing her. He went to touch Willow's face, but the child buried her face in her mother's shoulder. 'I want to be here for you, Ava. If you need me.'

'I've had a crap night,' she said again. 'We'll talk tomorrow.' She rushed into the house, and up the stairs, leaving him alone on the doorstep.

*

Later, in bed, Ava listened as the village church bells chimed midnight and the roar of Rory's Ferrari made its way down the hill.

Before long, Jeannette and Peter climbed the stairs, and after a rush of whispers, taps running, toilets flushing, doors banging – the cottage was finally at peace.

Chapter 22

YOU

Sometimes you confided in me. Told me about your childhood. How you hated your father. How you would never forgive him. You would talk for hours about your mother, and we would drink wine, and hug. That's all. Nothing more. Those days I felt so close to you.

Other days you'd transform – flirty, feisty. You would go out, be the gorgeous one with the flashing eyes – charm everyone, win them over. I'm not going to lie, I was jealous as I looked on, watching as you shared yourself with everyone like an expensive bottle of champagne. They could never see how you manipulated them, moulding their egos like plasticine, only to crush them later. You always had your way, no matter who got hurt. You never cared about anyone but yourself. Never understood that people have feelings.

I saw the signs.

It almost became too easy, didn't it?

Bored you.

Chapter 23

ROSE

Now

'So Willow definitely visited her father,' I say, as I close the front door and see Becky standing at the foot of the stairs.

'Really?' she says biting on her nails.

'Really,' I repeat, imagining the effect it would have had on Willow, on top of everything else. 'She would never have coped,' I add in a whisper. 'Especially if she thought he may have killed her mother.' I take a deep breath and lead the way into the lounge. 'Anyway, the inspector is going to report Willow's disappearance at his end. He'll keep us updated.'

'What can the police actually do?' Becky says.

I fiddle with my earlobe, thinking. My only knowledge of police protocol is gleaned from TV. 'I guess they'll check hospitals.' I pause 'Maybe I should tell your grandpa and Eleanor she's disappeared,' I say, already knowing it's a bad idea.

'Leave it for a bit, Mum,' Becky says. 'She could turn up today. We don't want to worry them – especially Grandpa.'

'Yes, you're probably right. What good would it do, anyway?'

Becky glances out of the front window. 'Jeez, it's that boy again,' she says. 'The one in the yellow cap.'

I join her at the window, sensing there's something suspicious about him. His stance. The way he stares.

'I'm going to speak to him,' she says. Before I can reply, she dives into the hall, and shoves her feet into my flip-flops. 'He may know where Willow is,' she adds, throwing open the front door, and racing down the path.

I head out after her, bare feet slapping crazy paving. 'Becky,' I call.

I expect the boy to run, like he did before, but he doesn't, and moments later Becky is standing next to him.

'What do you want?' she says with a bite in her voice. 'Who the hell are you?'

The boy is taller than Becky, almost six foot, older than her, I suspect. His faded yellow baseball cap covers shiny black hair, a long fringe hangs over one of his mud-brown eyes – eyes that are vacant, as though he doesn't see what's in front of him. He doesn't speak.

'Are you looking for Willow?' I say.

'Do you know where she is?' Becky adds, but he just looks up at the house, then down at his feet.

'Who are you?' I ask.

He lifts his gaze once more, studies us for a few seconds, before taking off, sprinting until he's out of sight.

'What the hell?' Becky looks at me wide-eyed.

'I've no idea,' I reply, leading the way up the path, feeling emotionally battered. 'This just gets weirder and weirder.'

*

After a morning of going over everything and constantly checking my phone, I suggest a walk to the village shop. Becky declines. She says she's going to watch TV to take her mind off things.

Slathering sun cream on my arms, I head down the road in my white vest-top and knee-length shorts, feeling guilty that I'm enjoying the sun on my face – the sounds of the countryside. Again, I wish I was here on holiday.

The village store is in dire need of renovation, and the amalgamation of smells – spices, bread, vegetables – that greet me as I head up the aisle of the shop, confuses my senses.

I place two pints of milk in the wire basket I'm carrying and open a small chest freezer. I grab a box of chicken in breadcrumbs, and some frozen veg – it's not very exciting so I doubt I'll tempt Becky to eat. I keep hoping her food obsession is a phase she's going through – that nagging too much will only make it worse. But then I don't want her ending up like Willow did.

The woman in her sixties behind the counter smiles as I return with the basket and unload it.

'You on holiday?' she says, blowing a tendril of ginger hair from her tanned, plump face. She's wearing a pale pink short-sleeved blouse, over black trousers. A necklace with a large pink stone hangs around her neck. 'You've picked a gorgeous week.'

'Yes, the weather's perfect,' I say. 'We're staying at Ocean View Cottage.' Her hand freezes on the till.

'Really? She pauses for a moment. 'Are you a friend of Willow's?'

'She's my stepsister, but she's not there at the moment.'

'Nice girl,' she says, continuing to ring up the items. '£6.95, please, love.'

I hand over a ten-pound note, and with a deep breath, I say, 'Do you remember the Millars?'

'Ooh, I got a tingle of déjà vu just then,' she says, with a shudder, pressing her ample chest. 'That's exactly what she asked. Willow, I mean.' She hands me my change and rams the till drawer closed. 'Well, of course I remember the murder. Everyone around here does. Young Ava Millar's death was a terrible tragedy.' She shakes her head and bites her lip as she stares into space. 'I hadn't been here long when it happened.' She rubs her neck, avoids eye contact. 'You just don't expect it in a quaint little village like Bostagel, do you? Only good things should happen here.'

She's right. The village is stunning. Picture-postcard perfect.

'Taking over the shop,' she went on, 'meant I got to know people quickly.

The mother, Jeannette Millar, didn't mix much with us village folk, kept herself to herself mostly, even before Ava's murder. The older daughter, Gail, was a beauty. Full of her own importance, God rest her soul. Now I liked Ava well enough, but she had another side to her. In fact, my son Dexter worked with her for a bit at the big DIY in Newquay. Took her out once, he did.'

'Dexter?' My mind swings back to my conversation with the inspector earlier. 'Dexter Powell is your son?'

'Uh-huh. Yes.'

Trying to keep my voice even, I say, 'Does he still live here?'

'Lord no. Hasn't lived with me for years. In fact, he doesn't come to Cornwall often.' There was a sudden sadness in her voice. 'Though he calls me every Sunday without fail. He's always been a good boy.' She pauses for a moment before adding, 'It was a crying shame what happened to those young Millar girls.' Her eyes tear over. After all these years, it still distresses her. 'How can such a terrible tragedy happen to two young girls?'

'It's truly awful,' I agree, tears filling my eyes too. This is getting to me. Just as it got to Willow.

Chapter 24

AVA

2001

'Gran will look after you,' Ava said, stroking Willow's cheek.

'No! No! No!' Willow cried, banging her legs against the high-chair, and throwing Marmite soldiers across the room. It was getting harder to leave Willow with her mother. The problem was, Jeannette tended to plonk her granddaughter in front of the TV while she went about her day, which may have worked for her own children, but Willow needed so much more. She was an imaginative child, who needed constant stimulation.

'Hey, what's all the racket?' Peter appeared in the lounge doorway, looking pale and smelling of last night's alcohol, his eyes bloodshot.

Ava lifted Willow from the highchair. 'She doesn't like staying with Mum while I'm at work,' she whispered, glancing through the patio doors at Jeannette hanging out washing, battling with a sheet in the wind.

'Well, I'm here,' he said. He turned his attention to Willow,

'We can play together.' He tickled the little girl's tummy, making her giggle.

Ava felt a rush of confusion. He sounded so genuine. Kind.

Willow reached out her chubby arms to him, and Peter winked at Ava as he took the child from her. 'Now go get ready for work, aye?'

'Thanks,' she said, but she didn't move.

'Go, before I change my mind,' he said with a laugh, kneeling down on the floor with Willow. He grabbed a cardboard box with her toys in with his free hand. 'We'll be just fine.'

Ava still waited, watching them play for a while. She had to admit, Peter had a way with Willow, and an oddly comforting memory flooded into her mind. Peter reading to her when she was a child. He must have been about fifteen. The book was *Little Red Riding Hood*. Peter was doing all the voices – so scary as the Big Bad Wolf – and making her giggle. She'd felt secure snuggled in his arms, hadn't she?

*

'This is Dexter.'

Ava turned from loading five-litre tins of magnolia emulsion onto the shelves at the DIY store where she worked, to see her boss Eric – short, chubby, looking far too stressed – with a dark-haired man of about twenty. Despite being anti-men at that moment, her traitor heart gave a leap. She'd seen him before – the son of the woman who'd taken over the village shop – but she'd never spoken to him.

'Dexter started this morning, Ava,' Eric continued, shoving an apron at Dexter. 'Can I leave him with you? He'll need to get up to speed in the garden centre. We're expecting a rush on bird tables at the weekend.'

Ava wiped her hands, grubby from the tins, down her bright-blue apron, and held out her hand. 'Hi,' she said, conscious of her tatty jeans and sweatshirt, her lack of make-up. 'I'm Ava Millar – bird table expert, it seems.'

He smiled. 'I've seen you about,' he said, shaking her hand a little awkwardly, before putting on his apron.

'Great.' Eric dabbed his sweaty forehead with a cloth, looked from Ava to Dexter, before dashing down the aisle towards plugs and sockets.

'So how long have you worked here?' Dexter asked, as they walked through giant double doors into the cold air – it had snowed earlier, not enough to settle on the ground, but enough to turn the shrubs and trees wintery white.

'Too long,' she said, as they walked towards the newly delivered bird tables. 'It's crap money, the job is boring, and some of the customers are rude, but the people who work here are nice enough – well, some of them.'

'Way to sell it to me,' he said with a laugh.

'No, it's OK, honestly.'

'Well, I won't be here long, anyway,' he said, as they passed some sad looking plants on offer at ninety-nine pence.

'Yeah, that's what I said when I first arrived.' She tucked a curl behind her ear, trying not to catch his gaze – he was nice-looking, with deep blue eyes and a cute nose.

'No really,' he said. 'I'm going to uni next September. I wanted to go when I left school, but Mum couldn't afford it. So I've been saving.'

'That's impressive.' She meant it. She envied his determination.

'Thanks.'

'I'm hoping to study from home soon,' she said, recalling her conversation with Gareth Jones.

'Good for you.' A smile dimpled his cheeks. 'Education is our ticket out of here, Ava.' They had reached the bird tables. 'So what's the low down on these?' he said, nudging one with his trainer.

'Ava!' The yell came from the double doors they had just walked through. She turned to see Peter, his arm raised in the air.

'Excuse me,' she said to Dexter, and raced towards her brother whose panicked look sent her heart racing. 'What's wrong?' She cleared her throat. 'What are you doing here?'

'It's Willow,' he said, catching his breath. 'You need to come. She's had an accident.'

*

'What happened?' Ava raced across the DIY store's car park, trying to keep up with Peter, her eyes filling with tears. 'Is she OK?'

'He just appeared at the house. Said he wanted to see her.'

'Who did?'

Peter unlocked his car doors, and they climbed in.

'Who did?' she cried, wrestling with the seatbelt, dashing away a tear from her cheek. 'You're scaring me.'

'She's with Mum at the hospital. She was unconscious for a while.'

'Oh my God!' She pressed down her skull with her hands. 'Oh my God!'

'They said she'll be OK,' he went on, starting the engine. 'Try not to worry, Ava.' He rammed the car into first gear and pulled away.

'Try not to worry?' It was a ridiculous statement. Of course she was going to worry about her darling girl.

'She'll be OK. Honestly.'

'Who was it? Who turned up at the house?' she snapped. 'How the hell did this happen?' Had her brother neglected Willow? She should never have left him responsible for her. What had she been thinking? She hardly knew him. 'Peter?'

'Justin.'

'Justin came to the house?'

'He said he wanted to see Willow.'

'And you let him in?'

'No! Mum did. She thought everything was OK between you two. He is Willow's father.'

112

'But it's over.' Tears dripped from Ava's chin. 'I told him last night that he couldn't see her anymore.'

'Well, you should have told us.' His knuckles were white on the steering wheel.

She nodded. 'I just can't believe he came to the house.' The thought brought on fresh tears. 'How did it happen?' She sniffed and rubbed her eyes with the tips of her fingers.

'Well, I was playing with her in the lounge when he appeared in the doorway, like he owned the place. Mum introduced him as Willow's dad, said he'd come to see her. I had no choice but to leave them to it. I went upstairs. Next thing Mum's yelling at Justin, saying he couldn't take her, so I raced down again. There was a bit of a set to. Justin yelling, Mum crying – normal stuff really.' He half-smiled again, but it disappeared when his eyes met Ava's. 'Willow wiggled and fell from his arms, cracked her forehead on the coffee table as she went down.'

'Oh my God,' Ava cried, covering her mouth.

'We couldn't get her to come round, so rushed her to hospital. But she's going to be OK, you'll see.'

Ava stared again at her brother with his sallow skin and scruffy hair. A sudden sharp memory of him punching his fist through the lounge door came and went. Had he really changed that much?

'Where's Justin now?' she asked.

'He took off as soon as Willow fell. Couldn't see the bastard for dust. Honestly, Ava, you need to get him out of your life.'

'I know. I really didn't think he'd turn up at the house.' She covered her face with her hands, rubbed away the tears. 'He hasn't wanted to see us for months.'

'You want my opinion, Ava?'

'Not really.' She glanced out of the side window, watching the frosty world pass her by.

'He's a psycho. In fact, how did you ever get mixed up with him in the first place?'

'I was only sixteen when we met. I believed fate had thrown us together at the right time. His mum had died. My life was crap. We were meant for each other.'

'So what went wrong?'

'His dad started drinking, couldn't cope with life without his wife – had some sort of guilt trip too. Justin got mixed up with the Bristow brothers – got into drugs. I stuck with him for ages though. I don't know why.'

'Maybe you were rebelling against Mum.'

'Maybe. She thought I was a failure, so I proved her right.' She gave a strangled laugh.

'Mum cares too much what people say about our family, and we've let her down, Ava. I reckon we'll always be the black sheep.'

'I know.' She tried for a smile, feeling slightly calmer. 'Safety in numbers though, aye? Anyway, as far as Justin's concerned, it's over.'

'I'm sorry, Ava,' he said, sounding genuine. 'Although you should never trust a bloke whose eyes are too close together.' He looked at her and smiled. He couldn't help the way he was, but this was no time for jokes. 'Sorry,' he said. 'Joking is my go-to when I'm stressed.'

'And alcohol?'

'Uh-huh, that too. What can I say? I'm not proud of that fact. I want to change, but it's hard.'

He was facing forward now, concentrating on the road.

'I thought I loved Justin, you know,' she said quietly, remembering the moment they'd met by the sea in Newquay.

There was a silence for some time, before they pulled up at a red light. 'Your turn,' she said.

'What?'

'Tell me about your love life – you said you were married.'

He glanced her way, and she saw, for the first time, pain in her brother's eyes. 'I told you before, she didn't want kids,' he said. 'Anyway, I don't want to go there right now.'

She looked through the front windscreen, the hospital now in view. Her stomach flipped with anxiety as Peter pulled into a space in the car park. She threw off her seatbelt and opened the door. 'Are you coming in then?' she said, jumping from the car.

They ran to the entrance and through the automatic doors, into the hospital.

'So do you still love her?' she said, trying to keep her mind occupied as they raced towards the lifts.

'Who?

'Your wife.'

He shrugged. 'I suppose so. What is love anyway?'

'If you're lucky it's the best thing ever. But it's still something you have to work at.'

'And you're the expert.'

'Clearly not – but I was young, and thought I loved Justin. I tried to make it work – at first, anyway.'

'He wasn't worth a moment of your time, Ava.'

'I know.' She paused, as they reached the lifts, fear rising at the thought of seeing her little girl in a hospital bed. 'Did you work at it, Peter? Did you work at your marriage?'

'I wanted kids, Ava, she didn't.'

'Maybe she would have changed her mind in time.'

'Maybe,' he said.

They took the lift, and as the doors whooshed open at the correct floor, Ava moved fast.

'Darling girl,' she cried, on seeing her daughter. She raced to her bed and took her in her arms. 'Whatever have you been up to?'

Willow touched the dressing on her head. 'Got bump,' she said, and Ava's eyes filled with tears of relief.

Chapter 25

ROSE

Now

Back at the cottage, the shopping put away, I perch on the edge of the sofa.

I'm getting so caught up in the past – just as Willow did – far too curious about who killed Ava Millar. But it's all connected. The more I know, the more likely I am to find Willow. I believe that.

'Mum?'

I jump, stupidly, like a child caught with her hand in a biscuit barrel.

'Jeez, I didn't mean to startle you,' Becky says, a thick eyebrow arched. 'Are you OK? You seem jumpy.'

'Yes, I'm fine. Just trying to make sense of everything, that's all.'

I'm turning my phone over in my hands when a message appears on the screen. I read it, and look up at Becky, 'Oh God, Eleanor's asking why we haven't called her. She wants to know how Willow is. What the hell am I going to say?'

'The truth.' She plonks down next to me.

'But it will only worry her. Willow may turn up soon.'

'You don't really believe that, Mum.'

'No. No I don't,' I say, shaking my head. 'In fact, I'm worried sick about her.'

'I feel the same. But if Grandpa knows he'll worry, and he's not well. There's nothing he can do anyway.'

'But you just said to tell the truth.'

'What I meant was, don't lie. Say Willow's not here yet. That we'll get her to call her when she arrives.'

'Yes. Yes. I'll do that,' I say, typing out the words on my phone as she says them. 'No point in worrying them too, is there?' But still I feel guilty.

*

We've been sitting around for hours, unsure what to do.

'I'll give Inspector Jones a call,' I say at around five o'clock, picking up my phone. 'In case he has any news.'

The call goes straight to voicemail, and I rattle off a message asking what the police are going to do, asking him to call me as soon as possible.

Unable to face cooking, I suggest we eat at the pub. 'It's still hot out there, we could go for a nice meal.' I nod through the patio doors, where the sky is a brilliant blue and the sun a bright yellow, as though painted by a child. 'A nice walk into the village will do us good.' The words feel too normal. Willow is missing. Before she disappeared she was hunting for a killer. And now we're going for a *nice* walk into the village for a *nice* meal. But it's not the only reason I'm going. I need to ask questions. Interrogate villagers. I can't wait around for the police.

'OK,' Becky says, getting up.

*

The pub garden is noisy with chatter and laughter. Children play on a brightly coloured slide and climbing frame. The pub itself is ancient, with a lopsided roof, the red brickwork crumbling. I'm amazed it's still standing.

It's quiet inside; you can almost hear people slurping their drinks. It's gloomy too, after the bright light of the sunny evening – the tables are dark wood, the curtains deep burgundy, but I want to stay inside. Becky drops down on a seat at a table in the corner. She feels the same way.

A young lad serves me at the bar, and I carry a glass of wine and an orange juice to the table, menus wedged under my arm.

Before looking at what I fancy to eat, I pull out my phone – obsessively checking for calls or messages.

'No signal,' I say. 'Oh God, what if Willow tries to get through?'

Becky leans over, reaches for my hand, her eyes meeting mine. 'Stop worrying for a moment, Mother,' she says. 'You'll spontaneously combust, and it will make a terrible mess.'

I smile at her efforts to ease the tension. 'Easier said than done, I'm afraid.'

'I know. But seriously you'll be no use to anyone if you don't relax a bit.'

She sounds far too grown up.

'Are you OK sitting inside?' she goes on. 'I thought we could chat easier in here.'

I glance beyond the window towards the pub garden at a group of women in bikini tops and shorts who are throwing back their heads in laughter, clutching large glasses of wine. A couple of lads are jabbing each other playfully, slopping lager. A child lies on her stomach crying and thumping the ground. I haven't room in my head for the liveliness through the window.

I turn to Becky. 'I prefer it in here,' I say, turning my phone over in my hands.

'OK. Good.' Becky picks up one of the menus. 'Then let's pick what we want to eat.'

*

I'm about to tuck into battered cod and triple cooked chips, when Becky leans over the table, our foreheads almost touching. 'He's been watching us for ages,' she whispers.

'Who?' I say, shuddering. I lower my cutlery and go to turn.

She grabs my hand. 'Don't look,' she snaps. 'We don't want to scare him off.'

'Who?' I repeat, my heart picking up speed.

'Some idiot, he's giving me the creeps, is all.'

'Let me look then,' I say.

'No. If you turn, he'll leave.' Her eyes are far too wide. This is getting to her.

'You don't know that. He's probably a regular. What does he look like?'

She glances past me, and bobs back. 'Light brown hair, forty – quite good-looking for an oldie but a bit weird too.'

I whiz round. Whoever this man is, he's staring right at us.

I look back at my daughter.

'Flip's sake, Mother, talk about obvious.'

I look over my shoulder again, to see he's standing now, downing the last of what looks like a gin and tonic.

I jump to my feet.

'What the hell are you doing?' Becky crosses her arms over her chest and slides down in the chair.

'I'm going to ask him why he was staring.'

'No. No, please don't.'

'But it could have something to do with Willow.'

'Yeah, right, like he could be Ava's killer, or something. Mega reason not to go right up to him.'

119

I take a gulp of wine.

'Too late, he's gone,' she says, sounding relieved.

I see through the tiny front window he's getting into a red car. I sit back down and look at my food, my appetite gone.

Becky silently pushes her salad around her plate.

'Are you OK, sweetheart?' I reach across the table and touch her cheek. 'Maybe you shouldn't be here in Cornwall.'

'Well, I'm not going home if that's what you mean.' She spears a cherry tomato with her fork. It splits and splatters across her plate.

*

'Was everything OK for you?' The man collecting our plates has a ready smile. He's in his fifties, and I suspect he's the landlord.

'Oh, yes,' I say, looking at the meals we've barely eaten. 'We weren't as hungry as we thought we were. Eyes bigger than our bellies, that's what my mum used to say.'

Becky glares at me. She's of the opinion that if we pay for our food, we don't have to explain ourselves if we don't eat it. *They only ask because they're afraid we'll put a one-star review on Trip Advisor.*

'Have you been here long?' I ask, as he's about to walk away.

'Since two,' he says, looking at the huge clock on the far wall.

'No, I mean, have you worked here long?'

'Ah, no, not long. The wife and I took early retirement to fulfil our dream of running a little pub in Cornwall a couple of years back. Turns out it's more of a nightmare at times.' He laughs.

'I wonder ...' I fumble with my phone, getting up a photo of Willow. 'Has this woman ever been in here?'

He furrows his forehead, studying the picture for a few moments. 'Yes, I've seen her. Don't ask me when. One day's the same as any other.' He shrugs. 'She certainly looks familiar.'

I would never make a private detective. I've no idea what else to ask.

'The man sitting by the door a few minutes ago,' Becky says, pointing to the seat the stranger vacated. 'Does he come in here regularly?'

He peers over his shoulder, and back at us. 'He's been in a couple of times.'

'Do you know his name?' Becky is on a roll.

He scratches his head, and his salt and pepper hair stands up with electricity. 'No, sorry.'

'Not to worry,' I say.

'Well, I hope you'll be back,' he says, as he carries away the plates. 'We do a catch of the day on Monday, a lovely midweek roast on a Wednesday, and if the forecasted storm stays away, we've got a BBQ planned for Friday.'

*

We head up the road towards Ocean View Cottage, and my phone springs into life as the signal returns: two messages and a voice-mail from Inspector Jones.

'Oh, thank God,' I say, stopping in the middle of the road. 'There's a message from Willow.'

'Oh, Mum,' Becky says, as our heads touch and we read it together:

Hey, Rose. So sorry I'm not there to greet you. I'm in Newquay, staying with a friend. I've discovered something important. Please make yourself at home. I'll give you a call soon. Love, Willow X

'Well that explains it,' I say, sighing with relief as I close the message. 'Thank God she's OK.'

'Is she?' Becky says. 'How do you know she even sent the message?'

'Oh, Becky, you watch far too many thrillers on Netflix. Of course she did. It's from her phone.'

'Yeah, but someone could be holding her kidnapped and forced her to type the message.'

I don't want to even consider Becky's theory – that something so awful could have happened. I need to believe Willow is fine.

We continue up the road, my phone pinned to my ear as I listen to Inspector Jones' voicemail:

'Hi, Rose,' he says. 'I got your message. I've filed a missing persons report for Willow, and we'll circulate her as a missing person on the Police National Computer. Some officers will ask about in the village. Can you send a recent photo of her to my email address, please? Plus we'll need to do a search of the cottage too. And, Rose,' he goes on, 'try not to worry.'

I fight against the fact Willow is a missing person. We've had a text from her now. She said she's OK. But as I link arms with Becky and we make our way up the hill, I still can't get it out of my head that Willow's in terrible danger.

Chapter 26

ROSE

Now

It's ten o'clock. Becky has gone to her room. I'm restless – anxiety bubbling under my skin, waiting to boil over.

Sick of pacing the same stripped wooden floorboards – sick of the hum of the fan whirring, the feeling of helplessness – I grab my jacket and leave the cottage. I make my way down to the beach, the darkness swallowing me as I head across the sand with the aid of my phone torch, hopeful the sea will calm me.

A cool breeze tickles my face, as I sit on my jacket a few yards from the rolling waves, my arms wrapped around my knees, squeezing, my chest rising and falling as I focus on my breathing – in, out, in, out. My eyes fix on the sea; in places shimmering metallic in the full moon. The current moves and shifts, as black as ink – impossible to know where the sea ends and the sky begins.

It's lonely here, but the crash of the waves against the sand sooth my jangled nerves and confused mind – comforting. I've always loved the sea. I visited Crantock as a child, and loved to race down the hill from the caravan site where we stayed to the beach, swinging my bucket and spade. There was nothing quite as beautiful as Cornwall in the sunshine.

I glance over my shoulder, raising my eyes to Ocean View Cottage. There's a light on in Becky's room. This is all too much for her, and I was pleased when her dad texted earlier, reminding her once more she's got so much to look forward to.

My eyelids grow heavy. I close my eyes for a moment, running my fingers through the sand.

Justin … Rory … Peter. Had one of them killed Ava? Or had someone else ended her young life? Dexter? Is Dexter the man in the yellow cap in the fourth photo? Would the inspector have recognised him if he was, or is the picture quality too bad?

My phone rings out too loud, bouncing off the cliffs. I open my eyes and pull it from my pocket.

'Aaron,' I say, answering the call, and a surge of relief rushes through me.

'Hey, how's it going?'

It's so good to hear his voice, and I want to tell him everything. 'It's all a bit odd,' I say, my voice sounding lost on the deserted beach. 'Willow's not come back, and I'm worried.'

'Have you tried calling her?'

'Of course, loads of times.' I rake sandy fingers through my hair, depositing grains onto my scalp. 'We've even told the police.' I desperately wish he was here by my side, holding me close. 'But then I got a text from her earlier today saying she's staying with a friend in Newquay.'

'Well, there you go. Mystery solved.' He sounds far too certain. 'It's what Willow does, Rose. When it gets too much, she takes off. Disappears. You know that.'

'Maybe,' I say.

'So you're still there? At the cottage?'

'Mmm. I've come out for some air. There's a beautiful bay nearby, and I'm sitting here in the darkness. Thinking.'

'You sound exhausted.'

'I didn't sleep well last night. I'm not sure I will tonight.'

'Listen, sorry, I've got to go, darling,' he says. 'I'll call you when I can. Love you.'

'OK,' I say, and when he ends the call, my heart sinks.

I shove my phone into my pocket. I need him right now more than I've ever needed him, and feel so close to tears my head throbs. I close my eyes again, and after some moments I hear the sound of stones crashing down the cliff face some distance away.

My eyes spring open, and I look around, a shudder running through me. Over on the far side of the bay, standing on the cliff edge is a figure silhouetted against the night sky. I can't be certain, but whoever it is seems to be watching me.

My chest tightens. I jump up and grab my jacket, eyes glued to where the person is standing. I head up the beach towards Ocean View Cottage, my legs heavy in the sand. I'm about halfway when I look over my shoulder. I can't see the figure. I stop to fumble in my pocket for my phone and flick on the torch. The light picks out someone at the foot of the steps that are cut into the rock face. I can't see their face.

Fear thuds in my chest, and something inside me tells me to run. But my feet sink into the sand even more, slowing my pace. I stumble, falling onto my hands and knees, my breath catching in my throat.

I pull myself up and flash the torchlight around the area. I can't see anyone, but they couldn't have gone. They must be somewhere.

I turn and head onwards, but within moments I sense someone behind me. Before I can twist round, I feel a sharp pain in the back of my head. I stagger forward, and the ground rises up to greet me. I fall hard on the sand. My vision blurs but I know someone's still here, hovering over me, crouching – touching my hair – stroking it. I feel their breath on my skin.

'Leave.' It's a muffled whisper. I try to lift my head, but before I can see my assailant, everything goes black.

*

I have no idea how long I've been unconscious, but when I come round, whoever hit me has gone. I rub my head – there's a bump, blood on my fingers. The shock of what's happened hits me. I need to get back to the cottage.

I take a deep breath, and ease myself up, wobbling precariously, trying to get my balance. Once I feel stable, I move up the beach, heart thudding. I'm not far from the cottage now – almost there – looking over my shoulder every few moments.

Once inside, I fumble with the bolts on the front door, pulling them across, one, two, three, and rest my forehead against the opaque glass.

Someone is trying to scare me away. Is this what happened to Willow?

I hear Becky lumbering down the stairs behind me. She flicks on the hall light. 'Mum?'

'Oh God, Becky,' I say, turning to face her, blinking in the brightness. 'We need to go home. Now.'

'Why? What's happened?' Her eyes look browner than ever – wide and worried.

She puts her arm around me, and guides me into the lounge, where she clicks on the side lamp. We sit down on the sofa. I'm shaking – can barely see through the blur of tears.

'You look really white, Mum. What's happened?' she says again.

'Someone knocked me out,' I say, my voice cracking. 'They told me to leave.'

She covers her mouth. 'Oh my God, Mum. Are you OK? Are they still out there?' She looks towards the door.

'No. No. They're long gone.' I fumble with my phone, and she takes it from me.

'Shall I call an ambulance? The police?' Her eyes are back on me, her voice full of concern. 'What were you doing out there on your own in the dark in the first place, Mum?'

'I needed some air. I didn't expect someone ... shit!' I say, burying my head into my hands, feeling the lump under my fingers. It's so sore. 'What the hell's going on, Becky?'

She taps my phone. I hear her voice, calm and crisp. 'Police, please,' she says, and I look up at her. She's just a child, and yet she's so grown up – I desperately need her right now.

*

The police arrive as the village church bells chime midnight: a woman officer of around thirty, a younger male PC, both in uniform, both look as though they've been on duty for a week.

'I'm PC Lewis,' the female cop tells me, showing me ID. 'This is PC O'Timoney.'

Holding Becky's hand, unsure whose benefit it's for, I lead them down the slope towards the beach, their flashlights lighting the area.

'It happened about here,' I say, stopping. 'But it's a waste of time. Whoever hit me has long gone.' I look towards the cliff. 'He was over there at first, staring down at me.'

'You know it was a man?' she asks.

I shake my head. 'Well, no. Not really.'

The officers walk towards the steps in the cliff. PC O'Timoney climbs up them and onto the cliff top, searching the area with his torchlight. PC Lewis remains below, angling her torch over the steps.

But they're shaking their heads as they walk back, their torches making me squint. I cover my eyes, look down at the sand.

'There's nothing that we can see,' PC O'Timoney says. He's Irish, has a look of Ronan Keating. 'There's nothing much over that side of the bay. No houses for about quarter of a mile. Did you hear a car?'

I shake my head. 'No, I don't think so.' But I can't be sure.

We make our way back to the house in silence, and I realise Becky is still holding my hand.

'Are you OK?' I whisper. It's a silly question.

'You'll need to come down to the station to make a statement, Mrs Lawson,' PC Lewis says over her shoulder, as we reach the cottage and they make their way down the path towards their car. 'Try to recall anything at all about your assailant. In the meantime, get your head checked out.'

'I will,' I say, and because there is nothing more we can do, Becky and I step inside the house and close the door.

Chapter 27

ROSE

Now

It's 2 a.m. I can't sleep. I throw back the quilt and sit up. A yawn and stretch later, I get up and pad towards the window.

From a patchwork wing-backed chair, I look out across the bay for almost half an hour. It's a full moon and I watch the tide going out, taking the events of earlier with it.

'Where are you, Willow?' I whisper.

A memory floats in of Willow, around twelve years old, telling me she'd seen someone hanging about Darlington House wearing a mask. It was just one of her stories, but it scared me. Despite the fact I was twenty-five at the time and a mum who should know better than to listen to her crazy stories. I remember sleeping with a cricket bat by my bed for about a year after that. And round about now, I wish I had that bat.

I get up from the chair, return to bed, and squeeze my eyes closed. But my brain still won't close down, and for the rest of the night I barely sleep. When I do, vivid nightmares where Willow is trapped in a white room by a faceless man invade.

I get up early, shower, dress in shorts and a stripy blue and white T-shirt, and tie my hair up in a ponytail. I poke my head around Becky's door to see she's still sleeping, and close her door gently, deciding to let her have a lie in.

I make some coffee, and sit on the sofa, going over and over what's happened. Still making no sense of any of it.

'Morning, Mother,' Becky says, and I turn to see her slouching into the room, her hair a fizzy mess, her dressing gown tied tightly.

'Did I wake you, sweetheart?'

She flops down next to me, smelling of sleep. 'Not really, I couldn't sleep anyway,' she says. 'How are you?' She touches my head gently. 'Are you going to the hospital? I really think you should.'

I shrug. 'I'm fine,' I say. 'In fact, I'm wondering if we should go home, let the police do their job.' But even as I say it, despite my fears and lack of sleep, I know I must stay at Ocean View Cottage. I can't let Willow down. She turned to me for help, and I need to find her.

It's clear Becky feels the same way. 'No! No! We can't, Mum. Don't you see? That's exactly what whoever's doing this wants us to do.'

She's right, but we're hardly Rizzoli and Isles.

I realise I haven't let Inspector Jones know about Willow's text saying she's in Newquay. But even as I type the words into my phone, I don't believe them.

When Becky goes upstairs to shower and change, I get out the photographs of the four men. Surely one holds a clue to Willow's whereabouts.

I stare at Willow's father, Justin. If he recently came out of prison, where would he have headed? I recall the conversation with Inspector Jones – the way he hinted that Justin has abducted Willow. If anyone knows where Justin is now, it will be the gossiping owner of the village store.

I climb the stairs and poke my head around Becky's door. She's sitting on the bed with her laptop. 'I'm going out,' I say.

'Where?'

'Just to the shop.'

'OK,' she says with a smile. 'I'd come, but I'm about to Skype Tamsyn.'

'Don't for God's sake tell her about Willow,' I remind her. 'I don't want it all over social media.'

She rolls her eyes. 'I won't,' she says. 'Although maybe it wouldn't be such a bad thing, Mum. Someone may have seen her.'

'Yes, but Eleanor may see it,' I say, raising my hand in a wave. 'I won't be long. Bolt the doors after me.'

'Later!' she calls, as I hurry down the stairs. It's good to hear despite everything, she sounds upbeat.

*

A bell rings out when I open the door to the village shop. There's nobody behind the wooden counter, and nobody in the store buying up the dusty tins.

'Hello?' I call through a beaded curtain, which would look more at home in the Seventies.

'Hello again.' The woman I saw before appears through the beads, bringing with her an aroma of heavy perfume. She's wearing a flowery sundress, her ginger hair pulled back, fastened with a slide. 'Lovely day, isn't it?'

'Beautiful ... sorry, I can't recall your name.' It wasn't strictly true. I had worked out she must be Mrs Powell.

'I don't think I told you it,' she says, eyes narrowing. After a pause, her face breaks into a bright smile, revealing a smudge of red lipstick and something green on her teeth. 'I'm Megan Powell. And you are?'

'Rose Lawson,' I say, unsure whether to go on. But I have to

– for Willow's sake. 'I wondered if you know or knew Justin Havers. He used to live around here.'

She nods. 'Yes, I know Justin – well more knew of him really. He went down for armed robbery about eighteen years ago, just after Ava died.'

'That's a long sentence …'

'Mmm, I read in the paper a long time ago how he lost his chance for parole. Smuggling drugs into prison, apparently. He was a wrong 'un, and no mistaking.' She pushes a tendril of hair from her face, revealing a sprinkling of freckles.

'I heard he was released recently,' I say.

'Well, God save us all,' she says, crossing her chest. 'Are you looking for him?'

I lift my gaze to her face again. 'I am, yes. But I haven't got a clue where he might be.'

'Nor me, I'm afraid.'

The door opens, the bell ringing once more throughout the shop. A young woman with a baby in her arms walks in.

'Morning, Sue,' Megan calls out, with a flurry of her ringed fingers.

'Morning!' the woman says, grabbing a wire basket, and heading down the aisle towards the chest freezer.

Megan turns and struts into the back of the shop without a word, returning a few moments later. 'My hubby says Justin and his dad lived on Cranberry Close before he went down.' She says it in a whisper, as though it's a secret. 'So if you're looking for him, that would be the first place I'd try. Hubby says Justin's dad, Ian, died around the time his son went to prison. Cirrhosis of the liver, some say, although there was some talk that he took his own life.'

I feel my eyes widen. 'How tragic.'

'Mmm,' she says, her tone unsympathetic. 'The house would have gone to Justin, him being the next of kin, like. Apparently Justin got left a bit of money too, although I bet he's injected the lot by now.' She pauses for a moment. 'Be careful though, love. As I say, Justin's a wrong 'un.'

'Do you know what number on Cranberry Close?'

'Well, there's only a couple of semis and a farm down that way. I'm sure you'll find it.' She touches her necklace. It's the same one she had on before with the large pink stone.

'That's a lovely necklace,' I say, meaning it. It's pretty.

'What, this?' Her chin doubles as she looks down at it. 'My son bought it for me years ago now. I always wear it.'

'You said he went out with Ava.'

'Yes, that's right. And I know it's awful to speak ill of the dead, but she hurt him. He had such a crush on her, but she treated him terribly.'

'I'm sorry.' I take a deep breath. 'I guess it must have made things worse when he was suspected of her murder.' I'm aware I'm pushing my luck.

'Dexter?' Her voice cracks up a notch. Her eyes fired. 'He was with me the night she died,' she snaps. I've hit a nerve. 'His father was away, and we went to the wedding together, both of us left early. We watched *The Office* and *Eastenders* when we got home.' It sounded like a well-rehearsed speech. 'I can't believe, even to this day, that Dexter was questioned. My little angel wouldn't hurt anyone!'

'Of course he wouldn't.' I step backwards, unable to think of anything else to say, my heart thudding, glad the counter separates us. 'I'm so sorry for bringing it up.' But she hasn't finished.

'Have you any idea what it can do to a family, to a young man, to be considered a murder suspect?'

'I'm sorry,' I say again, turning to leave, her eyes burning my back as I dash through the door and into the heat of the day.

I make my way to Cranberry Close. I had the sense to print out a map of the area before I left Old Stevenage. I know where I'm going.

Megan Powell is right; two semi-detached houses and a farm

make up Cranberry Close. For some reason, even from a distance, I know which house is Justin's, and the rundown appearance of the place makes me uneasy.

I make my way up the gravel road, pebbles crunching under my feet as I go. The sun disappears behind a cloud as I reach the gate, which is barely attached to the post, and head up the path.

Once under the porch, stepping from foot to foot, I knock on the front door. After a few moments I sense movement inside.

'Who is it?' It's a male voice behind the glass, a silhouette of someone hovering.

'I'm looking for Justin Havers,' I call out.

'That's not what I asked.'

'My name is Rose Lawson. I was hoping to talk to Justin about Willow.'

The door opens six inches and a man with white-blonde cropped hair looks me up and down. I know immediately he's the man in the photo Willow sent me. He's older, with heavy lines around his eyes and a greying complexion, but it's definitely him.

'Justin?' I say. His name almost lodges in my throat, my heart thuds. 'Listen, I'll come back another day if it's a problem.'

I go to turn, but he opens the door wide. 'Come in,' he says. My chest tightens, and I freeze on the step.

'What are you waiting for?' he goes on.

I take a deep breath and step inside.

The lounge smells of a combination of smoke and body odour. The surfaces are thick with dust, and an ashtray heaving with cigarette butts is on the coffee table next to a pack of Marlboro and a lighter. The sofas are worn down to the thread, and there's no carpet, just grubby, patterned rugs scattered over scratched and battered parquet flooring. He doesn't offer me a drink, for which I'm thankful. I prefer not to think about the state of the kitchen.

I take another deep breath and clear my throat, wishing now that I'd told Becky where I was going.

'I'm Willow's stepsister,' I say. 'She's been staying down here at Ocean View Cottage.'

He nods. 'I know.' His voice is husky. 'She's searching for her mother's killer.' He stares down at his trembling hands. He's nervy, and there are dark rings around his eyes. I think of the young lad in the photo Willow sent me. He's now a husk of that boy. He's wearing grubby denim shorts and a sweat stained black vest-top that reveals a tattoo on his left shoulder – it says 'Willow'.

'Willow asked me outright, when she visited, if I killed Ava.' His blue eyes are on me. 'I told her. Why would I kill the mother of my child?'

He's not asking me, but I answer anyway. 'Maybe Ava wouldn't let you see Willow?'

He laughs, a sad laugh that doesn't reach his eyes, and I realise I'm not threatened by him. 'Well, that bit's true,' he says. 'Quite honestly, I didn't blame her. I was a bastard back then.' He stares at me for some time, then picks up a cocktail stick and pushes it between his yellowing teeth before continuing. 'You know what? When Willow came here, I felt a false sense of pride when I saw her. That I had a part in creating someone so vivacious, spirited – so beautiful. It did my heart good. I'd wanted to see her for years, a chance to explain why I couldn't keep her.'

'That you'd rather commit armed robbery?' It was out before I could think straight.

He throws the stick on the coffee table. His swift movement makes me jump.

'I'm not proud of what I did,' he says. 'My gun wasn't loaded. I had no idea the Bristows were carrying loaded firearms.' He lowers his head. 'That they were going to shoot.'

'They killed someone?'

He shakes his head. 'The woman survived, thank Christ. But it was still attempted murder. I'd thought if I had money I could care for Willow, but it all went tits up. At the end of the day, I knew someone else could give her a much better life than I could.'

'Eleanor's been a good mum to Willow.'

'Yeah, Willow said. I wish even now I could have been *that* person who gave Willow a decent life. But I wasn't a good man. I treated Ava terribly, was a crap dad to Willow – I know that now. But you have to understand, I had nothing at the time.'

I nod, feeling a mixture of sadness and disgust for the man. A man who still has nothing.

'Were you surprised when she visited you? Turned up after all these years?'

He shook his head. 'I sent her a message on Facebook, attached an article about the murder.'

'That was you?'

He nods. 'I set up a fake account. I wasn't sure she'd come here to meet her crap father. I haven't exactly got a lot to offer her. In fact, some still think I killed Ava. But I thought if she knew what happened to her real mother, she might come – and with luck on my side, I would get to know her slowly.' He shakes his head. 'I was a bloody idiot. I just thought ...' He drags his fingers through his hair. 'I don't know what I thought.'

I stare for some time, unable to take in that he drew Willow to Cornwall the way he had. 'How did you find her?'

'I saw her in the newspaper back when she was modelling. I didn't know it was Willow first off. But the photo haunted me. I couldn't believe how much she looked like Ava. When I saw her name was Willow and that she was the right age – I knew it had to be her. My daughter.' He touched his forehead. 'The scar clinched it for me. The scar I caused.'

'Did you book the cottage?'

He nods. 'Dad left me a bit of money when he died. I put it down on the cottage. I should have been more open with Willow, but instead—'

'You lured her into danger.'

'What do you mean?'

'Nothing. It doesn't matter.'

'Of course it matters.' He's suddenly animated, his eyes full of concern.

'I just meant you lured her here with information about her mother's murder. It could have been dangerous.'

He lowers his head. 'It was a long time ago,' he says.

A suffocating silence falls, covering more angry words lodged in my throat.

'I spent all those years in prison thinking about Willow and Ava,' he says finally, his knees bouncing. He rubs his forehead with the tips of his fingers. 'They never really knew who killed Ava.'

'I know,' I whisper, looking at my hands. I should go.

'They thought it was her sister, Gail – that she topped herself after she'd killed Ava. Apparently they rowed. Someone even said they saw Gail take the cake knife, and a few witnessed her slap Ava across her face that night. Others said it was Dexter Powell. I mean his mother was his alibi, for Christ's sake.'

I think of Megan in the store. How angry she was that he'd been a suspect. Was she the mother of a killer? Would she have given him an alibi?

'I guess it was odd that he turned up in Cornwall with his mother, took Ava out, and she ended up dead,' he says. 'But I've had a long time in prison to think about it. I don't reckon it was Dexter or Gail. In fact, I know who killed Ava.'

'You do?' I wait, but he doesn't go on. 'Tell me! Tell me who you think it was.'

'Everyone will know soon enough,' he says.

I wonder if it's a bluff – if he killed her and is misdirecting me. But his silence says he's finished talking. I get up and loop my bag over my shoulder. 'Just one more thing,' I say. 'Have you seen Willow in the last few days.'

He shakes his head. 'I've called her a couple of times, but her phone goes to voicemail. She'll call me back when she's ready. I'm not going to rush her. Our relationship – if you can even call it that – has a long way to go.'

I open my mouth to tell him she's missing and close it again, deciding not to involve him.

He doesn't get up as I leave the room and head into the hallway, just rests his head back in the chair, and closes his eyes.

I look up the stairs, suck in a breath, and make my way up, needing to be sure Willow isn't here.

'Willow?' I whisper, when I reach the landing and cross towards one of the bedrooms. I turn the handle and open the door. Inside there's a mattress on the floor, with an old blanket over it, and a pillow. Is this where Justin sleeps?

Back on the landing I attempt another door handle. It's locked. 'Willow? Willow are you in there?' I call softly.

'What are you doing?'

I twist round and let out a scream. Justin is far too close. His eyes are fired up with anger. 'I was just ...' But no words form.

'Leave,' he says in a horrible whisper.

I dash past him, and down the stairs, almost falling on my way through the front door.

Chapter 28

AVA

2001

'You can take Willow home, Miss Millar,' the young nurse said, handing Ava a letter. Ava had stayed at the hospital all night, lying on a mattress on the floor next to Willow's bed. Despite the doctor insisting it was only precautionary, she had been too worried to sleep. Although there hadn't been much chance of sleep anyway with little ones crying, nurses giving out medication, the hum of staff talking, and just when she was dozing off, the breakfast trolley had rattled onto the ward.

Now, she sat in a chair with Willow on her lap. 'Thank you,' she said, taking the release letter from the nurse.

'And here's a list of things to look out for,' the nurse went on, handing it over. 'But, I'm sure she'll be absolutely fine.' She leaned forward to check the dressing on Willow's forehead, and touched her cheek. 'You're a little beauty, aren't you?' she said. 'And now you'll have your very own Harry Potter style scar,' she concluded, before walking away.

Fifteen minutes later Peter dashed onto the ward. 'I've parked as close I can,' he said, tweaking Willow's cheek. 'You don't have to worry, Ava,' he went on, lifting Willow from her arms. 'I won't let anything bad happen to her ever again.'

*

Ava didn't want to go to work the following day, even though Willow seemed bright and happy. But she had no choice. Peter hadn't found any plumbing jobs yet, so it was up to her to earn money.

The thought of leaving Willow with Jeannette made her uneasy, and despite her not blaming Peter for what happened, she couldn't shake that Willow was his responsibility when it did. Would he even notice if Willow took a turn for the worse?

'Stay, Mummy,' Willow cried, grabbing Ava's legs as she attempted to put on her duffle coat and boots.

'She'll be fine,' Peter reassured, crouching down and reaching out his arms to Willow.

'She loves you,' Ava said, as the little girl went to her uncle, and Ava fastened the toggles of her coat, blinking back tears. 'You'll keep a good eye on her for me, won't you, Peter?'

'Of course,' he said. 'And before you ask, I won't let Justin anywhere near her.'

*

Ava went about her workday in an almost trancelike state. By afternoon she'd called Peter three times to check on Willow.

'She's absolutely fine,' Peter said again when he picked up for the fourth time, before she'd even said a word. 'Stop worrying.'

She'd been put on bathrooms, which she didn't mind – it made her feel important when customers asked her opinion. She imagined now she was in charge of the whole department – what it would be like to manage her own store.

'Hi there.' She turned from her daydream to see a man in his early twenties. She'd seen him before. Maxen. Yes, Maxen that's what he'd said his name was that day in Kathy's café. It had been a few years since she saw him last, and she wasn't sure he recognised her. She wouldn't jog his memory.

'Can I help?' she said, in her best voice, trying to push the last moment he'd spoken to her out of her mind.

'I'm looking for taps, please, Ava,' he said with a wide smile.

She passed her hand over her name badge, feeling strangely uneasy.

'This way,' she said, leading him down the correct aisle, sensing his eyes on her back as she walked. She pointed out the selection on display.

'Thanks,' he said, with a hint of a Welsh accent. 'I haven't a clue what I'm doing.' He scanned the shelves. 'We've got a faulty tap – sprung a leak – Dad's at home controlling it while I save the day. Plumber-man to the rescue.' He clenched his fists and playfully raised his arms at the elbow, like he was Superman.

She smiled, her feeling of unease lifting.

'Except—'

'You haven't got a clue.'

He laughed and rubbed his temples. 'Dad's always rattling on about how Mum was the whiz in that department. Well, all departments really. There wasn't much she couldn't turn her hand to, apparently.'

'Wasn't?' It was out before she could tell herself it was none of her business.

'She left when I was three.'

'I'm sorry.'

'Thanks, but it was a long time ago. I barely remember her.'

'But I shouldn't have poked my nose in. Sorry.'

'No worries, honestly,' he said. 'Now about these taps, I've got visions of my dad drowning if I don't get back soon.'

141

She helped him pick some out using what she hoped was a good sales technique.

'Cheers,' he said with a smile, picking up the box and heading away. Perhaps he hadn't recognised her. Had she really changed that much?

'If you have any problems let me know,' she called after him.

'Thank you, Ava, please send my love to Gail.'

And there it was.

He had remembered her too.

*

'Who was that?' Dexter said, coming up beside her.

As she looked up at him, her stomach twisted, like it had the day she met Justin. 'Just a customer.'

'You seemed very chatty.'

'I'm good at my job,' she said, smiling. But Dexter's eyes had fallen on the man. Her gaze joined his, and together they watched as he loaded the taps onto the counter, and laughed with the checkout operator.

'His name's Maxen,' she whispered.

'Sorry?'

'Nothing,' she said, deciding Dexter didn't need to know. 'Not important,' she added, heading away.

*

It was almost a week later that Peter and Ava sat in the lounge of Ocean View Cottage, the smell of a chicken roasting making her hungry. If there was one thing her mother could do well, it was cook a Sunday roast.

Peter was making Ava laugh about the antics they'd got up to on Rory's stag do the night before. She could tell Peter had had a few too many; he looked pale, his eyes red-rimmed, and he was swallowing down painkillers with a pint of water.

Ava tried to imagine her future brother-in-law tied to a tree, half naked, and stifled a laugh. 'He could have died of exposure. It's pretty cold out there for November.'

'Nah, one of his mates felt sorry for him. Went back to save him. Everyone else went home at that point. Anyway, it's no more than he deserved,' he said, plonking the half-drunk glass of water onto the coffee table. 'Rory can be a right prick at times.'

'Can he? He seems OK to me.' She wasn't sure she meant it. She was still conflicted by how she felt about Rory.

Peter picked up his cigarette packet, then put it down again as though he couldn't face going outside for a smoke. 'Admittedly Rory was trashed last night. He came straight from work, and we didn't eat until about ten, but he was chatting up loads of women. If Gail knew, she'd bloody kill him.'

'Maybe we should tell her, or Mum.'

'Tell Mum what?' Jeannette said, poking her head out of the kitchen, furrowing her forehead.

'Nothing,' Peter said. Then whispered in Ava's ear, 'It's not our place to interfere.'

Jeannette entered the lounge, both hands clutching a mug of tea, and plonked herself down on the sofa, her face shiny from cooking, and her hair flyaway. She put the mug down, and picked up the local newspaper that was folded on the coffee table, and began flicking through it – her presence rendering Peter and Ava silent.

'Oh my God,' she said, pausing on a page. 'This isn't good. This isn't good at all.'

'What's happened?' Peter said, glancing at Ava, and then back at their mum.

'A young girl was attacked near Crantock.'

'God that's awful. When?' Ava asked.

'Last Wednesday. A rapist far too close to home.' She lowered the newspaper, her eyes meeting Ava's. 'You must be careful at night,' she said. 'You never know who could be lurking about.'

'You're freaking me out, Mum. I'm always careful,' Ava said, rubbing her neck.

'Yes, well.' Jeannette closed the paper and placed it back on the table. 'Be even more careful from now on, Ava.' And with that, she rose and, with her mug in her hands, headed back to the kitchen.

*

Dexter was sitting under the bus shelter when Ava approached. It was the first time she'd seen him there as he was normally dropped off at work by his mum.

'Hey, Ava,' he said, taking off his headphones so they hung around his neck, his eyes meeting hers.

Ava's stomach tipped and her heart picked up speed. 'Hey,' she said, sitting down next to him. A silence followed, and she was relieved when the bus appeared.

Once on the bus, she plonked down in a seat next to the window, and Dexter sat down beside her.

'Fancy seeing *The Others* tonight?' he said, once they were travelling through the village.

She twirled her hair around her finger. 'At the cinema?'

'No, at the swimming pool.' He laughed, and she smiled. His hair and eyes looked darker than ever, so different from his mother with her ginger hair and freckles, who she'd seen in the local shop a few times. 'Nicole Kidman is meant to be awesome,' Dexter continued. 'It's supposed to be creepy.'

Ava hated the thought of ghosts. When she was little, Gail told her Ocean View Cottage was haunted. She'd slept with a torch under her quilt most nights after that, as Gail hadn't let her sleep with the light on.

'With you?' Excitement bubbled. She sounded ridiculous, but

couldn't quite believe he was asking her out. He couldn't possibly know about her past – about Willow.

'No, with Bugs Bunny.' He laughed again. 'Yep, of course with me.'

The giddy feeling evaporated, as Willow drifted into her thoughts. She couldn't leave her daughter all day and then go out in the evening, could she? But if she told Dexter about her daughter, would he still be interested? A wave of guilt that she was hiding Willow from him lowered her mood further. 'I don't think I can,' she said.

He looked surprised, as though he wasn't used to rejection. 'Fine,' he said, turning away from her, staring out of the grubby window.

'It's just, well …' Would Peter look after Willow? She would be in bed asleep before she even left the house. 'Well, OK then,' she said.

He turned. Looked deep into her eyes. 'Great. I'll borrow my mum's car, and pick you up at seven,' he said as the bus pulled up at their stop. 'OK?'

As he led the way down the aisle, grabbing her hand, her heart fluttered. Maybe he could share her journey towards a better future. He was going to university, after all. He wanted more too, didn't he? Maybe everything was going to be OK.

*

Willow and Peter sat on the sofa in the lounge, his arm around his niece, her head against his chest, thumb in her mouth, watching a cartoon.

'You look cosy,' Ava said as she shuffled out of her coat and hung it up. She kicked off her boots, raced towards them, and knelt down in front of Willow, who popped her thumb from her mouth.

'Mummy,' she squealed, leaning forward and grabbing Ava's neck, and placing a wet kiss on her mum's cheek.

'Have you had a good day, darling girl?'

Willow released Ava, nodded, and leaned back on the sofa, resting her head on Peter's chest once more.

'We've had great fun, haven't we Willow?' Peter said with a smile.

But Willow's thumb was back in her mouth, her heavy eyes on the TV.

Ava had never felt so torn. Would she be a terrible mother if she went out with Dexter?

'I've been asked out,' she said to Peter. 'Tonight. To the cinema.'

'Do you good,' Peter said with a smile.

'Yes, but Willow ...'

'She'll be fine. And, from what I've seen since I got back, it's all work and no play for you. Go Ava. Go have a good time. I'll keep a careful watch on this little lady.'

'She'll be asleep before I go.'

'Exactly. She'll be no problem at all.'

'Thanks, Peter,' she said. 'Thanks so much.'

*

As expected, Willow was in bed asleep by the time Ava was standing at the window watching for Dexter's car headlights. She was relieved to have an excuse to escape, as Rory and Gail had turned up to show everyone their wedding rings, and her mum was cooing over them, kneeling at their feet as though the couple were royalty.

'We're giving each other a piece of jewellery too. I've told Rory what I want. I'm getting him a necklace of some sort.'

Rory rolled his eyes. 'I don't wear jewellery, Gail. And it might be better if I choose something for you that comes from my heart.'

'You know what I want, Rory,' she said. 'It's that antique piece I showed you in the shop. Anyway, Mum, we're going to give them to each other at the same time as the speeches.'

'So you're not only giving rings, you're giving another piece of jewellery. Bit overkill if you ask me,' Peter said, looking up from a book he was reading.

'Nobody's asking you, Peter. It's my wedding—'

'Our wedding,' Rory corrected.

'Yes, well you know what I mean.' She slipped off her cardigan. 'It's really hot in here, Mum.'

Her mum grabbed Gail's arm, and glared at a large bruise on her upper arm. 'Jesus, what have you done there?'

Gail looked shocked for a moment and pulled her cardigan back on. 'You're never going to believe it; I tumbled over in the garden. It was icy, and my legs just went from under me. Thankfully Rory was there to pick me up.'

'And a good thing you'll be wearing a long-sleeved wedding dress, by the looks of things,' Peter said.

'Why didn't you tell me?' Jeannette asked.

'It was nothing Mum, honestly.'

'Are you getting used to the idea of having your wedding at the village hall?' Ava said, glancing over her shoulder. She knew it was a cruel thing to say. There was no way Gail wanted her reception at Bostagel village hall.

Gail glared at Ava. 'Well, it's not like I've got a choice, is it?'

'I've said I'm sorry, Gail,' said Rory. 'What do you want, blood?'

'So, who is this bloke you're going out with tonight, Ava?' Peter asked, cutting across Gail and Rory's simmering argument.

'Dexter Powell,' she said.

'Ooh, I know Dexter,' Gail said. 'He goes to my gym.'

'Well, I work with him,' Ava said. 'He's really nice.'

'Nice?' said Rory.

'Yes, nice,' she said. 'We're going to see *The Others* in Newquay. We shouldn't be too late.'

'It's a freaky film, Ava,' Gail said. 'I thought you hated ghosts.'

'Well, yes I do, but—'

'She'll be snogging in the back row,' Rory said with a laugh. 'I see you're dressed for it.'

'Rory!' Gail snapped, giving him a daggering stare.

But before Ava could respond, or consider changing out of her short skirt, a horn tooted outside.

'I'm off,' she said, picking up her coat, and escaping from the room at speed.

'Be good, and if you can't be good be careful – *this time*,' Gail called after her.

Chapter 29

AVA

2001

'Jesus, that was freaky,' Ava said, as she and Dexter left the cinema, and made their way towards the foyer, past huge posters of upcoming films. 'I had my eyes closed through most of it. I can't believe we ate a whole tub of popcorn.'

He laughed and took hold of her hand. 'You ate a whole tub of popcorn, you mean.'

'Sorry. My only excuse is I eat when I'm nervous,' she said, spotting Gareth Jones in front of them.

He turned as though sensing her there. 'Ava,' he called raising his hand, stopping to wait for her to catch up.

As Ava and Dexter caught up, she explained who Gareth was, noticing a familiar figure standing with him.

'Hello, Ava,' Gareth said with a smile, as they reached him. 'How are you?'

'Good thanks,' she said.

'This is my son, Maxen,' he said, gesturing to him.

'Your son?' Ava couldn't hide the surprise in her voice. But then she didn't know that much about the inspector, not really.

'Hey!' Maxen said with a smile 'We must stop meeting like this.'

'We really must,' she said with a small laugh, feeling herself flush. Dexter released her hand, and placed his on the small of her back, as though claiming her.

'Oh, do you two know each other?' Gareth said, surprise in his voice.

'Not really,' Maxen said, eyeing Dexter. 'We've just seen each other about.' He paused. 'Did you enjoy *The Others*, Ava?'

'Yes,' she said, nodding and glancing at Gareth, hoping he would chip in with the conversation, but he said nothing. This was all a bit stiff and awkward, but Maxen was on a roll.

'Freaky, isn't it?' he said.

'Yes, yes, it really is, yes.'

'And what a twist,' he added.

'Well, yes, what I saw of it from behind my hands.'

Dexter's face was set hard. 'We should go,' he said, and the pressure of his hand on her back, told her the conversation was over.

'Well, it was good to see you both,' she said, allowing him to lead her away.

'I'll get those courses to you as soon as I can, Ava,' Gareth called after her, as they pushed through the vacating crowd and out into the street.

A flurry of snowflakes fluttered down, and Ava turned her face towards the night sky, allowing them to dance on her skin.

'He's the guy who bought the taps, isn't he?' Dexter said, taking her hand and squeezing, as they headed down the street, past shops decked in Christmas decorations. She liked Dexter, but he suddenly seemed a bit possessive. 'How do you know him, Ava?'

'Maxen? I've seen him about, that's all.' Why was he making her feel guilty? 'I think they must live in the village. I hadn't

150

realised he was Gareth Jones' son though. I know Gareth better. He's a police inspector. In fact, he saved me from Justin the other night.'

'Justin?' Dexter stared down at her intently, his eyes dark. She hadn't meant to say his name. She didn't want him to know about Justin – not yet anyway.

'Ah, well … there's so much you don't know about me,' she said, with a small laugh. 'It's such early days.'

'I'd like to know more.' His face brightened and his tone softened. 'Fancy a drink? There's a bar round the corner.'

She glanced at her watch. 'I should get back.'

'Oh go on, one can't hurt.'

'Well OK then, just one – maybe it will calm my nerves after that freaky film. You do know I won't sleep tonight.'

'Not even with me?' he said, but before she could respond, he added, 'Maybe we should have seen *Serendipity*.'

'Now that's more my kind of film. I love John Cusack.'

'Next time?'

There'll be a next time?

*

The bar heaved with youngsters, the atmosphere loud and smoky. 'Mambo Number 5' played through speakers.

'Grab that table,' Dexter said, pointing, and Ava turned to see two women putting on their coats. 'What will you have?'

'White wine, please,' she said. He headed to the bar, and she raced towards the table, almost knocking one of the women over. 'Sorry.'

'Bet you wouldn't jump in my grave so quickly,' the woman said, giving her a foul look as they walked away.

She felt a pang of anxiety. Was she so fragile, so vulnerable, that random strangers could upset her? She sat down, pushed the used glasses away from her, and took a deep breath. She was happy here – out with Dexter, despite the fact the film would give her nightmares. *Yes*, she thought, as she stared at him pushing through the throng towards the bar, she liked him. She liked him a lot.

Her eyes drifted around the bar. She'd been here before with Justin, before she could legally drink in a pub. It was one of his favourite places, and a veil of anxiety attempted to lower her mood once more. He could be here somewhere in the crowd. But even if he was, he wouldn't notice her tucked away in the corner, would he?

'Here you go,' Dexter said, plonking a glass of wine down in front of her. He sat down with a pint of lager. 'Music's not bad,' he said. It had changed to a Beautiful South track.

'Yeah,' she said, taking a gulp of wine.

'You're my perfect ten,' he said, leaning forward and pressing his lips tenderly against hers. Yes, she really liked him.

'I'm more of a twelve,' she said, as he slowly moved away and picked up his drink. 'So which uni are you hoping to go to next year?'

'Not sure yet,' he said, his eyes on her as he took a mouthful of his drink.

'What do you want to study?'

'Not sure yet.' He smiled.

'What do you want to be when—'

'I grow up?' He laughed. 'Rich, hopefully.'

She laughed too, and sipped her wine.

'OK, you've asked me enough questions,' he said, reaching over and curling a tendril of her hair around her ear. 'It's your turn to tell me about Justin,'

'It's a long story.' She wasn't sure she was ready to tell him about Willow, but he seemed desperate to know about her life. 'The thing is, I've got a little girl. She's two.'

'What? God, you don't look old enough.'

'Well, I suppose I'm not. I had her when I was seventeen.'

He looked shocked, his eyes trapping her in a stare.

'I'd been seeing him – Justin – thought I loved him.' She grabbed her bag. 'Perhaps I should go home,' she said, sensing he disapproved.

'No. No. Don't be daft. Sorry. It's a bit of a shock that's all. But I like you, Ava. I like you a lot. Stay. Please.'

As he leaned forward and kissed her again, a man approached and tapped him on the shoulder. 'Dexter, mate,' he said, his heavy aftershave making Ava feel woozy.

Dexter turned. 'Mate,' he said, rising and hugging the man, as they patted each other on the back. 'Long time.'

The man didn't look Ava's way. It was as though she was suddenly invisible to both of them. 'The old crowd are over there,' he said, as they released each other. 'Come and say hello.'

'OK,' Dexter said, grabbing his drink.

'I won't be a sec,' Ava said getting up. She moved away, and headed for the ladies', certain Dexter didn't even notice her disappear through the crowd.

The loos were on the other side of the bar, down a narrow corridor. As she went to open the door someone grabbed her arm, and dragged her around a corner where it was quiet.

'Jesus, Justin, let me go,' she cried, but his fingers pressed deeper into her flesh. 'Please.'

'Willow's my daughter too,' he said. He was high, his eyes glassy. She noticed a tattoo on his shoulder, red and raw. 'Willow'. When had he had that done?

'You were the reason she ended up in hospital,' she said.

'That was Peter's fault, not mine. Listen, I want to do better by her, Ava. I've got big plans.'

'No! It's too late.'

'I'll fight you. She's my daughter too.' He looked towards the door to the bar. 'I see you've brought in a new daddy.'

'What?' He meant Dexter. 'No. No he's a friend. He doesn't even know Willow. Not that I owe you an explanation.'

She finally freed herself, and stormed away. Looking back over her shoulder, she called, 'I'm leaving Cornwall, Justin. I need to give Willow a better life, and there's no way in hell you'll ever be a part of it.'

She dived into the loos, and locked herself in a cubicle, breathing deeply, her chest tight as she tried to ward off tears.

When she finally ventured out, Dexter wasn't sitting at the table, and her eyes flicked around the room, searching for him, finally picking him out a few tables away, leaning over chatting with a group of men – some of them throwing their heads back, laughing.

She headed back to their table, sat down, and knocked back her drink at speed. She couldn't see Justin – she hoped he'd left.

Eventually Dexter approached. 'Sorry,' he said. 'They're great guys, but they'll keep you talking.' He looked into her eyes. 'Is everything OK?'

'Yes. Yes. Fine,' she said.

'Fancy another?'

'I should get home.'

'OK. Are you sure you're all right?'

'Yes. Fine. Actually, I will have another wine. It's my round.' She rummaged in her purse, a sudden rush of dizziness wafting over her, and handed over a ten-pound note. 'Do you mind getting them in?'

'No problem,' he said. He pushed once more towards the crowded bar, getting lost from view in the throng. He would be some time. Maybe she should leave – get a taxi home. But her heart was still racing from seeing Justin. And she felt odd too. She needed to calm down.

Her vision began to blur. Her head felt heavy.

A strong arm lifted her to her feet. 'Let's go, Ava.' But the voice was muffled. She couldn't be sure who it was.

'Dexter?' she tried to say, but her lips wouldn't form the words.

Her feet were moving, as whoever it was jostled her through the crowd who were up dancing now, a blur of bodies. 'Dexter?' she said, as the cold air hit her.

That was the last thing she remembered.

Chapter 30

AVA

2001

She was lying in a ditch in woodland, a watery sun low in the sky. A frost had settled during the night, and she was shaking from the cold, or was that fear? Tears flowed from her eyes, trickling down her cheeks, and into her ears. Her head throbbed. She didn't move. She was in shock.

Eventually she reached out her hand slowly to pick up her clothes, crushing the fabric in her fists. Whoever had done this had covered her with her coat. They hadn't wanted her to die of exposure. She wished she had.

She pulled herself up with the aid of a tree and gingerly put on her coat, wrapping it round herself like a shield. She went to move, bent over, and threw up – coughing, spluttering, crying – who the hell had done this to her? She let out a scream from the pit of her stomach, and birds flew – scared – from the tree-tops, flapping their wings, startled.

A small, royal-blue velvet box lay at her feet, calling to her. She kicked it away.

Sobbing, she stumbled through the wood, gripping trees for support, finally reaching the road. She wasn't far from home.

'Where have you been?' her mother called from the kitchen, as she stepped through the front door. She didn't respond. She climbed the stairs, and headed into the bathroom – numb now, as though this was a stranger's body that no longer belonged to her. She splashed her face with cold water, before taking off her coat and getting into the shower. She ran it as hot as she could bear, her skin turning red as she stood, motionless for over twenty minutes.

A knock on the bathroom door startled her. 'Shouldn't you be at work?'

'I'm not going, Mum.'

'Are you ill?'

She didn't answer, and eventually her mother's footfalls descended the stairs.

Ava turned off the shower and stepped out onto the mat.

There were bruises on her thighs – gashes on her legs.

Who had done this to her?

Once in the bedroom, dressed in clean pyjamas, she crawled under her quilt and hugged her pillow, squashing it against her, burying her face into its softness. Hoping it would take her breath away. Wanting the pain to stop.

She let out a sob, as she gasped for air.

The rumble of Peter's voice below and the sound of Willow giggling gave her little comfort.

How could she make a perfect life for Willow now?

Chapter 31

ROSE

Now

'Becky,' I call, as I step out of the sunshine and into the hallway of Ocean View Cottage. 'Becky?'

The cottage is silent. I sense already she isn't here, and my heart thumps.

I'm about to go upstairs, when I spot through the lounge doorway a note on the coffee table in Becky's handwriting:

I'll be back before dark. I'm going round to the other side of the bay to where you saw the figure. Becky X

'Jesus!' I turn and run through the front door and slam it behind me. Why would Becky do this? I race down the path, fumbling in my bag for the car keys as a gust of wind catches my hair and blows it in front of my face.

It hits me how our children are no longer almost-adults when we fear for their safety, instead becoming that child who we saw take their first steps; the little one whose hand we released on their first day at playgroup or nursery school, and then walked home in tears; the girl who finally learnt to ride her bike after months of us holding the seat – steadying her, praying she will never fall.

I jump into my car and pull away with a screech of tyres. At the bottom of the hill I see an ambulance parked outside Justin's house. *Is he OK? Do I care?*

I turn left and head for the other side of the bay – to Becky.

It's further by road than across the beach, and seems to take ages as I manoeuvre down country roads, my car scraping against the hedgerow as I hold back for oncoming traffic.

I finally pull up in a layby. Across the grass plateau I see Becky on the edge of the cliff, far too close, a silhouette against the pale blue sky. I climb from the car as a restless wind whistles across the land, the sound rising and falling – the cries of lost souls.

'Becky,' I call. Despite my voice struggling to beat the wind, she hears me and turns, raising her hand.

I wave too, as I set out across the wild grass towards her with determined strides. 'Becky, get away from the edge, sweetheart,' I call, as another gust whips across my face, swallowing my words.

As I get closer I pick up on the sound of the waves crashing against the sand. The sea is angry today.

Suddenly a figure appears at the top of the cliff steps, wearing a dark hoodie and tracksuit bottoms. He sets out, running towards Becky.

She looks towards him, stumbles. Her leg slips over the edge, and my body screams out in pain as the runner grabs her arm and yanks her back. He's talking to her now. Resting his hand on her shoulder for a moment, before setting off again.

'Mum,' she says, as I reach her. She's crying. 'God, if that man hadn't grabbed me—'

'What the hell are you doing here?' I say, letting out a breath

I hadn't realised I was holding. I grab her and hold her close, realising I'm crying too. 'I thought for a moment you—'

'Please don't be angry, Mum,' she says, eyes wide. 'I just wanted to help.'

I release her. 'What did you think you would find here, Becky? You shouldn't be up here on your own.'

'I know. You're right, there's nothing to see. The first house is at least a quarter of a mile away.' She moves from my embrace and points across the fields towards a house in the distance. It's the cottage I spotted on our way here – Floral Corner. The perfect cottage – where I'd half-hoped Willow was staying. 'We could go there, maybe,' she says. She's stopped crying now, and wipes her tears away with her hands. 'Ask if they saw anything last night when you were attacked.'

I shrug. 'Maybe,' I say.

'They may have heard a vehicle or something,' Becky goes on.

'I'm not sure, maybe we should leave it to the police. I'll mention the place when I give my statement.' As another gust of wind almost topples us over, I say, 'Come on, let's get back to the cottage.' And we link arms and make our way back to the car.

*

The wind is calmer as we head up the path to the cottage. It's a warm breeze, the kind that tans you quickly – may even burn you without you realising.

'Who's that?' Becky says.

I look down at the bay. A solitary figure is sitting close to the sea, hugging his legs, his back to us.

A chill runs through me, as memories of last night flood in. 'I've no idea. Let's go inside,' I say, thrusting my key in the door.

'It's that boy again,' she says, as he turns and looks up at us.

'Remember. The one we saw outside the cottage a few times. Look, he's wearing the same yellow cap.'

'Yes, well, let's leave him to it, shall we?' I'm super nervy right now, my hand trembling as I push open the door.

'We should speak to him. I reckon he knows something about Willow.'

'Not right now,' I snap, stepping inside. 'Later, maybe,' I go on, trying to sound calmer. She follows me in, and I close and bolt the door behind us.

'But he'll be gone by then, Mum.'

My vision blurs a little, and my head starts throbbing. Maybe I should have had my head injury checked out.

'Are you OK?' Becky asks, following me as I head for the kitchen. She fills the kettle, flicks it on, as I knock back a couple of tablets with water. This room is far too small for the two of us. 'Migraine?' she asks. 'Or is it where you were hit?'

'I'm fine, sweetheart. Just a headache,' I say, leaving her to make some coffee.

I sit down on the sofa, and lean my head back, going over and over everything. *Justin? Peter? Rory? Dexter? Justin? Peter? Rory? Dexter?*

'Here you go.' Becky plonks down a weak-looking coffee on the table in front of me, startling me. I'm far too jumpy.

'Thanks, sweetheart,' I say.

She sits in the chair, and takes a sip of her drink. 'So what have we got?'

'Sorry?'

'Let's try to piece it all together. Think like Sherlock.'

I know she's not deliberately trivialising the situation, but I'm irritated. I rub my temples. The pain is becoming intolerable, and I have a vague sense of nausea.

'Are you sure you're OK? You look so white? You been dating vampires again?'

161

I rise. 'To be honest I feel pretty rough. I think I'll have a lie down for a bit.'

'Is it where you were hit, Mum? Should we go to the hospital?'

'Let's see how I am after a little sleep,' I say, leaving the room.

It's gone 3 p.m. when I wake. I've wasted precious hours, when I should have been searching for Willow. I stumble out of bed, and into the bathroom, where I splash my face with cold water and clean my teeth, as my mouth tastes foul. I realise, as I pat my face with a towel, that the worst of my headache has dissipated, and I'm left with a dull fuzzy feeling, as though my brain is wrapped in cotton wool.

I step into the shower and turn the water up as hot as I can stand. My hair clings to my skull, and I squeeze my eyes closed as soapsuds roll down my face. They're there again. The four men swimming around my mind: *Justin, Peter, Rory, Dexter. Justin, Peter, Rory, Dexter. Justin, Peter, Rory, Dexter.*

I step out, wrap myself in a towel, and sit on the toilet seat.

Let's try to piece it all together, shall we? Think like Sherlock.

I half-smile at Becky's words – and now far less agitated I try to *think like Sherlock*. But it's no good. My head spins once more.

Still wrapped in the towel, I get up and head into the room Willow was staying in and pick up her leather jacket. I rummage in the pockets: a tissue, a till receipt from the local shop, and a screwed-up piece of paper. I hang the jacket on the back of a wooden chair, before smoothing the note flat on the top of the chest of drawers. My heart picks up speed. Just one word written in capitals:

LEAVE

I lumber across the room, and as I pass the window my chest tightens and a shard of panic plunges through me.

'Becky,' I cry, slamming my hand against the glass. She's out there. Sitting on the beach with the boy in the yellow cap.

*

Once dressed, I leave the cottage and dash across the beach towards them. Angry tears that Becky has been so stupid yet again, spilling down my face. 'Becky,' I cry, losing a flip-flop, but carrying on across the sand as though my daughter's life depends on me. 'Becky, what the hell?'

They both look up, innocent eyes on me as I stop a few yards from them and dash away tears with the back of my hand. Am I becoming paranoid? Surely I have cause to worry, after what happened to me the night before.

'What's up, Mum?' Becky says. 'This is Isaac.'

He doesn't smile, but continues to stare from under his base-ball cap.

'He doesn't seem to be able to talk,' Becky goes on calmly, as though I'm not standing here breathing heavily, with a tear-stained face. 'But I think he's eighteen and lives with his parents. When I showed him a picture of Willow, he said he knows her.'

'Really? Have you seen her lately?' I ask him, stepping closer. He looks far younger than eighteen.

He raises his shoulders in a shrug.

'You can hear me, can't you?' I ask, crouching down in front of him.

He nods his head.

'He hears perfectly well, I think,' Becky says, and starts nibbling at her thumbnail.

'Why do you keep coming to the cottage?' I say, staring into his worried eyes.

He makes his hands into fists, his thumbs up, and moves both fists up and down in front of his chest.

'What does it mean?' I ask Becky. We learnt a bit of sign

language several years ago, to help communicate with a deaf friend of mine. Becky picked it up better than I did, but there's a lot she doesn't know.

'I've no idea,' she says. 'He keeps doing it.'

'Have you seen Willow lately?' I repeat, sounding far too agitated.

He clambers to his feet, his face expressionless – difficult to read.

'Mother!' Becky snaps. 'You have to treat him gently.'

But it's too late. The boy – Isaac – takes off sprinting, sand spraying up in his wake, his long, thin legs taking him to the slope that leads to Ocean View Cottage and the village. Within moments he's out of sight.

'He's pretty good at running off, isn't he?' I say, rolling my eyes.

'Yes, and he knows something, I'm sure of it.'

'We should go after him,' I say, as Becky gets up, steadying herself with the aid of my arm, and brushing sand from her jeans.

'We'll never catch him, Mum. Anyway, he'll clam up if you pressure him.'

'How long have you been down here?' I ask.

'About an hour, it took me a while to work out why he wouldn't speak.'

As we head back across the sand, picking up my flip-flop on the way, I take hold of my daughter's hand.

'How are you feeling after your sleep?' she says. 'You look loads better.'

'Yeah, I feel it,' I say, touching my head, realising even the fuzziness has gone.

Back at the cottage, I want to tell Becky about the piece of paper in Willow's jacket pocket, and that I've visited Justin, seen an ambulance by his house. But I'm worried about the effect this is all having on her. I begin to wish Dad and Eleanor weren't away, that I could take her to them.

Her phone blasts out. She grabs it. 'Whoop, it's Dad,' she says, a smile stretching across her face.

I leave the room and head upstairs, listening to her laughter, her squeals of excitement as she talks about going to America, and I'm so grateful to Seb for making her happy – he's doing a far better job of it than I am.

Chapter 32

AVA

2001

It had been almost three weeks since Ava was attacked. She desperately needed to tell someone – to offload some of her pain. Explain why she'd been cooped up in her bedroom, barely sleeping, barely eating.

Maybe her mum would listen.

Jeannette had never been an affectionate woman – Ava knew that much – but maybe she would help Ava to cope with the continual panic she felt simply looking out of the bedroom window.

She hoped too that her mum would understand how her mind refused to veer from that moment when she'd woken, cold and scared. How she now felt so vulnerable. Afraid. Powerless.

She would tell her mum about the pains in her lower stomach, the feelings of nausea – and pray she would understand.

She got dressed for the first time, in jeans and a chunky jumper, and padded down the stairs, gripping the banister as she went to steady herself. She'd been violated physically and emotionally.

She had to tell someone before it ate her alive. Was her mother really the only person she could turn to?

She reached the bottom of the stairs, picking up on Peter's muffled voice and the tinkle of Willow's laughter behind the closed lounge door. Willow had slept cuddled up to Ava each night since it happened, but Peter had taken care of her during the day, seeming to believe that Ava was unwell. He'd even brought her food – sandwiches mostly – but she couldn't eat.

Jeannette was outside hanging washing that would never dry in the freezing air, when Ava approached.

'Oh, Ava,' Jeannette said, clutching a damp pillowcase to her face like a security blanket, when Ava broke down crying, after telling her what had happened to her. 'Are you sure?'

'Of course I'm sure, Mum.'

Jeannette didn't move, and Ava felt isolated. Cold. She wished her Mum would take her in her arms and hold her there, stroke her hair and caress away the tears. But her mother didn't seem to know how.

'But if you were passed out, how can you be sure?'

'I just know, Mum,' she whispered, her heart thudding, as she pushed away thoughts of waking up with nothing more than her coat covering her body.

'Well, we need to get you straight to the GP. You'll need to have a pregnancy test and checks for gonorrhoea and HIV.' She was talking too fast, her voice tense, her eyes not meeting Ava's. 'Who have you told?'

'Nobody.' More tears bubbled to the surface. Why couldn't she see her daughter was dying inside?

'Good,' Jeannette said. 'Nobody needs to know.' She finally met her daughter's eyes, and tilted her head. 'We can keep this within our four walls this time.'

'This time?'

'Well, we couldn't exactly sweep Willow under the carpet, could we, darling?'

'For God's sake, Mum. This is not the same thing at all.' She took a deep breath and dabbed her tears with the cuff of her jumper. 'Justin didn't rape me. I thought I loved him.'

'I know. I know.' Jeannette bent and picked up one of Peter's brightly coloured tops. She turned from Ava, and with quick sharp movements pegged it on the line.

'Will you come with me to the police, Mum?'

Jeannette glanced over her shoulder, and fixed her eyes on her daughter once more. 'It's a bit late for that, Ava. You should have gone straight away. Let's get you to the doctor's, shall we? I'll come with you.'

For a few moments Ava watched her mother continue to hang out the washing, before she headed away.

'Ava,' Jeannette called after her, and she stopped and turned – hopeful. 'Don't tell Gail. We don't want to upset her before her big day, do we? It's only three weeks away.'

Ava raced inside and slammed the kitchen door closed behind her.

As she passed the lounge, she heard Peter pretending to be an aeroplane, but she didn't smile. She grabbed her coat from the rack by the front door, and pulled on her boots. She would catch a bus into Newquay. She would tell the police what had happened.

*

As she walked across the reception area of the police station, she spotted Gareth Jones talking to another police officer behind the counter. He turned and for a moment she thought he didn't recognise her, but then a smile brightened his face, and he raised his hand.

'Hello, Ava,' he called over. 'I've got that information on those courses. Hang on.'

'No wait …' she said, as he dashed out of sight.

She made her way to the counter where a young officer with

bright ginger hair stood behind a desk. 'How can I help?' he said.

She knew instantly she couldn't tell him. Not a man. Not a stranger. Her heart thudded. Why had she even thought she could? What could they do anyway?'

'Nothing,' she said turning to leave. 'Thank you.'

As she opened the door, Gareth called her name. She looked back over her shoulder to see him walking towards her with a handful of papers. 'There you go,' he said when he reached her, holding them out to her.

She took them from him. 'Thank you,' she said.

'Now, make sure you have a good look at them, and let me know if there's anything you don't understand.' He paused for a moment, narrowing his eyes as he looked into hers. 'Are you OK, Ava?'

Within moments his kindly voice had reduced her to tears.

'Sit down,' he said, ushering her to a plastic seat in the corner. 'Let me get you some water.'

Grabbing a plastic cup, he filled it from a water cooler, and handed it to her. But her hand shook so much, he took it back, and placed it on the table beside her.

'What's happened, Ava?' he said.

She looked out through the window for some time, trying to form the words, trying to bring them up from the pit of her stomach, where they'd sat, festering. 'I was raped,' she said finally.

'Oh, Ava, when did this happen?'

'Three weeks ago – Mum says it's too late to report it. That I should have come sooner.'

'Well she's wrong. It's never too late to report rape.' His voice oozed with kindness. 'In all honestly, I'd have to say, yes, it would have been better to come sooner. But we can help you. Get you victim support. And if you can remember anything about the man—'

'I can't,' she cut in. 'He drugged me. Oh God.' She got to her feet, a panic surging through her. 'I shouldn't have come.

I wish I hadn't.' And with that she raced from the dreary grey building and onto the road where a thin icy rain fell from the sky, the sound of Inspector Gareth Jones calling after her fading into the distance, as she picked up speed, heading for the bus stop.

*

Ava stepped from the bus, and as she walked towards home, the rain stinging her face, another message from Dexter popped into her inbox. She'd received several while shut in her room, closed off from the world. He'd asked over and over if she was OK. Where she had disappeared to the night they went to the cinema. But like his other messages, she deleted it.

There was another message too. It was from Justin:

Can we talk, Ava? Sorry about the way I've been. I'm an idiot. I know that now. But I want to be part of Willow's life, even if it's a small part. I should be coming into some money soon. Please call me.

She deleted his message too, looked up, and caught her breath – realising she was walking past the area where she was attacked. A cold chill ran through her.

She hadn't taken in that she'd passed where it had happened on her way to the bus stop earlier, far too focused on racing away from her mother, determined to tell the police. But now she was frozen, looking through the trees, shivering as droplets of rain clung to her hair, her eyelashes, and dripped from her nose.

The box.

She took a deep breath, and pushed through the bushes, her heart thumping as she made her way through the wood.

The box.

Could the velvet box she'd seen that morning belong to the

170

man who did this heinous thing to her – the terrible act that would stay with her for the rest of her life?

There was a sudden noise behind her, a breaking of twigs. She gasped, and her inner voice shrieked, 'Run, Ava, run.' But she stood still, unable to move. The twigs cracked again, as though someone was approaching from behind, then a movement in the bushes. She turned to see a flash of orange fur. A fox.

She clasped her chest, relieved, but her heart still thumped as she made her way further into the woodland.

And then she was there: the spot where it happened. Panic set in, and her whole body shook. This wasn't helping her. She needed to get home, to the safety of her room. But as she turned to run, she caught sight of the velvet box.

She crouched down, picked up a thin stick, and poked at it like it was a decaying creature, before picking it up and prising it open. Inside was a silver bracelet. And she knew, as she snapped the box closed and pushed it into her pocket, whoever it belonged to was a monster.

Chapter 33

ROSE

Now

'Mum!' Becky's shaking me. 'It's six o'clock.'

My eyes fly open. 'Gosh, I must have been tired,' I say, pulling myself to a sitting position on the bed, and stretching. I can't believe I fell asleep again. Perhaps it's my body's way of healing after the attack. 'Fancy going to the local pub for dinner again?' I go on, knowing I'm incapable of cooking right now, and we may get to talk to some locals who remember Willow or Ava.

'OK,' Becky says. 'We might see scary-man again.'

'Maybe. Although why are we calling him scary-man, exactly?'

'Because he freaked us out,' she said. 'He's totally scarier than IT.'

'Hardly,' I say, laughing and getting up. 'Nothing's scarier than a psychopathic clown.'

We head downstairs, and I shove my feet into my flip-flops. Becky sits on the bottom step of the stairs and pulls on her Doc Martens, despite the heat.

I take the opportunity to stroke her hair, but she wiggles me away. 'Mother!' she says, flapping her hand as though batting away an annoying fly. 'Leave the hair.'

Outside, the sun seems triple the size it should be, and I slip on my sunglasses and hat.

Once at the end of the road, I stop. 'I'm going to make a little detour. Can you go on ahead? I won't be long.'

Becky widens her eyes. 'Why? Where are you going?'

I sigh. 'If you must know, I'm going to Justin's house.'

'You know where he lives?'

'Mmm. And ... well ... I've already been there.'

'What? When? Why the hell didn't you tell me?'

'I didn't want to worry you.'

'I'm already worried, Mum. I can't believe you went there on your own. He could be Ava's killer. Or have kidnapped Willow! Jeez!' She spins on the spot, rubbing her forehead. 'What the hell were you thinking?' Her eyes are watery, her lip quivers, but she takes a deep breath. 'So did he talk to you, mention that he's Willow's father?' It's as though she's swept my stupidity from her thoughts.

'Yes and yes.' I bite down on my lip. 'I was stupid to go. I know that. But I honestly can't imagine him killing Ava or hurting Willow.' I approach her with caution and link my arm through hers, pull her close. 'Come with me now,' I say, and she nods.

We're silent as we head for the house and walk up the path towards the front door. I knock three times, as Becky hops onto the overgrown front garden. She leans on the windowsill and peers through the grubby glass.

'Looks as though it's deserted,' she says, moving away. 'Yuk,' she adds, looking at her hands. 'Seagulls' poop, jeez, I need to wash this off.'

'Yes you do,' I say with a shiver, handing her a wet wipe from my bag, as she moves towards me bashing back a wayward bush.

'This place is pretty gross, Mum. In dire need of a makeover, that's for sure.'

I open the letterbox. 'Justin,' I call, but still nobody comes to the door. 'Maybe he was taken away in the ambulance,' I say.

'Ambulance?'

'Mmm, it was here earlier.' I shudder, giving the house one final sweep, my eyes falling on the garage set back from the house. The word 'killer' has been spray painted on the door in huge letters.

'Let's go,' I say. 'This place gives me the creeps.'

*

When we reach the pub, Becky heads into the loos to wash her hands, after I'd insisted the wet wipe wouldn't have removed all the germs.

'Glad we didn't scare you off,' the landlord says as I approach the bar. 'What can I get you?'

'A lemonade and an orange juice, please.' I reach for two menus.

'Leave the drinks with me,' he says. 'I'll put them on a tab and bring them over.'

'Thanks,' I say, and pad over to the same table we sat at last time, passing an elderly man in a cap folded over a newspaper, a young border collie asleep at his feet.

'What do you fancy?' I ask as Becky appears, and drops down opposite me.

'To be honest, I'm not that hungry,' she says.

'Oh come on, love. You must eat.'

'I'll eat later,' she says. 'There's stuff in the fridge at the cottage.' She looks deep into my eyes. 'It said killer on the garage door, didn't it?' she says, her voice a wobble. 'Do you think someone believes Justin killed Ava?'

'Sorry to intrude.' It's the old man with the border collie. His pale blue eyes, sitting under bushy white eyebrows, are fixed on us, his Cornish accent strong. 'Are you talking about Justin Havers?'

'Yes,' I say with a smile, eager to strike up any conversation with a local who might lead us to Willow. 'We've just been to his house, but he's not there.'

'Avee met him?' he says, pulling a handkerchief from his pocket, and blowing his nose.

I nod. 'Once, that's all.'

'Been in prison, he has. Armed robbery.'

'Yes, yes he told me.'

'Aye. Not surprising really. His mother died when he was sixteen, and his father turned to drink. He wasn't a bad father, just never recovered from the loss of his wife – guilt played a part, he'd been a bit of a womaniser over the years. Sadly, the boy – Justin – got mixed up with those Bristow boys,' he went on, as though I knew who he was talking about. 'Went off the rails like a train without a driver.'

I think for a moment about Justin – the man I met, unsure what to feel. 'Do you remember Ava Millar's murder?' I ask.

He takes a sip of his beer. 'I do. It was me who found her.' He shakes his head. 'Finding that young woman will live with me 'til the day I die – all that blood.'

'I'm so sorry. It must have been awful for you.'

'Aye, it was indeed. Bostagel has never been quite the same since it happened – for anyone. It was as if the ground cracked under the bloody lot of us, sending splinters everywhere.' He meets my gaze, his eyes watery. 'There was talk that Ava was dead even before the knife went in, but I don't know how true it is. Rumours, that's all. But what I do know is Inspector Jones had a terrible breakdown at the time. Convinced Gail didn't kill her sister, he became obsessed with the case. But I'm telling you this now,' he taps his large, red nose, 'those sisters never got on, and from where I'm sitting it was more than your normal sibling rivalry.'

'What about Rory? He'd just got married, he must have been devastated.'

He nods. 'Broken-hearted he was – poor chap. It was awful seeing him cry.' He shakes his head, as though trying to dislodge the memory.

'And Dexter?'

'Can't say I recall him too well. Bit of a mummy's boy by all accounts, left Newquay to go to university after Ava died, if I remember. In any case, he had an alibi – couldn't have killed the young woman if that's what you're thinking.'

The landlord appears and puts our drinks on the table. 'So what'll it be?'

I look down at the menu. 'I'll have the lasagne, please,' I say, before glancing back at the elderly man, hoping our conversation isn't over, but he's on his feet. He nods my way, taps his cap, and heads for the door, his dog by his side. His newspaper tucked under his arm.

'Lasagne,' the landlord says, scribbling on his pad. 'Good choice.' He moves his eyes to Becky.

'Nothing for me,' she says closing the menu, and handing it to him.

'I can't tempt you with our beef and ale pie? Battered fresh fish?'

'No, honestly, I'm fine.'

'OK,' he says shuffling the menus. 'You've picked a lovely week. It's been glorious again today, hasn't it?'

I nod. 'Yes, we've been lucky,' I say to be polite, but feel far from it.

'Though the weather forecast says a storm is on its way, I wonder what they'll name—'

'Has the man been in again?' Becky cuts in, looking up at the landlord.

'Man?'

'We asked you about him last time.'

He presses his finger to his bottom lip and furrows his forehead. 'Ah, you mean the Scotsman?'

176

'He's Scottish?'

'Mmm, I think so. Or maybe Welsh.' He tilts his head. 'Got an accent anyway.' He shakes his head. 'No, I haven't seen him since you were last here, I'm afraid.'

'He's Scottish,' I repeat to Becky, as the landlord walks away.

'Or Welsh,' she says with a roll of her eyes. 'How the hell doesn't he know the difference?'

'Shh! He'll hear you.' I take a wet wipe from my bag and swipe it over the table several times.

'I want to know why the man was staring at us, is all,' Becky says, sliding down in her chair, and folding her arms tightly across her chest.

'Perhaps he wasn't. Maybe we're a bit paranoid at the moment. Well I know I am. It's not every day your sister goes missing and you end up searching for a killer.' As I hear my own words, it confirms what I already know. I'm not only on a mission to find Willow, I need to find out what happened that night in 2001. I need to find out who murdered Ava Millar.

*

We're back from the pub, and it's much later. In fact, Becky is in bed asleep when, from the landing window, I see someone out in the darkness at the foot of the path. His hood is up, his face a blur of features. I realise I'm afraid, and acutely aware how isolated we are. My chest tightens. If someone wants to attack us, they can. If someone had wanted to abduct Willow, they could have.

I duck back as he takes sudden long strides towards the front door.

Heart thumping, I race down the stairs and thrust the three bolts across in time with his knocks. I can't believe I hadn't done so when we got back from the pub.

I dash into the kitchen and grab a carving knife from the

kitchen drawer. Am I overreacting? But it could be anyone. It could be the man who hit me on the beach.

There are two more ways he can get in, I reason: the patio doors and the back door. I need to check both. I race to the back door, which is locked and bolted, and return to the lounge. The light is off, but the moon highlights the figure now standing on the patio. Within moments he's thumping on the window, pressing his face against the glass.

The knife tumbles from my hand, and thuds onto the carpet.

I can see his familiar face now. Oh God, what the hell is he doing out there in the darkness?

Chapter 34

AVA

2001

Ava had been studying the bracelet for a while – it was made from heavy silver and studded with pretty coloured stones, beautiful and yet ugly – when there was a knock on her bedroom door. She could hear Willow making shushing noises and giggling, and Peter trying not to laugh.

She slipped the bracelet under her pillow and rose to open the door.

'What have you got there, darling girl?' she asked, trying for a voice that sounded somewhere near normal, as she crouched down in front of her daughter.

Willow looked at her with bright blue eyes, her golden curls making her look angelic. She handed Ava a handmade card, and a little box with spots on it.

Ava's eyes filled with tears as she took in the scribbled colours, swirling spirals of love across the page, 'Get Well Soon Mummy' written in an adult hand, the words sharing the space with far too much glitter.

'We made it,' Willow said, squeezing her hands into fists and grinning up at Peter.

Ava opened the box. It was a necklace. She pulled it out. 'It's beautiful,' she said, taking in the word 'Mummy' hanging on a chain. She put it on. 'I'll wear it always,' she said, taking Willow in her arms and hugging her close. 'I love you so much,' she said, as she kissed her daughter's hair, her cheeks, breathing her in. 'Mummy will be better soon, I promise.'

'Will you?' Peter said, as she finally released Willow.

Ava rose. She didn't answer him. She didn't have the energy.

Willow trotted away and bounced down the stairs on her bottom. 'Gran!' she called out. 'Drink, please.'

'What's happened, Ava?' Peter whispered, searching her face for answers.

'Nothing,' she said. 'I'm fine.'

'No, Ava, you're not. You're far from it. Talk to me. Please.'

She touched his face gently. Could he cope with knowing? 'Ava?'

'I was raped,' she said, as tears came. They always came.

'Christ, Ava, who did it?' His eyes flared with anger. 'I'll fucking kill him.'

She shook her head. 'I don't know,' she said softly, stepping backwards into her room. And with a quiet click, she closed the door.

*

A week later Jeannette put her head round Ava's door. 'Inspector Jones is here,' she said. 'He'd like to speak to you.'

Ava was curled like a foetus under her quilt. She didn't move. 'Is it OK to send him up?'

She didn't reply. It wasn't that she wanted him to come up, or that she didn't. She didn't care.

Moments later she heard soft footfalls on the stairs and across the landing – a tap on the door. 'Ava.' It was Gareth. 'Ava, can I come in?'

She heard the knob turn, the door drag across the carpet, and felt the presence of him in her room, the smell of his citrus aftershave. 'Ava?'

A silence seemed to stretch on forever, before she unfurled, and pulled back the quilt, to see him with his back to her, looking out of the window.

'Please go away,' she said, as he turned to look at her. 'I'm fine. Honestly.'

'It doesn't look that way from here, Ava. You need support. Even if you don't want to report what happened, you still need help.'

'I said. I'm fine.'

'Ava, have you any idea who might have done this to you?'

She shook her head, but her mind went to the bracelet tucked under her pillow. Should she show it to him?

'Peter's taking care of Willow,' she said, moving her mind away from the bracelet, feeling as if she should explain her neglect of her daughter. She didn't want social workers round the cottage, trying to take her darling girl. They used to come when she was a child. They made her mother cry.

'Peter?' Gareth looked surprised. 'He's certainly changed from the boy who ran away to Australia.'

'He has,' she said, believing in her brother.

'You haven't had it easy, Ava,' Gareth said, putting some leaflets on her bed, the words 'victim support' jumping from the pages. 'Call them please. You need help.'

After another lengthy silence he left, his feet soft on the stairs before the front door closed. She got up and looked out of the window. Beyond the windowpane, Gareth was at the foot of the path. Suddenly her mum dashed out of the house after him in her slippers, almost slipping on a patch of ice.

They stood by the gate for some time, Jeannette showing the

inspector what looked like a photograph. He studied it, shaking his head several times, before she shoved it into her pocket, and headed back inside the cottage.

*

'Mummy,' Willow cried as Ava stepped into the lounge later that day. Her little girl was kneeling in front of the coffee table, colouring, and Ava stroked her curls as she drifted past.

There'd been some attempt at putting up Christmas decorations in the room – a tree in the window, a fancy garland around the shelf above the fireplace – but Jeannette had never made a big thing of Christmas.

Rory and Gail sat on the sofa. Ava hadn't expected them to be there, and wanted to race back to her room. But if she did, she knew she might never come out again, never move forward, and she had to think of Willow.

'Mum told us you've been unwell,' Gail said, looking up at her. 'You'd better be OK for the wedding. I don't want you ruining my big day.'

Ava sat down. 'Where's Peter?' she said. He was her support, her rock, at least for the moment.

'Gone to the shop for some cigs,' Rory said. 'You look very pale, Ava. Are you OK?'

'It's an infection or a virus, that's all.'

'Well, which is it?' Gail said.

'Does it matter?' Ava looked down at her hands in her lap. They were trembling.

'Well, you might need antibiotics, Ava,' said Gail. 'Have you seen a doctor?'

'No.' She'd never gone, despite her mum insisting she should. She didn't want to be pulled about. Examined.

'Mum said you haven't been into work. If you don't see a doctor, they won't pay you.'

'For Christ's sake, what is this? The Spanish fucking Inquisition?'

Willow shot her head round to look at Ava, a crayon suspended in mid-air.

'Sorry,' Ava said, slipping from the chair onto her knees beside her daughter. She kissed Willow's cheek. 'Sorry. Mummy shouldn't swear.'

'We want to know you'll be all right for a week Saturday, Ava.' Gail gave a little squeal. 'I can't believe it's so close.'

Ava rose to her feet. 'Don't worry, I will be there,' she said.

'And what about your plus one, Ava?' Gail said. 'I need to tell the caterers his name. Please don't say it's Justin.'

'I'm not bringing anyone.'

'I would have thought they'd be queuing at the door to go with you, Ava,' Rory called after her, as she left the room.

Chapter 35

YOU

You told me you had raped her. Described it in detail. I ran home and threw up. But still I listened, pretending to enjoy your cruel words – just so you would love me.

'She was walking along a lonely road near Crantock – it was dark,' you said. 'She was gagging for it.'

Later, reading the article in the local press, you said, 'Recently married. Well that's going to fuck up their relationship.' You laughed, looked over at me narrowing your eyes. 'I hope she didn't see me,' you said. 'I need to be more careful next time.'

But nobody came knocking.

No one suspected.

No one would ever suspect you.

Chapter 36

ROSE

Now

Willow, dressed in yellow satin, screams as a featureless figure pushes her over the cliff edge. The trill of my phone snatches me from the vivid nightmare before she hits the ground. I pull myself up in bed, heart thudding, and answer the call.

'Rose, is that you?' Dad says, before I can speak.

'Yes, Dad, it's me.' I rub my forehead, fighting off the panic I feel from the dream. 'Are you having a good time?'

'Yes, we're staying in Inverness at the moment, it's beautiful, Rose. You really need to visit. Sorry. I digress,' he said, with a small laugh. 'I'm calling to let you know we've finally heard from Willow.'

'She called you?' My heart trips over itself with relief.

'No, no, not a call, love, a text message – this morning when I woke, but she says she's OK, and staying in Newquay.'

My heart sinks. 'Did she say where in Newquay? When she'd be back?'

'No, no, just that she's happy there for a bit, and will be heading to see you soon. That's good, isn't it? You sound worried, love.'

I drag my fingers through my hair, catching them in a tangle. 'No, I'm fine, Dad. I just thought she would be here by now, that's all.'

'Well, I'm sure she'll be back with you in no time.'

'I'm sure she will.' I'm trying to keep my tone even, cheerful, as though I believe Willow is exactly where the text says she is. But I don't believe she's in Newquay. I don't believe it for a moment.

'How's Becky? Is she enjoying Cornwall?' Dad asks.

'She is, yes.'

'Well that's good.' He pauses for a moment. 'Rose, if you need us we can come home.'

'No, Dad, honestly – we'll stay here a bit longer and wait for Willow.'

'Good. Yes. You've certainly got the weather for it down there. Scorchio, as they say. It's a bit chillier where I am. Chunky jumpers all the way.' He laughs – sounds in good spirits. 'Well, I'll love you and leave you, Rose. See you when you get back.'

'Love you, Dad,' I say before ending the call.

I rise, put on my robe and slippers, and shove my phone in my pocket. I go to leave the room, but I'm consumed with a sudden sadness. Once I would have turned to my dad. He was always my go-to in an emergency, or if I needed a good cry. Just after Mum died, he was always there, keeping me safe. Letting me talk until I ran out of words, telling me things would get easier with time. Now I wish I could pour everything out to him, and that he would put the world to rights. But I can't. He needs this holiday. And I know the anxiety he would feel if he knew the truth about Willow could make him ill.

I open the bedroom door, and head downstairs to where Becky is sitting in the lounge showered and dressed. She pulls out an earbud. 'I couldn't sleep,' she says, and I know I need to tell her who I saw in the darkness the night before – who I hid out of sight of for half an hour, until they left.

'I couldn't sleep either,' I say, padding into the kitchen. Before I can tell her, I need some coffee.

As the kettle boils, I send a message to Willow:

Give me a call, Willow. We're worried about you. Or tell us where you're staying in Newquay. Who with? When you'll be back? Please! Rose X

I press send as the boiling water reaches a crescendo, knowing already it's a waste of time. A sudden surge of anger pulses through me, and tears rest heavily in my chest. Why had Willow come here alone? Got embroiled in the mystery of her mother's death? Not asked for my help from the start? But I pull myself round. I love her, my silly, stupid stepsister, and there's no way I will ever abandon her.

'Do you want a hot drink?' I call through to Becky, but she's zoned out, listening to music as usual. I make her a cup of tea anyway, carry the mugs through, and put them on the coffee table. She pulls out her earbud once more, and smiles.

'Something happened last night,' I say, sitting down, resting my hands in my lap. 'When you were asleep.'

Her eyes widen as she waits for me to go on, but I'm suddenly unsure whether to tell her. Is she safer not knowing, or will she be on her guard if I tell her?

'What is it, Mum?'

'The man we saw in the pub,' I go on.

'Scary-man?'

'Yes, if you must insist on calling him that. He was here last night. He knocked at the front door and later I saw him on the patio, banging on the window.'

'Oh my God. You need to call the police, Mum. God, I've gone all wobbly.' She pulls out her other earbud. 'You will call them?'

'Well, I've got to go there to give a statement later today, I'll tell them then.' I take a gulp of coffee, and wince as it burns my mouth. 'Also, Grandpa called. He said he received a text from Willow.'

'Do you think it's from her?'

I shake my head, ridiculously close to tears. 'I honestly don't know anymore.' I fiddle with the handle of my mug, as a silence drops between us. It hangs there for some moments before I go on. 'I've been thinking about Justin Havers too. I thought I might call the nearest hospital. See if he's been admitted. I mean I saw an ambulance, didn't I?' My mind is taking detours, racing down different roads, arriving at dark dead ends.

'Good idea,' Becky says, nodding her head in approval, and picking up her mug of tea. 'This is all too weird.'

'I know, love. In fact, I've been thinking … maybe I should take you home.'

'What?'

'I can call Grandpa and Eleanor. They'd come home in an instant. Or perhaps you could stay with Tamsyn. I'm sure her mum—'

'But I don't want to go home, Mum,' she cuts in. 'I want to stay here with you.' Her eyes glisten with tears again. 'Please let me stay,' she goes on. 'Please. I feel safer with you.'

'Please don't cry, sweetheart.' I'm always sucked in by Becky's tears. I pull a tissue from my pocket and hand it to her. 'OK you can stay. But if anything else happens, Becky, we're leaving. Now make yourself useful and look up the number of the nearest hospital.'

'Thanks, Mum,' she says.

I wonder what Aaron would think of me letting Becky stay on here, but I know the answer. He would be horrified. But then she's not his daughter. I push the image of his concerned face from my mind, as I watch Becky's fingers dance on the screen of her phone. Soon she's reading out the number of the hospital.

I tap it into my mobile, and press call.

'Yes, he's on Ward 8,' the woman on the phone says, once I've asked if a Justin Havers has been admitted. 'Do you want me to put you through?'

'Yes, thank you.'

I sit with the phone pinned to my ear. The ringtone seems to go on forever, before a woman picks up. 'Ward 8, how can I help you?'

'I'm ringing to enquire how Justin Havers is,' I say.

'Are you a relative?'

'No, no, I'm …' *Who the hell am I?* 'A friend.'

'I'm afraid I can't give out information over the phone unless you're a relative,' she says.

'Oh. But he's OK?'

'I'm sorry, I can't give out information over the phone,' she repeats, almost robotic.

'OK. Well thank you.' I end the call.

I look at Becky. The sun shining in through the patio doors highlights the shadows under her eyes, and despite agreeing she can stay, I hear Aaron's voice in my head. *Take her home, Rose. This is no place for either of you.*

*

We've broken free of the winding country roads and I push down on the accelerator as we meet the main road heading into Newquay.

'So tell me again why we're going to the hospital,' Becky says, and I feel her eyes on me.

'I want to speak to Justin, that's all. I keep thinking about the garage door. What if someone attacked him.'

'He's probably ill, Mum. Maybe the shock of being released has caused his heart to explode. I think it's a waste of time, is all.'

189

I glance across at her. Her eyes are fixed on the passing countryside. She's hated hospitals since she had her appendix out two years ago, maybe it's that that's making her so negative. 'I'm sure going to Newquay won't be a waste of time. We may even find Willow.'

'She could be anywhere, Mum. Newquay is a pretty big place, and we don't really believe she's there anyway, do we?'

'No, I suppose not. But I thought we might visit Willow's grandmother too.'

'And you think she can help us find Willow? Why? Inspector Jones said Willow learned nothing from her mother, remember?'

'For God's sake, Becky, I thought you wanted to be supportive, be here with me.' My voice is rising, I take a breath, try for calm. Perhaps she's afraid. 'Have you got any better ideas?'

'No.'

'Well then, we'll go to the hospital, and to Green Pastures too, OK?'

She looks at me. 'OK,' she says. 'Mother knows best.'

'That's the first sensible thing you've said all day,' I say trying to squash the tension, and she cracks a smile.

Chapter 37

ROSE

Now

Green Pastures is easy enough to find with the help of the satnav, and once we're there, I pull into an allotted visitor bay and kill the engine.

We get out of the car, and head for the entrance. It's a heavy door, with a security lock. We either need a fob key, or the number of Jeannette Millar's apartment. We have neither.

"Told you. Waste of time," Becky reminds me, folding her arms. I ignore her and, blocking out the sun with my hand, I peer in.

'There's nobody about,' I say.

'Old people sleep most of the time,' she says. 'Or watch murder mysteries. Although many of their species can be seen on cruises and coach trips.'

'Stop stereotyping the elderly, Becky. You'll be old yourself one day. I'll have you know, your great-grandfather worked until he was eighty, and I only read the other day about a woman of ninety running a marathon.'

'I was only joking,' she says. 'I like old people.'

'Well, Jeannette Millar isn't exactly old – she's only in her early seventies.'

She's doing a Becky-eye-roll, when a smiling elderly man with a stick, looking smart in a purple polo shirt and cream chinos, appears. 'Can I help you young ladies?'

'Ooh, I hope so,' I say. 'We're looking for Jeannette Millar.'

'Number fifty-two.' He places his fob on the door entry pad. 'Come in,' he says as the door slowly opens. 'I'll take you there.'

We follow him down two carpeted corridors, all beautifully decorated, with flowers on display, until we come to number fifty-two.

He taps on the door, and after a few moments he leans in closer to the door. 'Jeannette! It's me, Godfrey Marsden from number nine.'

The door opens and a frail woman in a floral sweatshirt over black leggings, stands in front of us, looking older than her seventy years.

'You have visitors, my love,' the man – Godfrey – says with enthusiasm, pointing to us like we're contestants on a game show.

She narrows her eyes as she looks our way, and Becky steps behind me, as if the woman may shoot us, or batter us with insults.

'I don't want visitors, Godfrey,' Jeannette says, and goes to close the door.

'My name is Rose,' I say in a rush, placing my hand on the door. 'I'm Willow's stepsister.'

'Willow?'

'Yes. Could we speak to you for a moment? We won't keep you long.'

She opens the door, and steps back. As we enter, I thank Godfrey, who heads towards the IT suite.

'No problem at all,' he says, with a flurry of fingers. 'You girls have fun.' I'm instantly reminded of Dad.

'Whoa!' Becky says, as Jeannette leads us into her lounge. 'She's got all the radiators on. It's like a sauna in here.'

'Shh!' I say, hoping Jeannette didn't hear.

'You'll feel the cold when you're my age too, young lady,' Jeannette says, thumping down onto a squishy sofa, and I wonder if she's any idea that it's twenty-five degrees outside.

As I perch on the edge of an armchair, and Becky crouches at my feet leaning against my legs, I study the place. It's small and clean, the walls are cream, with vertical blinds at the window. A TV screen is frozen on John Nettles. Jeannette Millar shares the sofa with piles of books, magazines, and crossword puzzles. I notice a necklace around her neck with the word 'Mummy' on it.

'I'll tell you what I told her,' she says, before I can say anything. 'Willow?'

'Yes. She came round here asking questions about the past. I didn't want to be reminded. I lost two daughters on the same night, and my son took off back to Australia. I'd never felt so alone.'

'And Willow?'

'I could barely look after myself through such an awful time, letting Willow go was the kindest thing I could do for the child. That's what I tell myself daily.'

'I'm so sorry,' I say, my eyes leaving her creased face, and taking in the photographs on a display cabinet. There's no doubt they are her family when they were young – a boy, two girls – and there's one of Willow as a child, a Fisher Price phone pressed to her ear.

Jeannette caresses her dry lips. 'At the time, I thought things were getting better. Peter was back. We'd made our peace. He's doing well now, you know. Owns his own plumbing company in Australia.' She glances about her. 'He paid for this place. Bought it for me.'

I widen my eyes. 'That's very generous.'

She rests her head against the back of the sofa. 'I signed over the cottage to him, hoped he might come back and stay with me sometimes, bring his family. He never did. A few years ago he suggested I move here, so he could rent the cottage out as a holiday let. A man in the village does all the admin work for him.'

'Peter owns Ocean View Cottage?' I say.

She nods. 'It's worked out well. I'm happy here. Well, as happy as I'll ever be.' A tear rolls down her cheek. 'I never believed my Gail killed her sister and took her own life. I know she was angry that night, and someone saw her take the cake knife, but I don't think she had it in her, not to kill her own sister.' She pauses for a moment. 'They never found Gail's body, you know. I still dream she will turn up one day – walk through that door. Foolish, I know.'

'I'm so sorry.'

She looks out through the window at a well-maintained communal garden.

'It was the worst day of my life when they asked me to identify Ava's body. I went with Rory, and as he walked into the room where she lay under a sheet, I stood in the doorway, unable to move.' She pressed her hand against her chest, covering the necklace, breathing deeply. "I'll do it,"' Rory said, and

I rushed from the room, thousands of things I should have said to her when she was alive buzzing around my head, like wasps about to sting me over and over and over.' She buries her head in her hands for a moment, before looking up once more. 'From the corridor I heard Rory say, "It's her" and I knew at that moment I would never be the same again.'

'I'm so sorry,' I say, tears in my eyes. 'Would you like us to leave?'

She looks over at us and dashes a tear from her face with the cuff of her sweatshirt. 'Give me a moment,' she says, breathing deeply.

Becky looks up at me, her eyes watery too, and gives a little shrug.

'A lad had been hanging about,' Jeannette begins again. 'Always wore a yellow baseball cap pulled low so I couldn't see his face. I saw him before Ava was raped.'

'Ava was raped?' I say, unable to keep the shock from my voice, and Becky takes my hand. 'We didn't know.'

'Yes,' Jeannette says. 'A couple of months before she was murdered.' She looks down at her hands again. 'I wish I'd handled it differently.'

After a long silence, I ask, 'Do you think this man in the yellow cap could have been Ava's killer?' My mind drifts to Isaac – and away again; he's far too young.

'He hung about a lot,' she said. 'Never close enough to get a decent look at him. I took a photograph of him from the window once, but when I showed it to Gareth Jones he said it wasn't clear enough to work with. I gave it to Willow when she visited.'

I rummage in my bag, and bring out the unclear photo, and show it to her. 'Is this it?'

She nods, grabs a tissue from a box on the table in front of her, and dabs her eyes. 'I believe now he was stalking Ava or perhaps Gail. I should have done more.'

'You did your best,' I say, basing it on nothing.

'No, no I didn't, I'm ashamed to say. I only wanted the best for my children, but I was never very good at showing affection, particularly with Ava. I blamed her for why my husband left me. I deflected my anger onto an innocent child.' She pauses for a moment, seeming to gather her thoughts. 'I had a fling. Ava was the outcome. When my husband found out, he took off – so angry – rejecting us all. We never saw him again. And it was my fault. All my fault.' She shreds the tissue. 'I admit, after that, I was a rather cold mother, but I honestly wanted the best for all my children.'

I struggle to form the words, but I must know. 'Did Ava's real father know she was his daughter?'

She shakes her head. 'Not at the time.' She rises to her feet. 'I think you should go now,' she says, dabbing her cheeks, and fiddling with the necklace. She isn't going to tell me any more.

'One more thing,' I say, rising. 'I don't suppose you know where Rory Thompson lives? I'd like to talk to him.'

She rummages through the books and magazines next to her, and picks up a battered address book. She flicks through it. '48 Walton Avenue,' she says. 'It's on the other side of Newquay.'

'Thank you,' I say, as we head for the door, and open it. 'I'm so sorry,' I call to her once more, before we step out into the corridor and click the door closed behind us.

*

I pull into the car park, and once I've found a space and grabbed a ticket from the machine, we walk through the double automatic doors into the hospital, and head for the lifts.

When the doors swoosh open, we step inside to share the lift with a nurse, an elderly couple, and a mother with a baby. I hate lifts, and feel a migraine niggling – or is it the head injury? Maybe I should have got it checked out. But whatever it is, it fades as we step out onto the eighth floor.

'Can you smell it?' Becky says.

'What?'

'Iodoform. I watched a documentary a few months back about how clean hospitals are. It's the disinfectant they use.' She covers her nose. 'It's weird. I hate it.'

I shudder and look about me. 'Ward 8,' I say, using the hand sanitiser twice, before taking off down a corridor with determined strides.

'Wait up,' Becky calls after me, and I slow my pace. 'What are you going to say to him?'

'I'm going to wing it.'

'Wing it?' she says, as we reach the nurses station. 'You've never winged anything in your life, Mother.'

'I'm looking for Justin Havers,' I say, and a nurse looks up from her computer screen, and points to a side room.

Becky and I look at each other. 'Why not stay out here?' I say.

'No, it's OK. I'd rather be with you.'

I open the door, and peek inside to see Justin, his eyes closed. A monitor bleeps, and as we step inside I notice his head is bandaged.

A nurse bustles in and grabs a chart from the end of the bed. 'There's been no change,' she says, as though we know what she means, and I look back at Justin.

'What happened?' I whisper.

'You don't know?'

'We're old friends. I only heard this morning he'd been taken in. We got here as quickly as we could.' Becky looks at me wide-eyed, not used to me lying.

'He was attacked in his home, poor love,' the nurse says, writing something on the chart, and popping it back. 'He's in a coma.'

She leaves, and I lower myself onto the chair by his bed, and Becky hovers behind me. 'He's in a coma,' I say, repeating the nurse's words, as though Becky hadn't heard. 'Who the hell would do this to him?'

'I don't know, Mum,' she says, touching my shoulder. 'But we should probably go,' she says.

'We should, yes.' I touch his hand gently. 'But he hasn't got anyone else.'

Chapter 38

AVA

2001

Ava felt desperate. It was as though a vampire had sucked the life out of her. She'd been sick too. In fact, all she wanted to do was curl up in bed and hide from the world. But however much she and Gail didn't get on, she was still her sister, and today meant everything to Gail.

She stared in the mirror, her hand shaking as she held her red lipstick close to her lips, a sudden anger rising inside her. She struck each cheek with the lipstick, as though painting a picture. 'I hate you,' she yelled at her reflection. 'Why don't you just curl up and die?'

*

Later, after she'd scrubbed away the lipstick in the shower, Ava eased herself into her yellow satin dress, her body trembling. She'd hated the dress when she first saw it, and yet now she *almost* liked it – a blast of sunshine on the darkest of days.

She placed the ring of flowers on her head and took the stairs slowly with the aid of the banister. A rumble of excited voices radiated from the lounge, making her want to turn back.

She opened the lounge door. Jeannette was faffing with Gail's white gown, and Ava had to admit her sister looked stunning. Her hair was piled on top of her head, with ringlets falling softly each side of her perfectly made-up face. Her dress was delicate, feminine, the top half made from Victorian lace, the bottom silk.

'You look lovely,' Ava said, meaning it. Sometimes all she wanted was for her and her sister to get on, be friends. But she knew it would never happen.

'Yes, yes I know,' Gail replied, looking at her nails, distracted.

Willow was spinning in circles, her yellow satin dress flaring outwards from the waist. She was gripping a small bouquet, her hair decorated with tiny white flowers. *My darling girl.*

Peter looked good in a royal-blue velvet suit, his hair fastened in a neat ponytail. He'd scrubbed up pretty well.

Her mum looked the best Ava had ever seen her in an ankle-length dark green skirt suit, and a fascinator Gail had forced her to wear, pinned to her hair. Everything looked so normal – happy. *The book's cover – the real story inside.*

'Hey, Ava,' Peter said, catching sight of her in the doorway. 'Looking good, sis. Very nice.' She felt far from it but tried for a smile.

'Pretty Mummy!' Willow squealed and stopped spinning to run and grab Ava's legs.

'For God's sake, Ava, don't let her stain your dress,' Gail yelled.

Ava crouched down, and studied the flowers pinned to Willow's hair, touching them gently. The gash from Willow's fall had healed well, just a tiny scar now, as the nurse had predicted. Ava wished her own wounds would heal as well. 'You look like an angel, Willow,' she said, kissing her daughter's cheek.

Willow smiled, and touched her mum's face gently, and Ava took her small hand and kissed it three times.

'The car's here! The car's here!' yelled Gail, looking through the window. 'Oh God, should we leave now? I want to be a bit late.'

'Why?' Jeannette said. 'You don't want to give Rory a reason to change his mind, do you?'

'Maxen won't let him change his mind,' Gail said.

'Maxen?' Ava said uneasily. Surely it couldn't be the same Maxen?

'Anyway, Mum,' Gail went on, ignoring Ava. 'Why would he change his mind?'

'I was only joking, love.'

'Maxen?' Ava said again.

'Maxen Jones.' Gail narrowed her eyes, her tone irritated. 'Rory's best man.'

'Really?' She should have known. Maxen had mentioned Rory that day at Kathy's Café and again at the arcade. Yet she still found their friendship surprising. They were so different.

'Yes? Why are you so shocked?' Gail said. 'Do you know him?'

'I really think we should leave now, Gail,' Jeannette cut in.

'Yes. Well, OK, I guess we'd better go. Get me to the church on time,' she sang, raising her bouquet in the air as she headed for the door.

They poured from the cottage, and down the path towards the waiting limo – Gail holding onto Peter's arm, Jeannette a few steps behind, Ava and Willow following on hand in hand. It was chilly, but a watery sun shone high in the blue sky. Gail had picked the perfect day to get married.

Once in the car, Ava opened her silver clutch bag. The velvet box was at the bottom. Someone must have seen it before, and what better place to find out who than a village hall full of locals.

*

'Rory and I have been friends since we were kids,' Maxen was saying. He'd already told tall tales about their antics in their teens to raucous laughter, and now his tone was more serious. 'He had a much more exciting beginning than I had. Living in Italy for a while with his mum who adored him.' He looked over at Rory and tilted his head. 'I know the loss of his mother was traumatic, and his dad more recently – but they would be proud of you now, mate.' He smiled at Rory. 'Proud of everything you've achieved.'

Ava zoned out, her eyes falling on Dexter in a pale grey suit, sitting at a table with his mother, and a group of Gail's friends, looking a bit fed up. He caught her eye and smiled, dimples forming, and raised his glass to her. She shuddered. It was the first time she'd seen him since that awful night. She hadn't realised he would be here.

'And now we're the closest we've ever been,' Maxen was saying. 'I'd do anything for you, Rory. You're the best friend a guy could wish for. To the bride and groom,' he said, raising his glass.

There was a resounding echo of congratulations in the room, as Ava knocked back a full glass of champagne. 'To the bride and groom,' she said.

Next, Ava watched on with a pang of envy, as Rory and Gail presented each other with necklaces, and Rory told Gail how much he loved her, that he was the luckiest man in the world to have met her.

The only comfort for Ava was Willow, sitting next to her so well-behaved, throwing her mum looks every so often as if to say, 'Are you OK, Mummy?'

*

Later, Ava made her way towards Dexter. He was alone at the table now; his mother and Gail's friends had vanished to the separate bar area. It was that in-between time you get at weddings: the meal had finished, but the evening festivities hadn't started – although the band had almost set up.

Dexter looked handsome, as he always did, his hair tousled, his eyes on her.

She sat down, and he leaned forward, went to touch her cheek. She batted his hand away. He shot back, as though burnt.

'Christ, Ava, what's wrong with you?' he said, his dark eyes hurt.

'Who invited you?' she snapped. Being so close to him sent her body into meltdown. Had he raped her? Had he drugged her? If it wasn't him, where was he when someone put something in her drink? Why hadn't he seen someone take her that night? Why hadn't he protected her?

'Gail. We go to the same gym. I hadn't realised she was your sister until today.'

'So you brought your mum as your plus one?'

'Yes.' He looked over his shoulder. 'She's about somewhere. Probably gossiping.'

'I need a drink,' she said, rising, and he followed her through to the bar. 'Large wine,' she said to the barman, and turned to Dexter. 'What about you?'

'Think I'll pace myself,' he said, putting his hand up as though she'd offered him poison. 'I've already had a fair bit.'

'Fine,' she said, paying for the wine, and taking a mouthful.

'I messaged you,' he said, following her once more into the hall. 'They said at work you've been ill.'

'Yes. I have. Very ill.' Her words were clipped. She struggled to stay near him. Stay near anyone.

They sat back down, as the lights dimmed, and the band launched into a Beatles track. Within moments Peter was up on the floor, dancing with Willow and a little boy Ava didn't recognise.

Dexter and Ava sat in silence until the song ended, and the dance floor cleared.

'Are you going to speak to me?' Dexter said, his voice cracking.

She drained her glass. 'I need another one of these,' she said, getting up and leaving him. He didn't follow this time, and as she glanced over her shoulder at him sitting alone, she wanted to cry. She'd liked him. She'd liked him a lot. But the overwhelming fear the attack had left her with had set up home. She knew it would never leave.

At the bar she downed another wine. Dutch courage, that's what her mother called it. Fake strength. But heading back, she felt unsteady. She dropped down at a table and buried her head in her hands, as the band played a cover of 'Yesterday' and Gail's friends at the bar sang along, out of tune. She lifted her gaze to see them swaying in time with the music – all fascinators, posh frocks and heels – and wished she could remember what it felt like to be that happy. In fact, she wasn't sure she ever had.

Chapter 39

ROSE

Now

The police visit didn't take long. I gave a statement to PC Lewis, going over what happened the night on the beach, and mentioned the stalker from last night. But what can they do? Whoever hit me is long gone, and so is the stalker. I asked if there was any news on Willow, and they said they'd checked hospitals, but no news as yet. I hadn't expected anything else.

'Fancy something to eat before we go to Rory's house?' I ask Becky, as we pull out of the car park, and onto the main road. 'I've set my satnav for 48 Walton Avenue, and it informs me we're five minutes away.'

'I'm not fussed,' she says, tapping her fingers over her phone screen, her black nail varnish chipped.

'I worry you don't eat enough, sweetheart,' I say, as I pull up at a red light and look over at her.

'Not this again, Mother.' Her fingers freeze on her phone, eyes on me. 'Stop worrying, I'm fine. I like to look after myself, is all.'

'By not eating?'

'I eat. For God's sake stop hassling me.' I can hear by her voice she's getting upset. I know this isn't the right way to deal with it.

I pull into Walton Avenue, where beautiful Edwardian detached houses sit either side of the tree-lined road. I park up, and we climb out.

'We're looking for number 48.' I press my key to lock the car, as we walk down the road. 'These houses are stunning,' I say.

'Yeah,' Becky says. 'Rory must have loads of money.'

We find the house, with its sweeping drive leading to the front door, and large bay-fronted windows, and stand at the gate. I rummage in my bag for the photograph of Rory, just to remind myself of what he looks like.

'Come on,' Becky says, opening the gate, and I follow her up the drive, pebbles crunching under our shoes.

We ring the bell, and the door swings open. A blonde woman in her early twenties, wearing a white T-shirt and jeans, raises a perfect eyebrow. 'If you're going to try to sell me something, I'm not interested.'

'No, sorry,' I say. 'My name is Rose, and this is my daughter, Becky. We're looking for Rory Thompson.'

She shrugs. 'And?'

'We believe he lives here.'

'Nope! Never heard of him.' She crosses her arms.

'He's probably moved, Mum,' Becky says, looking at me. 'It's been a long time.'

'Have you lived here long?' I persist.

'Dad's been here for five years,' she says. 'Not that that's any of your business.'

'Who is it, Jess?' A man of around forty appears behind the woman.

'Oh, hi,' I say, raising a hand. 'We were wondering if you've heard of Rory Thompson. He used to live here.'

'Yes, I know Rory,' he says, grazing his chin with his hand. 'He owns the place. I rent from him. Although I rarely see him – he lives in Italy, so we mainly deal with the estate agent. Nice chap though. I can give you his email address if you need to get in touch. Hang on!' He disappears, returning with a little card. 'Here, have this. It's his card. I've got a couple.'

*

'Will you email Rory Thompson?' Becky asks.

'I guess so. Although I'm not sure he'll be able to help with Willow's disappearance, but you never know. It's got to be worth a try. He was in the box after all.'

'Mmm,' she says.

We drive in silence for some time before she says, 'Let's go to the house.'

'House?'

'Cottage. Floral something-or-other. You know, the place on the other side of the bay, we said we would go there, remember? See if the owners saw anything the night you were attacked.'

'Maybe we should leave it to the police, Becky.'

'You're not scared, are you?'

'Yes. I suppose. A bit. And you should be too. This whole situation is getting out of hand.'

'Oh go on,' she says. 'At least then we can rule it out.'

Becky's right, we should ask the owners if they saw or heard anything the night I was attacked. But there's truth in my words. I am scared – scared for Willow's safety. Scared for ours. In the end I drive towards the house, my desire to know outweighing the dangers.

Becky doesn't notice which way I'm going, her eyes closed as she listens to her music, so when I reach the house, and pull onto the cobbled drive, she looks surprised when she opens her eyes.

'Oh my God,' she says, pulling out her earbuds.

'It's so pretty, isn't it?' I say. 'I wonder who lives here.'

We get out of the car. There are no other vehicles on the drive, and the house is quiet, looks deserted. But there's no doubt someone lives here. The garden is immaculate. Rose bushes are in full bloom, and the grass is plush green, a sprinkler on, showering the lawn and surrounding shrubs and flowers.

'Shall we knock?' Becky says, heading for the door, which is art deco, and doesn't quite match the rest of the house. The brickwork is painted pale green, the roof thatched. It's much bigger than I'd first thought, with views on every side of open countryside. It's perfect – a dream house.

I follow Becky, noticing a bell situated inside a pitch-roofed porch, the kind that might be used to ring last orders in a pub. 'Maybe try that,' I say, pointing it out, the aroma of the roses around the door bombarding my senses.

She's on it immediately, ringing the bell several times. 'Bring out your dead,' she says.

'Shh!' I say, and despite my angst, I laugh – wondering if it's more hysteria.

Nobody comes to the door. I peer through the opaque glass, then turn and look about me. There's a separate garage, and a gate leading around to the back of the house. I shiver. What if whoever hit me lives here?

Becky takes off towards the garage. 'It's an electric door,' she says, observing it. 'Very fancy pants.'

'There's a side door,' I say, picking up on her investigative tone, and following her. She tries the handle.

'Should we be doing that?' I say, but it's locked too.

'We could go round the back of the house,' Becky says, as a cloud blocks out the sun. 'Or look in the windows.'

'No. I really think we should leave this to the police.' I'm beginning to feel odd, a prickle on my neck as though someone is watching us. What felt so beautiful moments ago, now gives me chills. 'It's far too quiet,' I say. There isn't even any birdsong. 'We should get back,' I add, fiddling with my car keys.

207

'OK. Just one more thing.' She grabs a log and pulls it towards the garage. There's a high window. I know what she is about to do.

The log wobbles as she climbs onto it, 'Nothing much in here,' she says, screwing up her nose and squinting, as she peers into the garage window. 'There's a red car, a couple of old bikes – that's about it.' She almost falls from the log.

'Let's go,' I say, and she trots to my side, and we get into the car.

It's as we pull away I notice a face at the upstairs window, and a flash of blonde hair.

Chapter 40

AVA

2001

'Is everything OK, Ava?'

She looked up to see Peter standing over her, and nodded weakly.

'You're necking it pretty quickly, maybe slow down a bit, aye?'

She scraped her chair back across the wooden floor, putting space between them. 'I'm fine,' she snapped. 'And you're one to talk.'

'Think about Willow, Ava,' he said, leaning over and placing his hand on her arm.

'I always think about her,' she cried. 'Always.'

'I know. Sorry. You must be in a living hell right now.'

With a deep intake of breath, she reached into her bag and pulled out the box with the bracelet inside.

He sat down, and furrowing his forehead, picked it up. 'What is it?'

'I found it.'

'Found it?' He lifted the lid, and stared at the necklace, and back at Ava. 'Found it where?

Her mind whirred and tears rolled down her face. 'I found it the night I was attacked.'

Gail appeared beside them, and Ava dabbed her tears away with the heels of her hands.

'You should go home,' Gail said. 'It's the first dance soon, and we've got to cut the cake, and if I'm honest, Ava, I really don't want you here ruining everything with your continual self-destruction. This is my wedding day for God's sake. It's meant to be the best day of my life.'

'I know,' Ava said. 'I'm sorry.'

'Sorry isn't enough. People keep asking me if my sister is OK. Go home, Ava.'

'Leave her, Gail,' Peter said. 'You know what she's been through.' Ava's eyes widened. 'You told her?'

His eyes met hers. 'I'm sorry. She was just so angry with you. I wanted her to understand.'

'I don't care what she's been through, Peter,' Gail snapped. 'If she can't put it on hold for one fucking day, then she can piss off home, quite frankly.'

'Shut up!' Ava banged her hands palm down on the table, and a splinter of wood pierced her skin. She pulled it out, and blood oozed from the small wound, but there was no pain. She was too numb to feel pain.

'Where the hell did you get that?' Gail snapped, snatching the open box from Peter, the bracelet glinting inside.

'I found it,' Ava said, glancing at Peter.

'I don't believe you.' Gail snapped the box closed. 'You took it, didn't you? You've always been jealous of everything I have, but I didn't think you were capable of taking the gift Rory bought for me. The bracelet I chose.'

Anger shuddered through Ava's body, her stomach churned. *Rory?* She rose, needing to throw up.

She tried pushing past her sister, but Gail wouldn't budge. 'He had to get this ridiculous thing instead,' she said, pointing at the necklace around her neck that Rory presented her with at the top table. She rammed the box into her bag. 'I'll have this thank you very much, you little bitch.' And with that she stormed into the main hall.

The noise that came from Ava was close to a wild animal in distress.

Peter got up, attempted to hug her, but she shook him away, fell back into her seat, and buried her head in her hands. *Had Rory raped her?*

Peter sat down and attempted to pull her hands from her face. 'What can I do?' he said sounding desperate. 'Let me help you.'

'Just leave me alone, Peter,' she said through her fingers. 'Please.'

He sat for a while longer, before kissing her head and leaving. After sitting as though in a trance for some time, she got up and followed him into the main hall where the band boomed out a cover of 'Cotton Eye Joe', and a row of guests were attempting line dancing.

'Ava!' It was Megan Powell, dressed in a pink floral dress, hurrying towards her, a cream fur coat over arm. As she got closer, avoiding guests who had taken to the dance floor, Ava could see she was angry. 'Can I have a word with you?'

'It's not a good time, Megan.' Ava could see Gail talking to their mother. Peter and Willow were dancing some distance away.

Megan grabbed Ava's arm, her neck flushing red.

Ava shook her arm free. 'What's this about?' she said, the waft of Megan's heavy perfume making her head ache.

'How could you be so cruel to my boy? You ignored his messages and now barely speak to him. The poor boy's devastated. He's gone home.'

'I'm sorry,' Ava said. 'I didn't mean to hurt Dexter. It's just—'

'There's no excuse for being so cruel, Ava Millar,' Megan snapped, thrusting her arms into her fur coat. 'I've got to go home now. Leave the party. Make sure he's OK.' With that she stormed towards the door, getting lost in the crowd.

Ava approached her sister. 'Line dancing,' Gail was saying. 'It's a wedding not a bloody barn dance. They need to play something more cultured, like a Grease medley or something.'

Ava took hold of her sister's arm. They were the same height, but Ava was running on adrenaline – she was stronger. 'Where is he?' she demanded. 'Where the hell is he?'

Gail spun round. 'Who?' She was wearing the bracelet. Brazen. Bold. How could she?

'Rory?' Ava yelled, trying to make herself heard over the music. 'He needs to pay for what he did.'

'What the hell are you talking about?' Gail's eyes were wide and full of anger.

'I think he raped me, Gail,' Ava cried.

Gail's slap across Ava's face stung like pins plunged into a pincushion. But as Ava looked about her, holding her cheek, tears filling her eyes once more, nobody seemed to notice. Or if they did, they politely ignored what they'd seen.

'Go home, Ava. Go!' Jeannette said, pointing to the door.

'You're unbelievable, Mum,' Ava whispered, before rushing away, diving through the crowd, knocking into a man who jabbed her chest with his elbow.

'Ouch,' she cried, clutching her breasts, as she headed for the ladies'.

She didn't want to walk home on her own. Afraid. Yes. He'd made her weak. He'd made her helpless. He'd made her vulnerable.

She continued through the throng of dancers, and someone touched her arm. She swung round.

'Join in, Ava.' It was Maxen, yelling above the music, as he tried to follow the steps.

She ignored him, throwing open the door to the ladies' instead. Women applying make-up and spraying perfume were lined up in front of the mirror. There was a wooden chair in the corner, and three cubicles. She raced into the vacant one, locked the door, and leaned her body against it, taking deep breaths until her heart resumed an even beat. She sat on the seat, lid down, cradling her knees, and rocking backwards and forwards. She would stay here. She would stay here until this fucking fiasco was over.

An hour went by. She cried. She got angry. She threw up. And repeat.

Music vibrated the walls. Women came and went. Trying the door. Accepting it was engaged.

She looked at her watch. Quarter to eleven. Gail and Rory would head to the airport soon in his stupid Ferrari.

Suddenly the outside door was thrown open, and she listened for the usual clatter of make-up, the giggles, the whispers, but there was nothing.

'A-va!' The voice was haunting, deliberately creepy. 'Ava, are you in here?'

Panic shot through her. It was Rory.

The cubicle was enclosed. He wouldn't know she was here if she stayed quiet. But her whole body trembled, and her neck prickled as though a spider was scurrying across it. He would hear her fear.

Something scraped across the floor and banged against the outside door. *The chair?* He was trapping them in.

'Gail told me you came in here over an hour ago. Are you still here?'

Silence, as though he was listening. She felt sure he could hear her heartbeat, her rapid breathing.

'She said you had the bracelet, Ava.' Rory went on. She could hear his footfalls, slow, calculating, as he banged open the doors of the other two cubicles, before thudding on her door three times. 'What's going on, Ava?'

Bile rose in Ava's mouth. 'Bastard,' she whispered.

'Now, now, Ava, is that anyway to talk to your brother-in-law?'

A rap on the outside door startled her. The sound of the chair scraping on the floor gave her chills.

'Sorry, lovely ladies,' Rory said, his voice jovial. 'Got caught a bit short.'

And then he was gone.

A rush of women's laughter filled the room. Ava sighed with relief, opened the door, and hurried out of the toilets, not looking their way. She had to get out of this place. She would run and run until nobody could find her.

She bolted across the hall, and into Peter. 'Look after Willow,' she said over the music, her mouth close to his ear. It was a slow dance – and she glimpsed Rory and Gail swooning into each other's eyes, him pushing a tendril of her sister's blonde hair, that had escaped her bun, from her cheek.

'Promise me, Peter, please,' she continued.

'Why? Where are you going?'

'Never let anything bad happen to her, Peter. Please. I'm trusting you.'

'Of course,' he said. 'But—'

'Promise me. Say it. Say it!'

'I promise.'

She bobbed down in front of Willow, who'd been dancing on Peter's shoes, and touched her little girl's face – so soft, so pure. 'Always remember I love you, darling girl,' she said, and kissed her cheek.

Willow touched her mum's face, 'Are you crying, Mummy?'

Ava held her daughter's hand and kissed it three times, trying to hold back tears. 'Mummy's going away,' she said, looking into her eyes. Certain her daughter would be better off without her. 'Peter will take good care of you. You will be good for Peter, won't you?'

Willow looked up at her uncle, and back at Ava. 'Yes,' she said, tilting her head.

Ava straightened up, and threw her arms around Peter for a

few moments, breathing in the smell of him – stale smoke and aftershave.

'Stay, Ava,' he said. 'I'm here for you.'

'I can't,' she said, and dashed away, barging past guests. But before she could reach the door, Gail was beside her.

'You're finally leaving then,' she said, fiddling with the bracelet on her wrist.

Ava nodded. 'And I'm not coming back.'

'For the best,' she said. 'I still can't believe you stole the bracelet.'

'I didn't steal it.'

'What? You just happened to find it, and didn't realise it was mine?'

'No.'

'Then what?' Her eyes were wide, refusing to let Ava escape from her stare.

'Rory dropped it when he raped me, Gail,' she said, so calmly, as though she was talking about the weather.

Gail's eyes widened further. 'Are there no end to your lies, Ava?' she cried. 'Do you really hate me so much that you'd resort to this kind of evil?' she yelled. She turned and rushed away, disappearing onto the dance floor, where everyone was now singing along to a cover of 'Don't Look Back In Anger', waving their arms in the air.

Chapter 41

ROSE

Now

'Shall I email Rory Thompson now?' Becky says, as we head for home.

'Yes, I guess so. The quicker we send him a message the better.'

Becky opens her email account on her phone. 'So what shall I say?'

'Mmm. Well.' My mind goes blank. 'Just ask him if he's been to the UK recently. Ask if he's seen or heard from Willow. The card is in my bag.'

'OK,' she says, retrieving the card, and typing a message into her phone.

It's as we reach the village that Rory responds. Becky reads out the message.

'Hi Rose and Becky. I haven't heard a word about Willow since she was adopted, and haven't been to Cornwall in a couple of years. I live in Italy with my wife and two sons.

I'd love to see Willow, so please drop me a line when you catch up with her. Best wishes, Rory.'

Becky looks up from her phone. 'Well, that's him out, I guess,' she says.

'Unless he's lying,' I say, as we pull up outside Ocean View Cottage behind a Fiat I don't recognise. I kill the engine, and we get out of the car. There's a man by the front door, his back to us. He's looking out at the bay, a holdall at his feet. Is it the man who knocked on the patio door last night?

'Oh God, is that scary-man?' Becky says, echoing my thoughts as we hover by the car. 'Call the police, Mum. Now!'

He turns, and I breathe a sigh of relief. 'It isn't the same man,' I say. This man is at least ten years older, with short dark hair, a goatee beard, and glasses.

On seeing us he raises his hand. 'G' day,' he calls, and heads down the path. He stops as he reaches us, his face bright with excitement. 'Willow?' he asks.

'No,' I say, aware I sound blunt. There's something familiar about him. 'Willow isn't here right now. And you are?'

'Peter Millar,' he says, and I recall the photo of him that Willow sent in the box: the hippy with unruly hair and glasses like Harry Potter. He's smarter now, tanned, and carrying a little more weight, which suits him. His glasses have trendy red frames, and he's wearing narrow-legged checked trousers and a white polo shirt with a Kookaburra motive. 'Willow wrote to me,' he goes on, and I remember Inspector Jones telling me how she'd got in touch with her uncle. 'I haven't seen her for about eighteen years. It was a shock to hear from her.' He paused. 'So you are?'

'Rose Lawson,' I say. 'Willow's stepsister, and this is my daughter, Becky.'

'Willow mentioned you both in her letter,' he says with a smile. 'She said she was trying to find my sister's killer.' His eyes seemed to evaluate us, as though deciding whether to go on. 'Did you know?'

I nod, and glance at Becky.

'I promised Ava before she died that I would look out for Willow. But her custody went straight to my mother – her gran – who put her into care after I'd gone back to Australia.'

'Yes, we heard about that.'

'I was never told who adopted Willow.' He bit down on his lip. 'But I never stopped thinking about her – hoping she was OK. When I received her letter I was blown away and booked a flight over.' He glances back at the cottage. 'So where is she?'

'She's not here right now,' I say again.

There's an awkward silence before Becky says, 'She's disappeared.'

I glare at her, and she shrugs.

'Disappeared?' He raises an eyebrow.

'Uh-huh,' Becky goes on. 'She asked us to come, but when we arrived on Friday she wasn't here.'

'I've had a couple of messages from her,' I say, deciding to go along with Becky's revelation. 'She said she's fine, but—'

'You don't think she is,' he cuts in.

'Exactly,' Becky says. I can tell she likes this man, and I think I do too – but my hackles are still up, protecting us.

'Have you spoken to the police?' he asks.

'Of course,' I say. 'They've put out a missing persons report. Checked the hospitals.'

'I'll stick around,' Peter says. 'Find somewhere to stay. I'm not leaving until I know she's OK.'

'You could stay here,' Becky says, and my eyes widen. 'There's a spare room.'

He looks up at the cottage, and it hits me it belongs to him – that's what Jeannette Millar told us. 'I'd rather not,' he says. 'Thanks all the same, but I haven't got the greatest memories of living there, if I'm honest.'

'Well, come in for a cup of tea or coffee then,' Becky says.

'No, sorry,' I say. 'We've got to go out again, Becky. Remember?'

'What? Where?' She knows I'm lying.

'It's fine,' Peter says, as Becky throws him an apologetic look. 'I need to find somewhere to stay, anyway.'

'Come on, Becky,' I say, glaring at her before storming towards the cottage, feeling far too hot, but she doesn't follow, and the arrival of Peter Millar makes me wonder if I can cope anymore. Maybe it's time we went home.

Chapter 42

AVA

2001

Ava passed Rory and Gail's wedding cake, now cut into pieces, unrecognisable as the beautiful thing it once was, and pushed open the door, a blast of cold air hitting her. She stepped away from the village hall, recalling how Rory had messed up booking the venue. Gail had been so upset that her big day would take place *in a pathetic village hall.* It was as though he'd done it on purpose.

Ava took off her heels, and the thrum of music faded as she ran across the cold ground, the wind whipping her hair, icy rain stinging her cheeks. It was so much colder than earlier.

She stopped, picking up the sound of voices on the village green some distance away, making out the shape of two people sitting on a bench.

'Mum wouldn't want this, Dad. You're going to kill yourself.' It was Justin, sounding distraught, and Ava felt a pang of pity for him. They'd been so close at first, lost souls looking out for each other.

'You're hardly one to judge, son,' came the reply from the figure now rising and staggering away.

'It wasn't your fault, Dad. The only thing to blame for her death is fucking cancer,' Justin cried after him, before burying his head in his hands.

Ava continued across the car park, darkness covering her like a cloak. She could hear the sea crashing against the shoreline in the near distance, calling to her like a friend. She would go there, to the sea – her favourite place.

She was about to move on, when she heard the slap of heavy footsteps behind her. Before she could turn, a strong hand gripped her shoulder.

'Maxen,' she said as she twisted round, and made out his face in the darkness.

'I saw you dash out of the hall. Are you OK?' he said. 'You looked upset.'

'I'm fine. I need air, that's all.'

'I'll keep you company, if you like.' His eyes shone glassy in the moonlight, but she couldn't read them.

'I'm OK, honestly. The fresh air will do me good.' She stepped out onto the road, but he was soon beside her, too close.

'I'll walk with you, shall I?'

'No! Honestly, I'd rather be alone,' she said, picking up speed. 'But thank you.'

'Well, it's up to you,' he said, keeping up with her. 'But it's so lonely out here. And there are some right weirdoes about. People do the most awful things, Ava. People you least suspect.'

'I'll be fine once I'm on the beach. Nobody will be down there this time of night.' Her voice cracked as she spoke. 'I want to be alone for a while, Maxen. Please.'

'You deserve so much better,' he said. 'That's what my dad says.'

'Your dad is a kind man.'

'Yes, yes he is.' He slowed, and she kept going, glancing over her shoulder to see he was being swallowed by the darkness. Almost out of sight.

'I saw Gail has the bracelet now,' he called after her. 'I'm angry about that.'

'What?' She stopped and twisted round. She couldn't see him, but he was there. 'What do you mean *now*?'

'I left it for you,' he said. 'I covered you with your coat to keep you warm.'

Panic pumped through her, and her heart began to race. 'You left the bracelet that night?' she cried. 'It was you?'

'Yes,' he called. 'I took it from Rory on his stag party. I wanted you to have it.'

'It was you?' she cried, taking off, sprinting, her feet scraping on the rough ground. 'Oh my God, it was you.'

'No. Don't go. The bracelet was meant to make you happy,' he called after her, his words haunting her as she ran. She'd accused Rory. Argued with Gail. Ruined their wedding day. She needed to put things right. Turn back. But her legs carried her away into the night, her head spinning with confusion. She'd felt so sure it was Rory who'd attacked her.

'Ava wait, please,' Maxen cried, as she continued to put distance between them, her chest breathless as she headed for the sea, her eyes streaming with tears.

Chapter 43

YOU

Everything changed in the summer of 2001.

You announced you were getting married. I didn't think, even then, you would abandon me. I'd always been naïve, that's what you said. But still I had thought we would last forever – that nothing would come between us. As far as you knew I'd always done exactly what you'd asked of me.

'You'll need to move out,' you said, so cold, so cruel. 'Gail will be moving in in a couple of weeks.'

I moved back in with my father. And, yes, I admit I hung about Gail's cottage in Bostagel. I wanted to see where the woman who was replacing me lived.

That's when I saw Ava again.

I shouldn't have gone into the cottage, and climbed the stairs. I hadn't intended to watch her sleeping. But it was as I watched her snuffle, snuggled on her red beanbag, I felt a connection, almost as strong as the one I felt for you.

Chapter 44

ROSE

Now

Becky doesn't follow me towards the house. She stays with the man – Peter Millar. They're talking and I want to stop her. Drag her inside where it's safe. There's no denying I'm getting more and more paranoid. But then anyone would be. Wouldn't they?

As I reach the door, my phone blasts, making me jump, demonstrating what an anxious state I'm in.

It's Aaron.

'I'm home,' he says, before I can say a word. Becky is calling me from the end of the path, but I can't hear what she's saying. 'Are you still in Cornwall?' Aaron goes on.

'I am. Yes. But I'm thinking of heading home. I've had enough of this place.' I meant it.

'Has Willow turned up?'

'No, no she hasn't – not yet, but it's awful here, Aaron. I can't stay, my head's all over the place. I don't know what to think anymore.'

'Hey, love, slow down,' he says. 'Just tell me what's going on.'

I push the key in the door, and once inside I climb the stairs, feeling hot and clammy. The weather is turning, and I desperately need a shower. But as I tell Aaron about the night on the beach, the lad in the yellow cap who's been hanging about, the beautiful house where I saw someone at the window, my mind slips and slides, and I burst into tears. 'And now Peter Millar's turned up, Willow's uncle,' I say, passing the room Willow slept in. There's a box of tissues on the bedside cabinet, so I drift in, sit down on the bed, and snatch one from the box. 'And I've no idea if I can trust him,' I say, sniffing into it.

Dexter, Rory, Peter, Justin. Dexter, Rory, Peter, Justin.

'I'm on my way,' he says. 'I'll be with you in under five hours.'

'No, I think we should come home, Aaron.'

'But what if Willow's in danger? I'm on my way.'

'OK,' I say, gathering my strength. It's not like Aaron. His usual go-to is keeping Becky and me safe. 'I'll leave the key under the rabbit by the front door, if we're out.'

'Great, I will be with you soon. I love you,' he says.

'Love you too,' I say, but he's ended the call.

I stand up and grab another tissue.

'Where are you, Willow?' I whisper. It's then that I notice her jacket isn't on the back of the chair where I left it, and my heartbeat quickens. I fling open the wardrobe, but there's nothing but mismatched hangers. The drawers are empty too. Someone's been here. Someone's taken it.

But my panic shifts as I pass the window, and glance out. Becky and Peter have gone.

'Oh God, oh God, oh God,' I cry, racing down the stairs, almost falling, and throwing open the door. I run down the path. 'Becky!' I yell. 'Oh my God. Where the hell are you?'

Chapter 45

AVA

2001

Ava lowered herself onto a rock, and looked out to sea. The icy wind howled through the reeds, whipping her hair in front of her face.

Maxen had raped her on that awful night. Taken away her future with one awful act.

She pressed her hands hard against her face, holding in tears. She didn't want to live carrying these thoughts like a ball and chain. She couldn't take it anymore.

If I wade into the freezing sea, will death come soon?

But what would become of her darling girl? Would Peter take care of her as he promised, or would he head back to Australia, leaving Willow with Justin, or worse, her mum and sister – Rory – in a world where Maxen would always be far too close.

She rose and padded across the sand towards the sea, away from the quiet country road behind her. She felt sober now – her thoughts coherent.

'I can't stay, Willow,' she whispered, mist hovering for a

moment in front of her chapped lips before disappearing into the velvet black sky.

She reached the sea, and a froth of cold waves covered her feet. 'Peter promised he would take care of you, darling girl,' she said, hoping her words carried the truth, that they would reach her daughter's ears.

She closed her eyes, and waded into the cold sea, her dress wrapping itself around her legs. She shivered and stumbled, but held her balance.

As she continued, deeper into the ocean, guilt swirled.

You should tell someone – someone who will listen.

Inspector Jones? But I could never prove it. And Maxen is his son. He'd never believe him capable.

He'll do it again, Ava. You need to protect Willow.

She was a fair way out, the sea in control, when she looked back at the shoreline to see the haunting sight of her sister running along the beach, the light of the moon catching her flowing white dress.

Ava turned back and fought the sea with the little strength she had left, heading towards the beach – towards her sister. She needed to ask her forgiveness. Tell her it was Maxen. To be careful – he was a dangerous man.

Chapter 46

ROSE

Now

'Becky,' I yell, looking down the road. The sky has darkened, the air heavy. A storm is heading our way.

There's no sign of Becky or Peter, and my heart gallops. But his car is still here. They couldn't have gone far I tell myself as I call out, 'Becky!'

I hurry down the slope towards the beach. It's deserted. 'Becky!' I call into the silence, spinning on the spot.

Back on the road, I race past Peter's car. That's when I notice it. Written on my car door in red lipstick:

LEAVE

I look about me, into the nearby wood. Had someone done this while I was in the house? Or had it been there earlier, and I hadn't noticed?

My heart thumps, as I crouch down and try to rub it away

with my hand. It smudges but won't come off. I'm not sure it ever will.

I rise, and race down the road. 'Becky,' I call again, suddenly spotting her with Peter in the distance. She turns. They stop to wait for me.

'What the hell are you doing, Becky?' I say, as I reach them, grabbing her arm. I exhale heavily – almost out of breath and sweating in the heat.

'Mum! You're totally embarrassing me.' She shakes me free. 'I told you we were going to the pub to talk.'

Peter has stepped away. My eyes are on him, but my words are still for my daughter. 'After everything that's happened, you walk off with a total stranger.'

'I'm not five – and he's not a stranger. Peter is Willow's uncle, he told us that.'

I want to scream and yell, but I fear if I do, I may never stop.

'I called out to you that we were going to the pub. You said you wouldn't let him in the house.'

'This is all my fault,' Peter finally says, stepping forward.

'Yes, yes, too bloody right it is.' I fold my arms across my chest, feeling the thud of my heart speeding up again as I glare at him.

'Calm down, Mum,' Becky says. 'Please. Peter may be able to help us find Willow.'

I look at her once more. 'How the hell can a man just back from Australia help to find Willow?'

'Come on,' Peter says, heading into the pub. 'I don't know about you, but I need a stiff drink.'

*

Once seated by the window, a drink in front of us, I feel a bit calmer.

'I'll do everything in my power to help find Willow,' Peter says, before taking a sip of his gin. 'I loved that kid. I would have taken her on in a heartbeat when Ava died. But it wasn't to be. I wasn't considered suitable. As I say, I didn't even know who adopted her at the time.'

'It was Eleanor Winter, my stepmother,' I say, fiddling with the stem of my glass.

'Yeah, Willow told me in her letter. Said she'd had a great life so far.'

'I'm glad,' I say, softening. I've never been sure what went on in Willow's crazy head at times, so it was good to hear it from a stranger.

He takes another sip of his drink. 'My mum got custody at first, but gave her up quite quickly, unable to cope after losing Ava and Gail, plus she was never very maternal.'

My mind drifts to the sad woman we met in the apartment in Newquay – so different to the one Peter's describing. 'And you took off to Australia.'

He narrows his eyes, as though warning me not to judge, and takes another mouthful of his drink. 'Originally I took off when I was in my late teens to get away from my mum. To be fair, she was glad to see the back of a difficult teenager with anger issues. Dad walked out when Ava was born, and we never saw him again. Didn't have a clue where he'd gone. I guess I was damaged goods after that. The anger festered, and inanimate objects suffered. The odd door or wall had it coming.' His smile is that of being lost in the past, almost childlike, and I find myself warming to him.

'One night I arrived home drunk,' he goes on, losing the smile. 'Mum was there, waiting for me.' He takes a deep breath. 'She attacked me with a bread knife for being pissed.' He rolls up his sleeve and shows us the scar. 'Admittedly I was rowdy – shouting, that kind of thing. It was my go-to when I'd been drinking. But I would never hurt anyone. I didn't deserve that. She told me much later she struggled because I reminded her so much of my father.'

'It's hardly an excuse though,' I say.

He shakes his head. 'Anyway, Ava came down the stairs that day, saw the blood. She scurried into the corner, squeezing as far against the wall as she could. I thought she would disappear.'

'Jeez,' says Becky. 'That's awful.'

'I'm so sorry,' I add – I didn't know Ava, but I could cry for her.

'Gail heard the commotion. Called the police. But by the time the cops arrived, Mum acted like she was the victim. Said I was dangerous, that it was self-defence, and at that moment I knew I had to get out of there. Ava was traumatised at the time – wouldn't speak for weeks.' He shrugs. 'I took off, never looked back ... well, not until Gail asked me to give her away at her wedding. We'd kept in touch over the years.'

'Did you know Willow had you on her list of suspects for Ava's murder?' I say. 'She had several men on her radar.'

He shakes his head. 'I would never have killed Ava. I loved her. She put me on the right road, I'll always be grateful for that. I miss her even now.'

'The right road?'

'She told me to try harder with my wife, that if I loved her, I needed to stop thinking of myself, work at it.' He smiles once more, as though bringing her to his mind.

'So you're married?'

He nods. 'Happily, two kids – well, teenagers. Both much better behaved than I ever was.'

'Oh God,' Becky whispers, suddenly looking past me. 'It's scary-man.'

Peter and I look round. The man is at the bar, handing over a twenty-pound note, and my stomach flips.

'Why scary-man?' Peter says, looking at Becky.

231

'Because he was stalking the cottage the other night,' she tells him.

Peter's eyebrows furrow. 'But that's Maxen Jones. He isn't scary. There must be some mistake. Hang on.' He rises. 'I'll introduce you. You can find out why he was there.'

'Oh my God,' Becky says, slipping down in her chair.

Chapter 47

ROSE

Now

'What the hell were you doing on my patio?' I yell as Maxen approaches, a few steps behind Peter. The couple tucking into gammon and eggs at the next table glance our way, and whisper to each other from behind their hands.

Maxen presses his body against our table, far too close. 'I was looking for Willow,' he says, his Welsh accent strong – how the landlord confused it with a Scottish dialect remains a mystery.

'I'll get another drink in, shall I?' Peter says, disappearing to the bar, and I wish he hadn't raced away so soon, leaving this stranger gazing down at us through narrowed eyes.

He's about forty, slim, his fitted grey T-shirt clings to his toned chest. He drags his fingers through light brown hair, and I notice an air of vulnerability about him.

'Why were you looking for Willow?' I've lowered my voice, but I'm aware I still sound snarky. I don't care. He's part of the reason my nerves are so frazzled. I turn from his stare, to notice the bar, so quiet a moment ago, is filling with people from the garden, covering their heads with their hands, and laughing. Through the windowpane I see the clouds have darkened, and splatters of rain hang on the glass.

'She contacted me about a week ago,' Maxen says, and I meet his eye once more. 'Asking what I remembered about the night her mother died. I came to Cornwall on Friday morning to meet up with her, but she didn't answer the door. She hasn't answered my calls or messages either. Last night I thought I'd come to the cottage again, see if she was there. I didn't expect anyone to be home, if I'm honest.'

'You could have picked a more suitable time. You scared me half to death.'

'I know, and I'm sorry. I'm a creature of impulse when I've had a few. Do you mind if I sit down?' Without waiting for an answer, he pulls out the chair next to Becky and sits down. Becky shuffles closer to the wall and looks over at me with worried eyes.

'Maybe sit here,' I say, rising. 'Next to Peter.'

'Fine.' He gets up, and we swap seats.

'You were staring at us the other day,' Becky says, nibbling on her nails, her shoulders hunched.

He nods. 'I was trying to muster the courage to talk to you both. I thought you might know where Willow is. I've been asking everyone.' He glances over his shoulder. 'Peter says you're her stepsister and niece.'

We nod, as he scrutinises us, the tension in the air tangible. 'That's right,' I say.

'Well, I was one of the last people to see Ava alive,' he says. His voice trembles. He avoids eye contact. 'I spoke to her when she was on her way to the beach.'

Peter approaches with a tray full of drinks, and Maxen grabs a gin with jittery hands. Knocks it back in one.

'Willow told me my father's helping her. He was the inspector on the original case.'

'You're Inspector Jones' son?'

234

'That's right, although I haven't seen him for years. We went our separate ways a long time ago.'

'I told Willow about Maxen when we chatted on the phone,' Peter says, once he's sitting down. 'I said he may be able to help her. Maxen and I stayed in touch for a bit after my sister died.'

'We met at Rory's stag do,' Maxen says.

'And later at his wedding,' Peter says. 'Kept each other's contact details, didn't we, mate?'

Maxen nods. 'I went back to live in Wales soon after Ava's death,' he says. 'I'd lived in Pwllheli until I was six, been happy there. So when a job came up that I couldn't turn down, I returned. My father stayed here and worked on the case for ages. He'd always liked Ava, felt sorry for her, and when she died he became a bit obsessed with solving the case. We barely kept in touch.'

'So you haven't been back to Cornwall in all that time?' I ask.

He shakes his head. 'But when Willow wrote to me, I decided it was the right time to return to Bostagel and set the record straight, and hopefully see my father.' And without another word, he knocked back the dregs from his glass, got up, and headed back to the bar.

Chapter 48

AVA

2001

Ava wrestled free from the sea's grip, and made her way up the beach, trying to catch her breath. Her sister was close – running towards her.

Gail glared at Ava as she reached her. 'You've ruined everything,' she cried, tears streaming her face, 'absolutely everything.'

'I'm so sorry,' Ava said, shivering, her teeth chattering. 'I didn't mean to.' She spotted the cake knife dangling from Gail's hand, and stepped back. 'Where's Rory?'

'Why? So you can accuse him again of raping you? Do you fancy him, Ava? Is that what this is about?' Gail spat.

'No! No! Gail I think—'

'You wrecked my wedding and accused my husband of rape. Why the hell would you do that?'

'I'm sorry. But I was drugged and raped, Gail. And I thought it was Rory – because of the bracelet – but I could have been wrong.' A tear zigzagged down Ava's cheek and trickled, cold, down her neck.

'Wrong?'

Ava held out both hands towards her sister. 'All I've ever wanted was for you to love me. Help me. Please.'

Gail stepped forward, and for a moment Ava thought her sister might hold her, but her eyes were filled with anger. With a sharp movement, Gail grabbed Ava's cheeks in one hand and squeezed. 'Wrong?' she yelled. 'You accused Rory of rape, and now you're saying you could have been be wrong.'

'I think it was Maxen.'

'Maxen? Rory's best friend? You're a fucking nightmare, Ava. You always wreck everything. You're the reason Dad left.'

Ava tried to punch herself free, but she was so cold and wet, her dress hanging sodden around her body, clammy, weighing her down. The sea had stolen her strength, and her mind whirred with confusion and anger. Why didn't Gail care what had happened to her?

'Maxen raped me, and you couldn't care less, could you?' she cried, the words like sparks in the darkness. Bile rose in her throat, and her mind whirred with confusion.

What if Rory wasn't innocent?

What if he'd been with Maxen that night? It was his bracelet after all. And he'd hounded her in the ladies'. Scared her. She gagged – could it have been both of them? She'd heard Maxen's speech at the wedding. He would do anything for Rory. 'And I can't be sure Rory wasn't there too,' she spat.

Gail's face morphed – ugly. 'You fucking bitch,' she yelled releasing Ava's cheeks and lunging towards her with the knife. Ava moved, and with the little strength she had pushed Gail hard.

As though in slow motion, her sister fell backwards, arms flailing. She dropped the knife, and crashed down hard onto the rocks.

Ava fell to her knees. 'Gail! Gail! Are you OK?' she cried.

'Bitch!' Gail screamed, staggering back to her feet, lashing out, and slapping Ava's face hard.

Ava rose too, tried to run, but Gail pulled her back to the floor, climbed on top of her, and reached for the knife.

Chapter 49

YOU

I saw Ava at the cinema. I talked with her, wanted to talk for longer, get to know her better. But Dexter wouldn't let us. He wanted her for himself.

I followed Ava and Dexter to the bar. I watched her for ages – the way Dexter left her alone to talk to his mates. He didn't care about her.

She went to the ladies', I remember. I thought about following, letting her know I was there, but I didn't want to come across as weird.

And then I saw you. Hovering near her table – waiting until she returned and taking her away.

I followed you out into the cold night, saw you get into your car, bundle her in the back.

I grabbed a taxi, asked the driver to follow, but he wouldn't go into the woods, didn't want to damage his vehicle, he said.

On foot I searched for you. But by the time I found Ava she was unconscious and you'd gone. I was too late.

I covered her with her coat and knelt down and wept at her feet. How could you? But then I already knew what you were capable of.

I'd taken the bracelet from you on your stag do, when I untied your half-naked body from the tree. The others had thrown your rucksack by your side, the bracelet had fallen out. It was for Gail, wasn't it? You'd told me that. But I'd taken it for myself that night. And then, on the night you raped her, I left it for Ava – poor, beautiful Ava. Destroyed by you.

I don't think I loved you in quite the same way after that.

Chapter 50

ROSE

Now

Rain hits the windowpane like marbles, startling me, and a flash of forked lightning stabs the sky. The storm is making my eyes ache, and the rumble of loud voices irritate me. I fear a migraine will set in.

Maxen returns from the bar. He's trembling, his drink sloshing onto the table. I resist the urge to clear it up, as he slides onto the chair next to Peter.

'Well hello again, ladies and gentleman.' We look up to see the landlord brandishing menus and a wide smile. 'Good to see you again, can I tempt any of you with a bite to eat? I can recommend the hunter's chicken and the sea bass.'

I realise we haven't eaten, and I need something to bring my blood sugar up to ward off this migraine. 'Do you fancy something, Becky?' I ask, turning to see her folded into herself, tapping on her phone.

'I'm not hungry,' she says, glancing over at Maxen, and back at her phone.

I have no idea what makes me flip. Tension? Stress? Lack of sleep? But I choose *now* to confront her – *now*, in front of Peter and Maxen, *now,* as the landlord is handing out menus, *now*, at a time when all our emotions are off the scale.

'You never eat,' I snap. 'I'm sick of this, Becky; it's getting out of hand. Look at you. You're far too thin. I'm worried sick.'

Her eyes fill with tears, and the landlord makes a quick retreat. Peter covers his face, and Maxen empties his glass.

'Why, Mum?' is all she says as she rises and shoves her phone in her pocket. She dashes a tear from her cheek with her palm.

'Sorry,' I say, and grab her hand. 'I'm so sorry. I don't know what came over me.'

She pulls her hand free and pushes past me. 'It's OK,' she whispers, but I know it's far from it. I should have known better. There's no doubt she has an eating disorder, but I've rushed in at the worst possible moment. I'm a terrible mother.

'Wait! Where are you going?' I call after her as she pushes through the throng, towards the door.

'I'm tired,' she calls over her shoulder. 'I'm going back to the cottage to have a lie down.'

'I'll come with you,' I say, getting up.

'No.' She stops and stares at me. 'I want to be on my own, is all. Please. Let me have that, Mum.'

It takes all of my power to let her go; to lower myself back onto the chair, and not run after her. But I feel sure if I don't let her have space, this will escalate. 'Text me when you're back safe,' I call, as she opens the door. A gust of wind almost knocks her off her feet and heavy rain splatters her thin frame. She doesn't reply.

'Teenagers,' Peter says, after a long silence. 'Not easy, are they?'

I shake my head. 'I need wine,' I say, getting up and heading for the bar.

I return with a giant glass of white wine. Alcohol isn't the answer, I know that, but it's the only one I have right now.

Peter and Maxen look up, as I take my place back at the table. The lights flicker and dip, and the sound of thunder cracking across the sky causes the locals and tourists to cheer and laugh.

I stare across at Maxen, who is tapping the table like a drum, and then take a gulp of my wine. It tastes bitter on my tongue.

He stops drumming his fingers. 'I can't keep it in any longer,' he says, rubbing the back of his hand across his mouth. 'It's killing me.' He picks up his glass, empties it, and thuds it down on the table.

'What is it, mate?' Peter says, his eyes boring into him.

The sudden silence between us gives way to the chattering and laughter around us, the sound of the rain hammering on the window.

'It's Rory,' Maxen says in almost a whisper. 'I gave him an alibi the night Ava died.'

'Yes. That's right. I remember,' Peter says, taking off his glasses and rubbing his eyes. 'You were with him at the time of Ava's murder.'

He nods. 'I said I saw him coming out of the hall looking for Gail. Said he seemed worried sick as she'd taken off after Ava.'

'And?' I say.

'Well that bit's true. I saw him, but rather than the two of us going into the village for a stiff drink, like I told the police, well … he took off in his car after Gail.'

'What the fuck?' Peter yells, shoving his glasses back on as though he needs them to see the truth.

The chatter around us falls away, and the couple enjoying their gammon earlier, and now spooning in sticky toffee pudding and custard, glare across.

'And it's worse than that.' There is a layer of sweat across Maxen's forehead, his face is chalk white.

'How can it be worse than that?' Peter says, rubbing his face frantically. 'For Christ's sake, Maxen, what if Rory killed her and got away with it?'

'He did.' He lowers his head and runs his finger hard around the rim of his glass, as though he wants it to slice through his skin.

'Fuck,' Peter cries, and I feel like I'm being whipped up in a storm.

'I took off after Rory on foot. I saw him on the beach that night. It was windy, and I was a long way from him, but there was a full moon, and I saw the glint of a knife in his hand.' He covered his pallid face with his hands, and took a deep breath. 'He stabbed Ava,' he said looking up, his voice breaking. 'He stabbed her over and over. I still see it so vividly in my nightmares – hear Ava scream. And there was someone else there. It must have been Gail.' He let out a cry, and buries his head in his hands once more.

'Christ, Maxen, what the hell?' Peter cries. 'Why would you keep that quiet? You saw him kill my sister, and you said and did nothing?'

I feel oddly numb – shock, I suspect. I have no words.

'I loved him,' he says, looking up, tears falling down his face, reminiscent of the fat raindrops on the windowpane beside me. 'I'd always loved Rory – always been there for him.' He covered his face with his hands again, and after some moments spoke through slim fingers. 'When he asked me to give him an alibi – said we'd never be together if I didn't – I agreed. I was a bloody idiot.'

'You selfish bastard,' Peter says, his fists clenched. His face – pale and tense – tells me exactly how he feels. I feel the same.

'I know. I know.' Maxen rubs his neck. 'I lost Rory anyway. I'd given the alibi, but wanted to retract it, knew I'd been a fool, but Rory threatened me, said he would kill my father – and I knew what he was capable of. I'd seen it for myself. So I moved away. My father continued working tirelessly on the case, but I knew he would never realise Rory had killed her – he trusted my alibi. God, how I've struggled with this knowledge for all these years.'

'You poor thing,' Peter said sarcastically. 'And what about the rest of us, Maxen? You didn't give a shit about us.'

'I'm so sorry, Peter. You've no idea how sorry I am.'

'Sorry? Is that it? Sorry?' He begins to rise, as though he's about to suggest taking things outside.

'We should call the police,' I cut in, pulling my phone from my pocket, hoping to prevent World War III.

'No, don't call the police,' Maxen says. 'Not yet.'

'Give us one good reason why not,' Peter says, lowering back down.

'Because I'm worried Rory may have taken Willow.'

'What? Why would he?' I say, trying to make sense of everything.

'He's capable of anything, Rose. Take my word for it. I think I know him better than anyone.'

'He lives in Newquay, doesn't he?' Peter says. He pushes back his chair. 'We should go there.'

'You won't find him there,' I say, recalling the woman who answered the door at 48 Walton Avenue. 'I've been. Rory rents the place out. He lives in Italy, apparently.'

Maxen shakes his head and casts a hand over his chin. 'I've my suspicions where he could be. His father left him Floral Corner when he died, and for a long time he said he rented the place out. But I have a real hunch he could be there.'

'I still think we should call the police,' I say.

'If they go in with their sirens blaring, he will disappear – or worse, kill Willow. I vote we go together to Floral Corner. Now.'

*

My phone bleeps as we leave the pub, and the signal returns. It's getting dark, and rain hammers down, soaking us within moments. I squint, trying to look at my phone screen through blobs of rain. It's a message from Becky:

Heading back to the cottage. Got a lift.

I quickly message back in a surge of panic:

Who with? x

'I'll drive,' Peter says, leading the way as we race up the road, feet squelching in puddles, heading for Ocean View Cottage where he'd parked his car. As I battle the rain, my head plays ping-pong with my anxieties. *Becky – Willow – Becky – Willow.*

A reply from Becky gives some relief:

Don't panic, Mum. I'm safe. X

The kiss on the message makes me hopeful that she will forgive me for my earlier outburst. That we will talk later – that I haven't done any lasting damage. And when we get home to Old Stevenage, I will handle things differently. I'll be a better mother.

As we approach Peter's car, rain trickles down the neck of my top, making me shiver. It's then that I notice Aaron's Mercedes parked on a nearby grass verge. *Thank God he's here.* But he's not in his car, and I begin to wonder why he hasn't messaged me to say he's arrived.

I look up at the cottage. Lights are on in most of the rooms, and I'm sure I see Aaron standing at the front window. He must be with Becky. He probably picked her up.

'Come on, Rose,' Peter says, through the open car window, his hands clenched round the steering wheel, his face splattered with rain, that drips from his nose and glasses. Maxen is by his side, so I get in the back, and pull out my mobile and call Aaron. It goes to voicemail. 'It's me,' I say. 'I'm going to look for Willow at Floral Corner. Please look after Becky, she should be with you.'

I end the call, and as we pull away with a screech of tyres it hits me, I'm in the back of a car with two men I barely know, on my way to confront a suspected killer.

Chapter 51

ROSE

Now

Rain hits the car window, so loud I fear it might shatter. Windscreen wipers whip across the glass. Thud. Thud. Thud.

Panic rises. Maxen stalked the cottage, and what do I know about Peter? Are these men even who they say they are?

It's so dark outside, and my heart is pumping hard, and I feel a dire need to escape. Are we going too fast for me to jump out? Yes! We're going too fast – far too fast for these twisting turning lanes.

'Peter,' I say, but he doesn't answer. 'Peter,' I repeat, louder.

Maxen turns. 'These roads are awful, Rose,' he says. 'Let him concentrate.'

'OK,' I say, drawing my legs up onto the seat. Looking out of the window, I realise I've no idea where we are. I suddenly spot the house in the distance and sigh with relief.

*

'We're here,' Peter says.

Most of the windows are lit up at Floral Cottage – someone definitely lives here. But as Peter pulls to a stop, fear won't leave me alone, niggling. What if they've brought me here to kill me? What if they've taken Willow?

Peter pulls on the handbrake. 'Let's go,' he says, throwing open the door, rain showering him.

I screw up my eyes against the weather as we run towards the cottage, mud splattering my legs, rain seeping into my canvas shoes. We gather under the pitch-roofed porch, our wet bodies huddled together, attempting to shield ourselves from the downpour.

Peter rings the bell, and I can see a light through the opaque door window, but no sound comes from inside.

Eventually a figure appears behind the glass, and bolts are pulled across. The door opens.

'Isaac?' I say, pushing my wet hair from my face as the boy stares at us, his face void of expression, the yellow cap he always wears pulled over his dark hair.

'My cap,' Maxen whispers. 'I thought I left it at Rory's house in Newquay.'

'We need to come in,' Peter says, pushing the boy aside so he stumbles against the magnolia walls, as he heads into the house. I follow, and Maxen, behind me, kicks the door shut.

The large hallway has four oak doors leading from it, and a wide staircase to a second floor.

We stand, rain forming puddles at our feet, shivering in our wet clothes.

A woman appears through one of the doors. 'Can I help you?' she says, and Isaac runs towards her.

She's about forty, with curly blonde hair to her shoulders. She's wearing a green dress, flared at the waist, with white polka dots, and her feet are bare, toenails painted pale pink.

'Oh my God,' Peter says, his eyes filling up. 'Is it really you?' I can tell he wants to rush over and hug the woman, but she stares at him for a long moment, her expression haunted – he doesn't move.

'Peter?' she says finally, as though she's worked out who he is, her voice flat, almost robotic. 'Is Gail with you?'

'No, Gail is …' He pauses. 'Christ, what are you doing here, Ava?'

My stomach tips as I take in his words, and I feel woozy. 'But … we thought—'

'We need to get you out of here,' Peter cuts in, his voice high with emotion. 'We need to take you home.'

Chapter 52

ROSE

Now

I'm reeling. Unable to take in that Ava Millar is standing in front of us – alive – and yet somehow not here at all.

The boy – Isaac – moves in closer to her, and she puts her arm around him protectively and pulls him to her.

'I live here,' she says, coiling her hair around her finger. Her face is made-up beautifully – lips blood red, eyelids shadowed with silvers and greys. 'This is my home,' she adds.

Maxen steps forward from where he has been hovering behind Peter. 'Ava, do you remember me?' he says.

She narrows her eyes and shakes her head.

'You helped me pick out some taps once at the DIY, didn't you?' He's talking to her like she's a frightened animal, who might bolt in a moment. 'The kid is wearing my baseball cap, Ava,' he says. 'Who is he? Who's the boy?'

She shakes her head. 'I remember a bracelet.' She touches her wrist, and I notice bruises on her arms. 'I think you should leave, now,' she says. 'My husband will be home soon. He won't be happy you're here.' Is that fear in her voice?

'Your husband?' I say.

'And I must feed Willow.'

'Willow?' There's so much wrong with this scene. It's as though Ava is talking about a child. 'Where is she?' I cry, looking about me. 'Where's Willow?'

'Her father put her in the basement, like he did me. Only for a while, until she understands this is the best thing for her. We'll give her all the love she deserves once she accepts things.'

'Shit,' Peter yells, and pushes past Ava, almost knocking her off her feet, and Maxen follows. 'Where's the fucking basement?' They open a door, and then another, finally disappearing, their feet thumping down steps. I go to follow, but Ava grips my arm.

'I missed her,' she says, but her voice is still void of emotion, her face chalk white, like a China doll. 'My darling girl – my Willow – it's so good to have her home.'

Suddenly the front door swings open.

'Darling,' Ava says. She looks at me, and smiles. 'This is my husband.'

I swing round, and my eyes widen. It's Inspector Jones.

Chapter 53

ROSE

Now

'What are you doing here, Rose?' Gareth says, narrowing his eyes.

'You have the audacity to ask me that?' I cry. 'We're looking for Willow, you know that.' I glance over at Ava, trying to work out her expression – it appears to be adoration for him.

Stockholm syndrome. I've read about it, and there's no doubting this is what I'm witnessing.

'Ava needs to see a doctor,' I say. 'Isaac too.'

'We do not.' Ava dashes to Gareth's side, and links arms with him. 'We're perfectly fine.'

It appears he hasn't got her held against her will.

He moves away from her and grabs my arm. He drags me to the corner of the hallway and whispers, 'Ava killed Gail, Rose. If you take her away from here, she'll go to prison. Do you really want that?'

'So Gail was the dead woman on the beach?' My head spins, as I look over my shoulder at Ava who is back with Isaac, straight-

252

ening his cap and tweaking his cheek as though he's five. She reminds me of a Stepford Wife.

A crashing sound comes from below us.

'Who else is here?' Gareth yells, taking off across the hall and through the door that Peter and Maxen went through earlier. His shoes sound heavy on the flight of stairs, and I hear someone cry out in pain.

I fumble my phone from my bag and dial 999. Ava watches, with tears in her eyes, as I speak to the police. The boy stands far too still.

'Why are you spoiling everything?' she says, once I've alerted the police, but I don't reply. I race past her, and head through the door, and down a dark staircase. Peter is lying at the bottom, lifeless. 'Oh my God!' I cry, bending down in front of him, his head is bleeding.

'Rose!'

I rise and head through the door, to see Willow tied to a chair at the far end of a long room with no windows and then I spot Becky lying on a bed. It looks as though she's unconscious.

'Becky!' I cry and go to run.

'Stop!' Gareth has a knife at Maxen's throat.

On a table I see Willow's and Becky's phones, and I realise Gareth must have given Becky the lift – so where is Aaron?

'I don't want to kill Maxen,' Gareth says. 'I love him. Always have. But I will.'

'You love me?' Maxen sounds so grateful, and part of me feels sorry for him. That he is so surprised to hear this from his father.

'Of course I love you,' Gareth goes on, but the knife is so close to Maxen's throat, a tiny slip would kill him in seconds. 'Why the hell did you come here?'

'You took Willow,' Maxen says.

'I had to. She got too close to the truth.' His voice is shaky, and I realise his Welsh accent has slipped away. 'She knew. She knew what I did.' His eyes are wild and fiery.

253

'Let him go Gareth, please,' I say, my voice wobbling. 'You don't want your son's death on your conscience too.'

He smiles, dimples forming in his cheeks. 'You have no idea, have you, Rose?'

'What?'

'You have no idea who I am.'

'This is Rory, Rose,' Maxen says, his voice cracking with emotion. He blinks, and a tear rolls down his face. 'This isn't my father,' he adds, his voice barely audible.

'I don't understand.' My eyes fix on who I'd believed was Inspector Jones. 'He's old enough to be your father.'

'He had me fooled too, Rose,' Willow says, her eyes puffy and red, and I wonder if he's had her tied to the chair ever since he took her.

'It doesn't matter now,' Rory says. 'You've ruined everything.'

I'm struggling to take in what he's saying. Why would Ava's brother-in-law, Gail's husband, masquerade as the inspector?

I'm aware the police will be here soon. My only option, if I want Maxen to live, is to keep *Rory* talking. There's a tremble in his hand now and I cringe, watching the blade hover close to Maxen's flesh.

'You told Willow you were Inspector Jones too?' I say.

'When she first arrived, I heard she was making enquiries in the village, so I went to see her at the cottage, told her I was Inspector Jones. Even made myself look older. You wouldn't believe what you can do with the help of a YouTube video and a bit of make-up. I intended to misdirect her, that's all. I gave her a photo of Justin, and told her I'd always thought he killed Ava, that I never trusted his alibi.

'I hadn't figured on some busybody telling her that *Rory Thompson* was briefly a suspect. Willow asked me what I thought, and I told her Rory's alibi was sound, that he was innocent. But she wouldn't let it drop. Asked me to get her a photo of *him*. So I did – well a photo of some random on the internet. I gave her a photo of Peter Millar too, hoping she might be more interested in him.'

'But how could you be sure the real Gareth Jones wouldn't turn up?' I say.

'Why don't you tell her, Maxen?'

I stare at Maxen, his Adam's apple rising and falling so close to the blade as he swallows. 'My father had a breakdown about a year after Ava's death. He was obsessed with catching her killer – blamed himself that he never did. I tried to talk him into coming to Wales with me. But he took off God knows where, said he wanted to be alone.

'When Willow contacted me saying my father was helping her, I was shocked he was back on the case. I came here as much to see him, as anything else. Hoping to set things right. I never dreamt it was Rory impersonating him.'

Rory laughs. 'I enjoyed being Inspector Jones.' He's putting on a Welsh accent again. 'I had to bring Willow here in the end. As I say, she was getting too close. But then you arrived with your daughter, asking the same fucking questions. I got a sense of déjà vu, as I gave you the same answers.'

'But you reported her missing. I spoke to the police about it.'

'Ah, yes, but I explained she'd done it so many times before, that we weren't too worried. I just covered my back, in case you called them. And then Justin turned up here. Ranting that he'd had eighteen years in prison to work out who killed Ava, said he knew it was me. He had no proof, of course, especially as Ava isn't actually dead.' He laughed. 'But I wasn't about to take any chances. I couldn't have him spreading gossip, snooping around.'

I know he's agitated. His eyes flash, flicking around the room, landing on each of us in turn. He won't hold out much longer before he loses it and slices the knife across Maxen's throat, and then God knows what else he will do.

'So you attacked Justin?' I say, still attempting to keep him talking, hoping the police will be here soon.

He nods slowly. 'I followed him back to his house in Cranberry Close, and cracked him over the head with a rock, if that's what you mean.' He's spitting as he speaks. 'I meant to kill him – but the coma will do for now. Spraying his garage door was a nice touch, don't you think?'

I sense someone behind me. I turn to see Ava at the foot of the staircase, standing next to Peter, who is stirring and rubbing his head.

'Was it you?' I say, eyes back on Rory, 'on the beach that night? Did you knock me out? Tell me to leave?'

'I tried to scare you off several times, but no. What is it with you and Willow? It's like you think you're a couple of super sleuths.'

Ava steps forward, her eyes wide and on Rory. She touches my arm. 'You should leave,' she whispers into my ear. 'While you still can.'

I look over at Willow, tears in my eyes. 'This is all my fault,' she cries, catching my eye. 'I'm so sorry, Rose.'

'I won't leave without you and Becky,' I cry. 'I promise.'

Rory moves the knife from Maxen's neck and plunges it into his shoulder. Maxen yells out in agony, as blood soaks his T-Shirt.

Heavy footsteps on the stairs startle me, and I turn. 'Aaron,' I cry on seeing him. 'Thank God.'

Maxen seems to find strength from somewhere. He thumps his elbow backwards into Rory's stomach, and Rory drops the knife, cries out, bending double. Within moments, Ava dashes over. She picks up the knife, and plunges it into Rory. A spray of blood covers her face – her polka-dot dress. She stares down at Rory writhing in agony – her silence is haunting.

The sound of sirens approaching snaps me from what feels like another dimension. I snatch a tea towel from the kitchen area, and hand it to Maxen who holds it against his shoulder, and slumps to the floor.

'Call an ambulance,' I yell at Aaron, as I race to Becky's side.

I sit on the bed beside her. 'Becky, Becky, please wake up,' I cry, shaking her, sobbing now.

'Mum,' she murmurs, stirring. 'Mum, I want to go home. Please take me home.'

Chapter 54

AVA

2001

Ava woke, shivering, shaking, feeling sand under her hands as she shuffled to a sitting position. She looked about her, eyes adjusting to the darkness. Any attempt to rub warmth into her arms was useless.

'Gail,' she cried, spotting her sister lying face down in the sand, and a sudden flash of memory invaded of her grabbing Gail's hair, throwing her down onto the rocks.

She crawled across to her. 'Oh my God, Gail,' she cried, covering her mouth as she turned her sister over to see her battered face. 'No, no, no.' There was so much blood. Had she done this? 'Wake up. Wake up, Gail. Everything is going to be OK,' she screamed, shaking her. 'Gail, oh my God, you're so cold.'

With shaky fingers, she felt her sister's neck, unable to find life under her fingertips. 'Oh God,' she continued, attempting to stroke the bloodied hair from her sister's face, then leaning over and hugging her.

'Hello, Ava.' She turned to see Rory, the knife clenched in his hand. He stared at her for some moments, his eyes liquid black. Suddenly, he bent down in front of her with quick jerky movements, and stroked her cheek, before placing the blade against her neck.

'Please, stop,' she cried.

'Shh,' he said, putting his finger against her mouth. 'I've heard you've been spreading rumours about me, Ava.'

Ava swiped away more tears with the heel of her hand and looked over at her sister – so still and lifeless.

Rory lowered the blade, and Ava attempted to crawl away. He laughed. Grabbed her leg. Pulled her back across the rocks like a sack coal. 'You really think I'm going to let you go?' he said. 'After you killed my wife?'

He straddled her body, so heavy, and placed the knife at her throat once more. 'I quite like you, Ava,' he said, his eyes dark, as though nobody was behind them, and her heart pounded with fear. 'It's a shame I have to kill you.'

'Please ...' she cried, words catching in her throat. 'I won't tell anyone.

And ...' She'd known for a few days. The feelings she'd had at seventeen were back – the nausea, the tenderness of her breasts. 'I'm pregnant,' she blurted. It was a gamble; she knew that, but if it had been Rory who raped her, she'd be carrying his child, and he might not kill her. 'I'm carrying the child of the man who raped me.'

'What?' He lowered the knife, and stared into her eyes. She noticed a change in him, a spark of something. 'You're carrying my child?' His lips quivered at the corners, as though they wanted to burst into a smile.

'Yes,' she said. He'd raped her. It had been Rory all along. 'I'm carrying your child.'

He seemed dazed, as though he'd just climbed off a merry-go-round. He shuffled off her, and sat for some moments, knees raised, the knife dangling between his legs.

Ava attempted to sit, and he turned sharply, and in a calm, almost kindly voice he said, 'Don't worry, beautiful lady.' He touched her cheek. 'Everything's going to be OK. I'm going to care for you and my child. I'm going to be a better father than mine ever was.'

'We need to call an ambulance,' she said, trying to match his calm voice, as she wrapped her arms around her knees, shivering – shaking. She could hardly believe he wasn't going to kill her. That *maybe* she could save her sister.

'Take off your dress,' he said suddenly, diving to his feet, and bending down in front of Gail's body.

'What?' A shard of fear stabbed.

He glared at her, a gust of wind whipping his hair. 'Take your fucking dress off, Ava.'

'I don't understand.'

'Just. Fucking. Do it!'

With shaking hands, Ava unzipped the sodden dress and let it fall from her shoulders in a heap at her ankles. She stepped out of it and handed it to him, goose pimples rising on her arms. He smiled as she folded her arms around herself, shivering, her body aching from cold and fear. Tears streamed down her face as he removed the lacy, once beautiful wedding dress, now stained with blood and beach debris, from Gail's limp, useless body, and fumbled her limbs into the yellow bridesmaid's dress.

Ava looked about her. Could she run? But she'd never get far. She was freezing and far too weak – he would catch her within moments.

'Give me your necklace,' he yelled, reaching out his hand.

'No!' she said, grabbing it with both hands. 'Willow bought it for me.'

He rose, ripped it from neck, and laid it on Gail's body.

Gail let out a groan. Or had Ava imagined it?

'Oh God, Rory, she's still alive. We have to call an ambulance. Now. Please.'

'No!'

'Please, Rory,' Ava cried, dropping to her knees, as he crouched in front of Gail, and pulled the wedding ring from her finger.

'If they think you're dead, they'll never search for you,' he said. 'You're my wife now, Ava. The mother of my future child.' He tossed the ring to her, and she instinctively caught it. 'Put it on,' he yelled. 'Put it on!'

She pushed it onto her finger, too scared not to, and watched as he folded Gail's wedding dress and laid it on a nearby rock.

He turned and touched Ava's face. 'You're so cold, my darling,' he said, and rose and raced towards his car.

Ava moved closer to her sister and grabbed her hand. 'Wake up, Gail. Please.'

But Rory was back within moments with a blanket. He draped it around Ava's shoulders. 'We don't want our unborn child suffering from the cold, now do we?' he said, and then placed a folded piece of paper on top of the wedding dress.

'Almost time to go home, Ava,' he said, a glisten of sweat on his skin, despite the freezing air.

'But she's still alive,' Ava cried. 'We have to do something.'

He picked up the knife. 'She never wanted to have my children. Just like my father. He never wanted children either,' he said, his tone calm. And as Ava screamed so hard she thought her lungs would burst, he plunged the blade into Gail's broken body.

Chapter 55

AVA

2001

Ava felt as though she was in another dimension. It was as if her mind had travelled to a safe place, and left her sad, useless body on the beach.

Was she dead?

No. No she wasn't dead. Her heart was beating. She could hear it – *thump, thump, thump.*

And Gail? *Is Gail OK?*

'You killed her, Ava. Remember? You killed your sister.' The voice was low. Male. Rory?

He caressed her face. Stroked her hair.

It was so dark inside her head, but she couldn't open her eyes. Was she safe inside her own mind?

As she drifted, as though on a rowing boat in the middle of the ocean, she could hear classical music playing way above her head – somewhere in the clouds. Or was that in her mind too?

'Willow!' she cried out, panic rising at the thought of her daughter – but her mouth wasn't moving. The words were inside, trapped, unable to break free. She tried harder, forcing them to leave her lips, 'Willow, where are you?'

The light behind her eyelids went out. Everything went black. Her silent scream went unheard.

Chapter 56

AVA

2008

Ava had no idea how long she'd spent with Rory. It was impossible to gauge time. But she knew Isaac was six now. She knew that much, because her husband had bought a cake with six candles, and they both sang Happy Birthday to him. He still wasn't speaking, and Ava was waiting patiently for the day he would. But Rory was teaching him sign language. Did he think he would never talk?

'He'll need to go to school soon,' she'd said. 'It will be good for him to mix with other children.' But Rory said there was no need for that. 'Isaac's a bright boy. I'll teach him all he needs to know.'

Ava had come to accept her strange existence – living in a room with no windows. It was almost perfect. And one day, Rory said, she would be able to live in the main part of the house, where he and Isaac lived, and she could cook for them, eat with him. But she had to understand she must never go outside. If she went outside, she would have to be punished. She didn't like being punished.

She couldn't remember much about before she came here. Sometimes memories floated in about a man called Peter, but they never stayed long. She remembered Willow though. She would never forget her darling girl.

'She died,' Rory had told her. 'Don't you remember?'

She couldn't recall her darling girl dying, and every time Rory reminded her she would sob for days.

'You must look after Isaac,' he would say, crashing his fist into her body. 'Willow has gone forever.'

Sometimes a flash of faces would appear in her mind – strangers, and yet somehow familiar. Her past was somewhere inside her head, but impossible to reach. Like she knew Isaac had grown inside her, and yet she had no idea how he got there. Rory said they'd made love. That's how he'd got there. But the memory was buried so deep, she felt sure she would never remember.

He was a good husband, most of the time, but she hated it when he slept with her. He was rough – hurt her. But if she tried to stop him, he got angry, would hit her, and worse, hit Isaac.

Ava had decided a long time ago she would accept her fate.

Chapter 57

ROSE

Now

Officers escort Ava and Isaac to a waiting police car, and I see in Peter's eyes the sadness of not being able to reach his sister, and I pray that one day he will.

'Will they be OK?' I ask a young PC. But despite his reassurances, this isn't a textbook case, something he may have read about or seen before. He has no more idea than I have how this will affect them going forward.

Rory and Maxen left in ambulances a short while ago, sirens blaring. Rory, the paramedics told me, is in a critical condition, and Maxen has lost a lot of blood.

Willow wraps her arms around me, and as we hold each other she whispers again, 'I knew you'd come, Rose. I knew you would never let me down.'

'We should go,' Aaron says as she releases me, closing the door on Floral Corner, and the five of us head into the night, my arm firmly round Becky.

We stop by the cars, and Peter reaches for Willow's hand. 'Hey there,' he says, speaking to her for the first time. 'I'm Peter.'

She takes his hand. 'I know who you are,' she says.

'You're so grown up,' he says, as she lets go of his hand as quickly as she took it and drops her arm to her side. 'I used to look after you when you were little.'

She shakes her head. 'I'm sorry, I don't remember.'

'Well, you wouldn't. You were so young when …' His eyes tear over. 'I can't believe we've found Ava. Your real mum.'

'My birth mum,' she corrects.

'Yes,' he says. 'I hope I'll get to see you again.'

'You will,' she says, but she doesn't raise a smile. None of us do. 'You can count on it.'

He hunches his shoulders and walks through puddles towards his car.

'Are you sure you don't want to stay at the cottage tonight?' I call after him.

'No, you're all right,' he says. 'I'll book in at a bed and breakfast.' He raises an arm in a weak wave.

'And get your head checked out?' I add, as he gets into his car.

Becky and I get into the back seat of Aaron's car, and I wrap her in my arms. She's still drowsy. As yet I don't know if Rory drugged her when he took her – time will tell, but I'm here, right by her side.

Willow sits in the front. She's silent now. In shock – as we all are.

'Are you all buckled up?' Aaron asks, before starting the engine. It's as he pulls away a delayed text arrives on my phone. It's from Aaron, and must have preceded my voicemail telling him where I was:

Just got here. Found the key under the rabbit. Where are you? X

We will stay at Ocean View Cottage tonight.
Tomorrow we will go home.

Chapter 58

YOU

You are still here inside my head. Will you ever leave? You are my addiction. However wrong you are for me, I'm still not sure I can walk away.

You said you loved me – that you've always loved me – and I cling to that. A lifeline.

'Mr Jones,' the nurse says, but I can't open my eyes. I'm locked inside my head with you.

Do you recall telling me about your mum? How beautiful she was. An Italian princess, that's what you said. She took you from Bostagel when you were four – do you remember? Ran away from your abusive father. He'd hit her, hadn't he? That's what you told me. Hit her so hard her bones snapped.

He tracked you both down in Italy. Took you back to Bostagel the day she died. A hit and run, they said. They never found the driver.

And then it started. The abuse. You cried that day. The day you told me everything. But I've never seen you cry since.

'Mr Jones.' The nurse. 'It's time for your medication.'

Am I as bad as you, Rory? I knew you raped Ava, and I saw you the night she died, when I not only ran, I lied for you.

I feel the touch of the nurse's soft hands on my arm. Pain in my shoulder as I stir. You would have killed me; I have no doubt of that.

I open my eyes, but I'm not sure I can do this anymore. Whether I'll ever get over you.

Chapter 59

ROSE

Four Weeks Later

Eleanor hugs Willow close when we arrive at Darlington House, as she has each time she's seen her over the last few weeks.

'I'm so sorry,' Willow says, not for the first time.

'No, it's me who should be sorry,' Eleanor says, as she always does.

Eleanor has cooked dinner for the six of us and after a glass of wine; we take our seats around the oak dining table.

As we tuck into roast chicken and vegetables, Becky talks about her friend Tamsyn – she's back with George, apparently – and about her pending trip to America, which had been delayed because of what happened; 'Dad's taking me to the Statue of Liberty and Central Park.' I know I have to let her go, but it won't be easy.

Dad, a roast potato suspended on his fork, animatedly tells us about their trip to Scotland, 'You really must visit Glencoe, Fort William and Urquhart Castle.' And his mates at the Fox and Hound. 'They fancy doing a bit of metal detecting. How much do you think a decent metal detector costs? Apparently a man found a coin worth thousands.'

'We're thinking of getting a gardener,' Eleanor says. 'It's getting too much for us now we're sixty. I keep wondering if we should downsize.'

'We've had such good weather, haven't we?' I say, when we lapse into silence.

'Global warming,' Dad says. 'We must listen to David Attenborough.'

'Hey, Rose,' Aaron says, waving his fork. 'There's a Frank Sinatra tribute act at the Gordon Craig Theatre, fancy it?'

'I'll come,' Becky says, moving her dinner around her plate, barely eating. Things are a long way from being right, but we'll get there.

'I like your hair, Mum,' Willow says to Eleanor. It's shorter. It suits her.

We talk, we even laugh, but we keep off the subject of Rory Thompson and everything that's happened. We desperately need to be a normal family again – for today, at least.

Chapter 60

ROSE

Two Months Later

Becky and I sit at the kitchen table. She bites into a piece of toast with Marmite I've made for her. As she chews slowly, I try not to stare as her mouth move, try not to become obsessive watching her swallow. But it isn't easy.

She's improving, though, and I'm here, ready to talk if she needs to, and her dad was a great support when she visited him. He and Jack are coming back to the UK for six months once the film is wrapped up – they'll get married here. It will be good to see them.

The psychologist we visited six weeks ago believes Becky's eating disorder relates to a fear of losing her dad and me. I think she's right. Seb met Jack around the same time that Aaron came into our life – after so many years where Becky had me and her dad to herself. Her sudden obsession with being overweight, despite being so slim, began around that time. It was her way of gaining control of her life, the psychologist said – when she thought she was losing her parents. It wasn't that she didn't love

Aaron and Jack – she just felt as though Seb and I were slipping through her fingers. Of course, Willow having been obsessed with keeping slim at sixteen hadn't helped, and the trauma in Cornwall made things so much worse.

'So what time are you heading off?' Becky says, taking another bite of her toast. She seems more mature since Cornwall, fifteen going on thirty.

'I'm picking up Willow shortly,' I say, glancing at my phone. I was about to face a long drive to Cornwall, but I didn't mind. Driving gave me time to reflect – time to be with Willow. 'In fact, I'd better get a move on,' I go on, rising.

'Good luck,' she says, and I lean over and kiss her forehead, then tuck a straying curl behind her ear. She throws me a sideways look, but she doesn't bat me away. 'I hope it goes well,' she adds.

I grab my jacket from the hall and open the front door.

It has taken a while for Willow to find the courage to visit her birth mother. Being abducted by Rory had left her traumatised, and the brief moments she'd spent with Ava at Floral Corner had been disturbing. But now she hopes she is ready.

I pull up at Darlington House, and Willow appears through the front door in stripy dungarees over a hooded top, and trainers, her hair in a high ponytail. She skips towards the car like a child, and I smile and lift my hand in a wave.

'Rose,' she says, as she climbs into the passenger seat, and we hug for ages. I read on Facebook that long hugs are medically beneficial, and I believe it.

'Ready?' I ask.

'As I'll ever be,' she says, taking a deep breath. And as she clicks her seatbelt, I start the engine.

*

We arrive to find Ava and Isaac in the visitors' room playing chess. Ava's in jeans and a pale blue cashmere jumper, Isaac's in black trousers, and a sweatshirt emblazoned with the name of a band, and the yellow baseball cap he always wears. They're so engrossed in their game they don't seem to notice our approach.

I've been keeping in touch with the hospital to find out how they are, and I know Ava is starting to recall her life before the trauma and that Isaac is beginning to talk.

Ava looks up and smiles. She's coiling her hair around her finger, and I turn to see Willow doing the same thing. It's as though this tiny habit connects them. Willow has twirled her hair around her finger from the first day I saw her. Is it something she recalls, or something genetic?

The necklace with 'Mummy' on it that Willow gave her hangs around Ava's neck. Jeannette's been here and given it back to her.

'Hello,' Ava says looking up, her eyes moving from me to Willow.

'I'm Rose,' I say.

'Yes, I've seen you before, haven't I?' She looks back at the chessboard. Moves a white bishop.

'And Ava,' I say. 'This is Willow. Do you remember? She was at Floral Corner.'

She looks up, her eyes watery as she stares at her daughter for some moments. 'My darling girl,' she says, reaching out her hand, and Willow takes it.

We all move away from the chessboard, to a corner with armchairs, and sit down. It takes a while to relax, and we begin with pleasantries about the weather – how we all seem to like autumn, the beautiful colours as the leaves fall. Eventually Ava talks about her time with Rory – it's as though she's been told the more she talks about it the better she'll feel.

'He never let me out of the house,' she says. 'For years, I was restricted to the basement, but eventually he trusted me upstairs – but he never gave me a key. He kept the doors and windows locked. Always.'

Willow places her hand over Ava's, tears in her eyes.

'I had no idea of time – my only gauge was watching Isaac

grow.' She smiles over at him. 'My boy.' Despite Isaac being Rory's, there's no doubt she loves him.

'Isaac got hold of a key to Floral Corner a few months back. Rory didn't know he had it. We could have left, but I couldn't find the courage. Rory was so kind to us most of the time.'

'You thought you loved him?' I say.

'Yes. Yes, I thought I loved him. He would disappear for ages.' She pauses for a moment before adding in a tone I struggle to read, 'It turns out he had a family in Italy.' Another pause. 'A normal family.' She twirls a curl around her finger once more. 'When he returned I was always pleased to see him. I was lonely, I suppose. We had no TV or radio for company, but we were allowed to watch videos and later DVDs. Isaac likes *Harry Potter*.'

The word 'allowed' hits me hard. She had been totally under his control.

'When Rory went away, Isaac would go out. I was worried he would find out, but he never did.'

'He never caught me,' Isaac says with a smile. It feels strange to hear his words, like hidden treasures, finally found. 'I got you your jacket, didn't I?' he goes on, looking at Willow.

'He was so worried you would be cold in the basement,' Ava says, squeezing Willow's hand, and a tear jolts its way down her cheek. 'He used Willow's key to Ocean View Cottage to get it for her.'

Isaac makes his hands into fists, his thumbs up, and moves both fists up and down in front of his chest. 'Coat,' he says. 'I wanted her coat.'

'I'm so sorry, Willow,' Ava says. 'I wanted the perfect life for you, always. But I messed up.'

'It was never your fault,' Willow says. 'I've been lucky. I've had a lovely life. And now ...' She pauses for a moment, looking into Ava's eyes. 'And now, I've got you and Isaac.'

*

As we head through the foyer, we pass a man with gold-rimmed glasses, greying hair, and a kindly face. He's talking to the woman on reception. There's something familiar about him.

I glance back over my shoulder. 'I'm looking for Ava Millar,' he says. 'My name is Gareth Jones.'

'Hang on,' I say to Willow, who seems oblivious. I stop and turn. 'That's Gareth Jones,' I say. 'The real Gareth Jones.' As we watch him chatting with the receptionist, I'm astonished at how close Rory came to replicating his appearance.

'Should we speak to him?' I say. 'I think he's going to see Ava?'

'You can,' she says. 'I don't think I could cope with it right now.'

I fish in my bags for my keys, and hand them to her. 'I won't be long,' I say, and she heads away.

'Inspector Jones?' I say, approaching him.

He turns. 'No,' he says, and then he smiles. 'Well, not for a very long time.'

'My name is Rose Lawson,' I say. 'I'm Willow's stepsister.'

'I know,' he says. 'I recognise you from the newspapers. You've all been to hell and back. I'm so sorry. How are you bearing up?'

'Getting there,' I say. 'Are you here to see Ava?'

'I am, yes. It all feels a little surreal. It's a long time since I've been to Cornwall. I'm here to support my son mainly. But there are people I want to see, and Ava is one of them. I hope to visit her mother too. I worked with her on a case in the early Nineties. She was part of the forensic team – we became good friends.'

'She's living in Newquay,' I say.

He nods. 'I know.'

'So have you seen Maxen?' I read a few weeks ago that he's awaiting trial for giving Rory a false alibi.

He nods again. 'He's doing OK. Knows I'm here for him. I just wish he'd come to me when he wanted to retract the alibi. But he was afraid, by then, of what Rory was capable of. Hopefully they will take that into account when they pass sentence.' He dashes a hand over his mouth. 'I should have been a better father to him.'

'I'm sure you did your best.' Thoughts of Becky and how I messed up fill my head. I should have left Cornwall long before things got so bad. 'None of us get it a hundred per cent right.'

'His mother left when he was three, and I buried myself in my work. He didn't stand much chance. But I'm here now, and I hope to put things right if I can.' He looks over his shoulder. 'Well, I'd better get on,' he says. 'It was lovely to meet you, Rose.'

'You too,' I say, as he walks away.

*

'Do you think you'll meet with Justin?' I ask Willow, as we pull up outside Darlington House, exhausted after driving from Cornwall.

'Perhaps,' she says.

He came out of his coma some time ago, and he's written to her several times. So far she hasn't responded.

'I'm not sure I can forgive him for not looking after Ava and me at that awful time. But I haven't ruled it out.'

I hug her goodbye, and she climbs out of the car.

'I'll call you tomorrow,' she says, raising her hand. 'Love you, Rose.'

Chapter 61

AVA

Now

'Is it true, Miss Millar, that you fought with your sister on the beach on the night of 21st December 2001?'

'We argued, yes.' Ava wasn't in the courtroom. They had linked her by a screen. Her lawyer said she wasn't strong enough to appear in court.

'What did you argue about?'

'She was angry because I accused Rory of raping me.'

'As we heard earlier from Dr Sandra Foster who did the autopsy on your sister in 2001, believing it to be you, she believes the deceased had been smashed against the rocks prior to receiving the knife wounds. Did you smash your sister's head against the rocks, Miss Millar?'

'No.'

'Did you put your dress on your sister?'

'No. Rory did.' Ava's voice broke. 'He took off her wedding dress. Replaced it with my dress.'

'But you took off your own dress so he could?'

'Yes.' She nods. 'I had no choice. He was going to kill me if I didn't.' She lowers her head. 'I didn't know what he was going to do to Gail. I said he should call an ambulance.'

'So it was a shock when he stabbed Gail?'

'Yes!'

'And what did Rory do after he stabbed your sister?'

'He folded her wedding dress and got a note from his car. He left it with her dress.'

'What were you doing all this time?'

'Screaming. I was screaming. Until—'

'Until what, Miss Millar?'

'Until he covered my face, and I struggled to breathe. I can't recall anything after that.'

Chapter 62

ROSE

Now

'He's been charged on two counts of rape, and one count of murder,' I say, unable to keep the excitement from my voice, although it feels wrong to be so delighted by something so awful. However I look at it, it's a tragedy – a mess – an awful waste of lives.

I'd been following the case, hoping to fill in the missing pieces, praying Rory would be sent down for a very long time.

'Yes, I heard,' Aaron says, dumping his bag in the hall, and rushing to sit down beside me on the sofa, kissing my cheek. He shoves a cushion behind his head, and I notice how relaxed he seems. He's cut back on his hours, and is home more often. We feel like a real family now.

'I can't believe he tried to blame Ava for killing her sister.'

'I know. Thank God for Maxen's witness statement, and Ava's memories returning. The bit I don't get is the suicide note,' Aaron says.

'It was a note from Gail to Rory. Apparently she was always

280

writing letters of apology for the things she'd said and done. It seems he was abusing her mentally and physically, and yet she loved him, found it impossible to walk away. He had a kind of power over her and Maxen.'

'So what did the note say?'

'It simply said, *Dear Rory, I'm so sorry. Gail.* But combined with everything else, it looked like suicide.'

'So Rory owned Floral Corner?'

I nodded. 'His father left it to him. It was Rory's childhood home. It's where his father abused him, whilst giving him all the riches anyone could wish for. You could almost feel sorry for him.'

'Never!' Aaron takes my hand. 'Tragically, lots of kids are abused, Rose,' he says. 'But few turn out with such deep psychological issues as Rory Thompson.'

Later, as I cook dinner, my mind drifts to work. I'm still the head of Mandalay Primary School. I decided a few weeks after I returned from Cornwall that if I can cope with everything that happened there, being a headteacher would be a doddle. It isn't, of course, but I'm managing for now, especially after a long talk with my dad when we got back from Cornwall.

'I'm proud of your achievements, Rose,' he said. 'But the most important thing to me is to see you happy. If you want to go back to teaching, or work in a fish and chip shop, it's fine by me,' he said. 'As long as you're happy, I'm happy.'

*

After dinner my phone blasts. I answer the call.

'So he's gone down for life.' It's Peter on the other end of the line, his voice upbeat. He returned to Australia in August – but we've kept in touch.

I rise and leave Aaron on the sofa. He aims the remote control at the TV and takes *Line of Duty* off pause.

I head for the kitchen. 'And good riddance,' I say, pulling myself onto a stool at the breakfast bar.

'Have you heard anything about Maxen?' he asks.

'I saw his father—'

'Gareth Jones?'

'Mmm. He's supporting Maxen while he awaits trial. Hopefully his sentence won't be too severe.'

'Yes, me too.' He's clearly forgiven him. 'Anyway, I'm looking forward to seeing everyone again soon.' He's returning to England in October and is hopeful Ava and Isaac will someday travel to Brisbane to meet his family. 'I guess some positives have come out of all of this – I have a bigger family. Even Mum and I are getting on reasonably well. It will never be perfect, but we're getting there.'

I realise Willow has a bigger family too – and I wonder, not for the first time, if she ever sensed when growing up that her mother and brother were out there somewhere in danger. She had always seemed unsettled, even when she was at her happiest.

'And I've got you guys too,' Peter adds.

'Yes.' *Every cloud,* I almost say, but know it will sound tactless.

But as I say our goodbyes, a bubble of happiness floats above us, and I hope, in time, everything will get better.

Epilogue

Ava sits on the sand near Ocean View Cottage, dressed in yellow shorts and a yellow T-shirt. She likes yellow.

Peter gave her the cottage. 'A place for you and Isaac,' he'd said. 'A place for Willow and me to visit.'

Now her blonde hair blows in the warm wind, and wild grasses stir. The sun shines over the Celtic Sea where seagulls cry.

Gareth Jones is on his way. He has so much more to say to her. Things she should have been told a long time ago. If only Jeannette had told him sooner.

He strides across the bay, coming closer, his greying hair flapping in the warm breeze. A golden retriever trots by his side, eyes on his master.

The man looks content, after years of sadness and regret. Mourning her loss.

When he sees her, his face lifts in a smile.

She smiles back and rises to her feet. 'Hello, Dad.'

'Ava,' he says, and takes her in his arms.

Gripped by *Traces of Her*? Don't miss *Her Last Lie*, another unputdownable novel from Amanda Brittany. Available now!

Want more?

To be the first to hear about new releases, competitions, 99p eBooks and promotions, sign up to our monthly email newsletter: po.st/HQSignUp.

Click here to sign up!

Acknowledgements

I have so many people to thank, not least my wonderful editor Cara Chimirri who has been absolutely amazing, and the team at HQ Digital. Huge thanks especially to Anna Sikorska for another fantastic cover design, to my excellent copy editor Dushi Horti and proof-reader Helen Williams, and to Alexia Thomaidis who works so hard to spread the word.

Thank you to my brilliant agent Kate Nash, her fantastic team, and her fabulous writers, for all their support.

Sending big thanks, as always, to my lovely friends Karen Clarke and Joanne Duncan for their endless support and feedback.

I've been so lucky to have so much support on Facebook, Twitter, and Instagram from so many lovely friends, readers, and writers. I would like to say a huge thank you to you all. I wouldn't have got this far without you, and I wish I had space to name everyone. I hope you know who you are.

As ever, I'm so grateful to all my lovely readers, and to the blogging community for all their support and brilliant reviews. Thanks too to the lovely Diane Jeffrey for all her support.

Thank you so much to my family and friends for listening to me go on about writing, and for being there for me. Again, you know who you are. I love you all.

Special thanks go to my daughter-in-law, Lucy, who once again bravely read an early draft of my novel, and to my sons Liam, Daniel, and Luke who tirelessly support me. Thanks to my mum who *still* tells everyone she meets that her daughter is a writer, and to Cheryl and my dad who I desperately wish were here to share the excitement of my third novel.

And last, but never least, a very special thank you to my husband, Kev – *I couldn't do this without you.*

Turn the page for and extract from Tell The
Truth by Amanda Brittany …

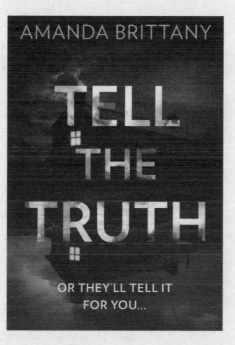

Prologue

Born or made? In my genes, or was it what happened to me as a child? Maybe I was dropped on my head at birth.

I laugh inside. They tried to find out once: the shrinks. They talked to me for hours, those who thought they knew. They couldn't see I would kill again.

I never meant to kill the first time – extinguish a life. Yes, the anger bubbled even then, but it wasn't meant to end in death.

The second kill was different. I sent David and Janet Green up in smoke like a Guy Fawkes effigy. They deserved to die. To scream as flames licked their bodies, and thick, black smoke invaded their lungs.

It was the same with Ronan, and again with Flora.

They all deserved to die.

Now there are more lives to take. But this time I'm going to make a game of it – have some fun. And when the game is over, I will drop off the edge of the world, into oblivion, my job here done.

Chapter 1

December 2017

The soft sofa felt as though it might swallow me. Suffocate me in its bright yellow fabric. I wasn't keen on yellow, unless worn by a daffodil or buttercup. It tended to reflect off my normally healthy-looking skin, giving me an unflattering jaundiced complexion that clashed with my blood-red hair.

It was hot in the TV studio, but it was too late to remove my hoodie. The clock said almost eleven, and Emmy – the nation's favourite morning presenter – had flicked me the nod. She was about to introduce me.

But I was crumbling, anxiety flooding through my veins. I had an excuse. Lawrence had left me.

A cameraman slid his heavy camera across the studio floor towards me. It seemed threatening somehow – a metal monster. I rolled my tongue over my dry lips, my throat closing up. Was I going to cope? I reached for the glass of sparkling water beside me, and gulped it back. I was about to talk about childhood memories to millions of people sitting in front of their TV sets at home. How was I going to do that, when I couldn't shake Lawrence's departure last night from my head?

Emmy finished telling the viewers about Stephen King's latest novel – another nod in my direction. She had a pile of hardbacks on the table in front of her: Stephen King, Paula Hawkins, and Felix T Clarke. If she'd asked for my opinion I would have told her I love them all. That I adored Inspector Bronte, Felix T Clarke's character who had come to life in over ten novels.

I scanned the studio, trying to stop my knee from jumping, still amazed Emmy had swung it for me to be here.

'You're perfect, Rachel,' the producer had said when I met her. 'The public will love your casual style, and your pixie cut is appealing – you've got a bit of a post-Hermione Emma Watson thing going on.'

I wish.

Five years ago, Lawrence loved my look, which, come to think of it, hadn't changed since then. Perhaps that's why he left. But then he'd once loved that I was a casual kind of gal, who lived in jeans, T-shirts, and hoodies. They say opposites attract, so when did I start to repel him? When did I pass my sell-by date in Lawrence's eyes? When was the first time he suggested I wore heels, or that I might look good in a figure-hugging dress?

'I want Grace in my life, Rach,' he'd said last night about our four-year-old daughter, folding his arms across his toned chest. He didn't have to say *but not you* – the words were in his eyes.

I admit I over-reacted, fired abuse at him, hoping to inflict pain. 'I'll move away. You won't see Grace, if I have anything to do with it.'

He said I was over-reacting – that I should calm down. 'I'll get my solicitor onto it right away,' he'd gone on, far too calm. 'We'll sort something out to suit us both. This can work. We can stay friends.' And then he'd disappeared through the front door without a backward glance.

I confess to getting pretty angry with some inanimate objects after a couple – five – glasses of wine. But the truth was I'd been thinking for a while that our relationship wasn't right. He worked long hours. I barely saw him. I'd wondered more than once if we were only together for Grace's sake. But it still hurt. The memories of when things seemed perfect kept prodding my mind. And his timing was awful. How could he leave when he knew what I was going through with Mum? Or was that partly why he left?

'We are lucky to have brilliant psychotherapist Rachel Hogan, who once worked for the prestigious Bell and Brooks Clinic in Kensington, in the studio with us today,' Emmy was saying, bringing me out of my reverie. She didn't mention that I now ran a private practice in a summerhouse at the foot of the long, narrow garden of my rented end-terrace in Finsbury Park.

The camera was on me, and my heart hammered in my chest. *You can do this, Rachel. You can do this.* The point was, if I did this right, they might ask me back for a regular slot – that's what Emmy had said – so I needed to throw a metaphoric bucket of cold water over my feelings, and get on with it.

Emmy had been one of my clients for about a year. Looking at her now – her pale ginger hair spiralling over her shoulders, her sparkly green eyes, the sprinkle of freckles on her nose, her beaming smile – you would never have guessed the torment she'd been through. The persona she'd created for TV never gave that away. Although for a time, the medication had helped pull it off.

'Hi, guys,' I said, waving at the camera, trying not to imagine the number of people watching. 'I'm here to talk about childhood memories. We've all got them, but how real are they? And what about those we've repressed, ones that lurk in the dark corners of our minds? In our subconscious.'

My confidence grew as I spoke – it was a subject I knew well.

Emmy chipped in. 'I remember my second birthday party. My parents bought me a toy monkey with a huge red bow. And when I was three I had a little pushchair for my dolls, and I would take them for walks round the garden.'

I was wrong-footed. She'd lost her mum when she was a child, and now, in front of millions, I was about to extinguish her recollections.

'Sadly, it's unlikely they are real memories,' I said, running my finger over my dry lips, as I looked her way.

'Oh,' she said, raising a brow, and giving a strange little laugh. 'So, you're saying I don't remember my second birthday party?' She'd lost her smile.

'Well, it is possible, but rare to recall things from before the age of three or four. In fact, few memories are stored before the age of six. You may have kept the monkey and pushchair for years.'

'I did, yes, Vanessa the monkey was my favourite toy until I was about twelve.' Her smile was back – always so professional. 'And before you ask, I've no idea why I chose that name.'

'Maybe you've seen photographs of you pushing the push-chair?'

'Oh yes, tons. My mum took mountains of pictures of me when I was little.'

There was a slight dip in her voice that only I would pick up on. I felt awful. I knew I'd hurt her, and wanted her to look my way so I could mouth that I was sorry, but she didn't catch my eye.

Once the camera was back on me, I said, 'I had a toy rabbit called Mr Snookum as a child.' I smiled. 'I still have him stashed away in my loft. My mother told me she gave him to me on my fifth birthday, and I'm sure I remember her handing him over and telling me to always take care of him.' My voice quavered, and a lump rose in my throat. *My poor mum. My poor, poor mum.* I swallowed, and took a breath. 'But I can't be sure the memory is real. Vivid recollections of my childhood start much later, particularly her painting on the beach at Southwold.' I gave a little cough to ward off my stupid emotions. 'She's an artist.' *Why am I sharing this with the nation?*

My slot seemed to go on for ages, as I continued to discuss childhood amnesia, and the different methods of retrieving infant memories. I did my best to put on a front, hoping I was making a good impression.

Then it was the phone-in. The bit I'd dreaded most.

A woman suffering from post-traumatic stress disorder came on the line, and I went through breathing and muscle relaxing exercises with her, and suggested meditation and yoga. 'Spending time with nature can be beneficial too,' I concluded.

Next, a man suffering with agoraphobia called in.

'Do you think it's something in my childhood that I can't recall, causing me to stay in my apartment day in, day out?' He sounded defeated, on the verge of tears.

What a ridiculous position I was in. How was I meant to answer someone I knew nothing about?

'Could be,' I said. 'Call your doctor as soon as possible. They can advise you.' *Pathetic!*

'We have John Burton on the line, Rachel,' Emmy said, once the agoraphobic man had hung up. She pressed her finger to her ear, as though listening through her earpiece.

'Hello, John,' I said. 'How can I help?'

'Polly put the kettle on,' he sang. 'Polly put the kettle on, Polly put the kettle on, we'll all have tea.'

'Do you remember that nursery rhyme from your childhood, John?' I said, feeling uneasy, and glancing over at Emmy.

There was a pause, before he said, 'Yes.'

Emmy furrowed her brow, and shrugged. Surely they would cut him off. Blame a poor connection.

'What age do you think you were when you heard it?' I asked, trying to sound professional.

'Suki take it off again, Suki take it off again, Suki take it off again, they've all gone away.'

The hairs on my arms rose, despite the heat of the studio.

'I'm crying out,' he said. 'But they won't listen. And now you must pay, Rachel.' The line went dead, and within moments we went to a commercial break.

'Oh my God,' Emmy said as soon as we were off the air, jumping up and dashing over. She plonked down next to me, and put her arm around my shoulder. 'Why the hell did they keep him on the line so long?'

I didn't reply; instead, I dashed off set, barely looking at the concerned faces following me through the door. I rushed through the labyrinth of corridors, desperately seeking an exit, my heart thumping. Eventually I spotted the automatic doors that led to the car park, and raced through them, freezing air hitting me like a smack. I stood for some moments, my eyes darting around the area, trying to catch my breath.

I drove home, relieved Emmy was still on the air and couldn't call me. I needed time to process what had happened, before discussing it. I collected Grace from Angela, keeping the conversation with my next-door neighbour brief so she didn't see how anxious I was. 'You knocked them dead, sweetie,' she said in her throaty middle-class way, as I dashed down her path, holding Grace's hand.

'Thanks,' I called back, certain she couldn't have seen the live show.

Inside my house, with the bolts pulled across the door and the deadlock on, my heartbeat slowed to a normal rate. Grace settled herself in the lounge, building with Lego, and I padded into the kitchen to make tea, the song 'Polly put the Kettle on' worming its way into my head on repeat, driving up my anxiety.

I rummaged in the freezer for fish fingers for Grace's lunch. As I closed the freezer door, I noticed a photo of Lawrence and me on holiday a couple of years ago, pinned amongst the magnetic letters. I couldn't tear my eyes away, and touched Lawrence's face with my outstretched fingertip. We were happy once. Weren't we?

'Mummy!'

I jumped at the sound of my daughter's voice, dropping the box of fish fingers to the floor with a thud. I fell to my knees.

'Are you OK, Mummy?' Grace said, running over and crouching beside me, as I shoved broken fish fingers back into the box with shaking hands. She craned her neck to see my face, touching my cheek softly, and I realised tears were filling my eyes.

'Don't cry,' she said.

'I'm not crying, lovely. I've got something in my eye.'

What the hell was the matter with me? Was it Lawrence taking off, or the stupid call? I took a deep breath, trying to escape the silly nursery rhyme in my head. *It's just some weirdo. A troll. Nothing personal.*

I rose and slipped the battered box onto the worktop, and lifted Grace up into my arms, burying my nose into her dark curls. She smelt of strawberry shampoo. 'So did you have a lovely time with Angela?' I said, as the kettle boiled.

*

The phone blasted on my bedside table. It was 7 a.m. Only one person would ring so early – someone who got up at five.

'Emmy,' I said as I answered the call, my voice croaky.

'I'm so sorry about the odd phone call yesterday, Rachel,' she said. If she'd been angry about my comments on air about her childhood, she'd let it go.

'It wasn't your fault. And I'm sorry too … for rushing off like that.'

'No worries. You dealt with it all amazingly while you were on air. After the break we had that cute contestant from *The Bake Off* on, and carried on as though nothing had happened. There's been a few tweets about it, but nothing major.'

'Thank God.'

'Live TV, especially phone-ins, can be a nightmare.' She paused for a moment. 'Are you sure you're OK?'

'I'm fine, honestly,' I said, pulling myself up to a sitting position, and propping myself against the headboard.

'I still can't believe they let him stay on the line for so long.' Her TV persona was confident, loud and bubbly, yet the real Emmy – the one on the other end of the line, was softly spoken. 'The guys handling the phone lines said he sounded upbeat and friendly when he called in. Had a great question to ask you.'

'It doesn't matter,' I said, raking my fingers through my hair. Despite 'Polly put the Kettle on' playing in my head during the night, I felt sure I was over the call. Lawrence had left. My mum was ill. I wasn't about to let some creepy caller add another layer of worry to my life. 'It was just some fool with nothing better to do,' I said, sounding strong. 'I'm sure the call wasn't aimed at me personally.'

'I'm not so sure, Rach,' she said. Words I didn't want to hear. The phone line went quiet for a few moments, and I imagined her twirling a curl of her hair around her finger, forming the words she sometimes struggled to get out. A trauma twelve months ago had triggered a childhood stammer, although she could mainly control it now and rarely stuttered on air. 'The thing is …'

'What is it, Emmy?' I leaned forward on the bed, and threw back my quilt, suddenly hot. 'What's happened?'

'Nothing's happened exactly,' she went on. 'And to be honest, I've been deliberating over whether to tell you – but then I feel you should know. Just in case.'

'Just in case what?' The hairs on my arms rose.

'The thing is, a man came to the studio looking for you earlier this morning.'

'Was it the man who called in?' *Is that fear in my voice?*

'No. Well, I don't think so. I don't know who he was, but he was quite normal, nothing like the bloke on the phone. He was waiting outside when I arrived. He'd been there a while, as he was soaked through.'

'It's raining?' I glanced at the window. Part of me didn't want to hear what she had to say. *Let's talk about the weather instead.*

'It's dried up now. Rach, are you taking this in? Did you hear what I said?'

I nodded, as though she could see me, before rising and pacing the room. 'Of course. Yes.'

'He didn't tell me his name, despite me asking several times.' Another pause. 'Just that he was desperate to talk to you. I hope I've done the right thing in telling you. I thought you should know.'

Just in case.

'Yes, yes thanks, Emmy. You did the right thing.'

'He looked nice. Normal,' she said. 'I'm sure it's nothing to worry about, Rachel. Listen, I must go, I'm back on the air in five. Talk soon. And please don't worry.' She ended the call before I could answer.

It's nothing, I told myself, continuing to pace the bedroom. *I'd been on TV. Things like this happen all the time.* But my neck tingled, and a chill ran through my body. Had it been the same man who called in to the studio?

And if it was, why was he looking for me?

Want to read on? Order now!

A Letter from Amanda

Hello!

Thank you so much for reading *Traces of Her*. I hope you enjoyed it.

I absolutely loved writing it. The thought of someone receiving four photographs of men and one being a potential murderer really appealed to my imagination. And I loved setting it in Cornwall. Somewhere I've had many happy holidays.

If you enjoyed *Traces of Her* it would be wonderful if you could write a review. It's always lovely to hear what readers think.

And I always love to hear from my readers. You can get in touch with me via my website, Facebook page or through Twitter.

Many thanks,

Amanda

www.amandabrittany.co.uk

Twitter @amandajbrittany

Facebook www.facebook.com/amandabrittany2

Instagram @amanda_brittany_author

Dear Reader,

We hope you enjoyed reading this book. If you did, we'd be so appreciative if you left a review. It really helps us and the author to bring more books like this to you.

Here at HQ Digital we are dedicated to publishing fiction that will keep you turning the pages into the early hours. Don't want to miss a thing? To find out more about our books, promotions, discover exclusive content and enter competitions you can keep in touch in the following ways:

JOIN OUR COMMUNITY:

Sign up to our new email newsletter: po.st/HQSignUp

Read our new blog www.hqstories.co.uk

: https://twitter.com/HQDigitalUK

: www.facebook.com/HQStories

BUDDING WRITER?

We're also looking for authors to join the HQ Digital family!
Please submit your manuscript to:

HQDigital@harpercollins.co.uk

Thanks for reading, from the HQ Digital team

DIGITAL

HQ

If you enjoyed *Traces of Her*, then why not try another dark and twisty thriller from HQ Digital?